F YOU
Above us o
Young-Stoi

ALSO BY MICHELE YOUNG-STONE

The Handbook for Lightning Strike Survivors

Above Us
Only Sky

MICHELE YOUNG-STONE

Simon & Schuster

New York   London   Toronto   Sydney   New Delhi

Simon & Schuster
1230 Avenue of the Americas
New York, NY 10020

First Simon & Schuster hardcover edition March 2015

SIMON & SCHUSTER and colophon are registered trademarks of Simon & Schuster, Inc.

For information about special discounts for bulk purchases, please contact Simon & Schuster Special Sales at 1-866-506-1949 or business@ simonandschuster.com.

The Simon & Schuster Speakers Bureau can bring authors to your live event. For more information or to book an event, contact the Simon & Schuster Speakers Bureau at 1-866-248-3049 or visit our website at www .simonspeakers.com.

Interior design by Joy O'Meara

Manufactured in the United States of America

10 9 8 7 6 5 4 3 2 1

Library of Congress Cataloging-in-Publication Data
Young-Stone, Michele.
 Above us only sky / Michele Young-Stone.
     pages cm.
 I. Title.
 PS3625.O975A64 2015
 813'.6—dc23
 2014016006

ISBN 978-1-4516-5767-8
ISBN 978-1-4516-5769-2 (ebook)

For Christopher Robin, my son

The reason birds can fly and we can't is simply because they have perfect faith, for to have faith is to have wings.

—J. M. Barrie

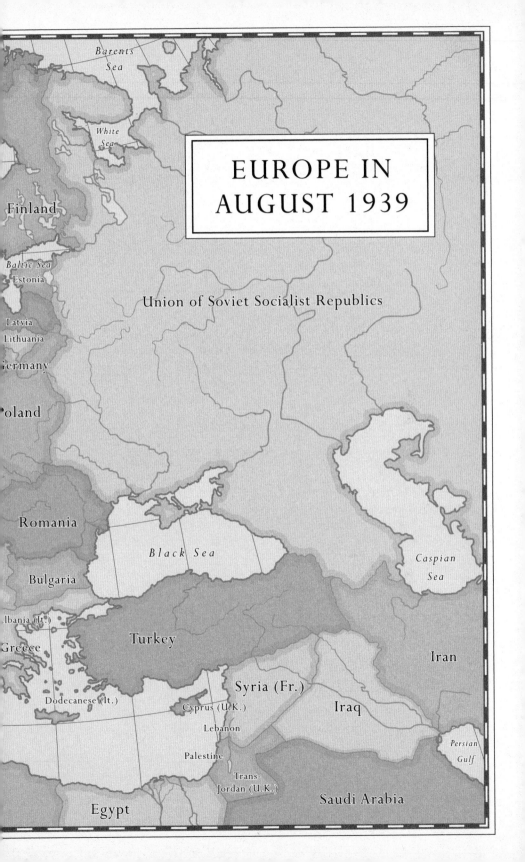

EUROPE IN
AUGUST 1939

Barents
Sea

White
Sea

Finland

Baltic Sea
Estonia

Latvia
Lithuania

:ermany

·oland

Union of Soviet Socialist Republics

Romania

Bulgaria

lbania (It.)

Greece

Black Sea

Turkey

Dodecanese (It.)

Cyprus (U.K.)

Syria (Fr.)

Lebanon

Palestine

Trans-
Jordan (U.K.)

Egypt

Caspian
Sea

Iran

Iraq

Persian
Gulf

Saudi Arabia

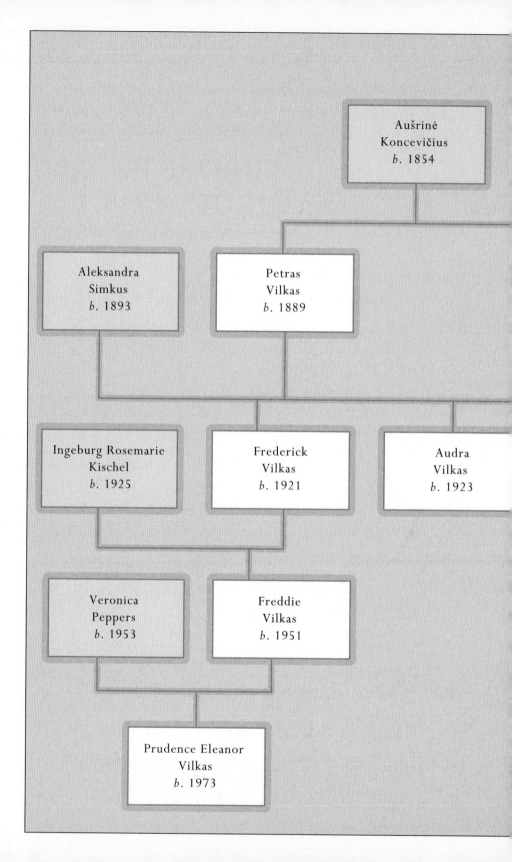

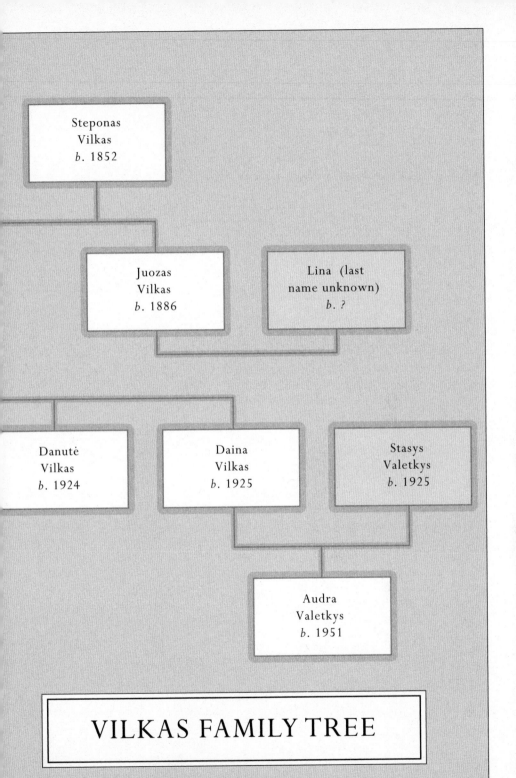

Steponas Vilkas
b. 1852

Juozas Vilkas
b. 1886

Lina (last name unknown)
b. ?

Danutė Vilkas
b. 1924

Daina Vilkas
b. 1925

Stasys Valetkys
b. 1925

Audra Valetkys
b. 1951

VILKAS FAMILY TREE

PART ONE

Much unhappiness has come into the world because of bewilderment and things left unsaid.

—Fyodor Dostoevsky

1

Prudence

*W*hen I was born, the doctor said, "I'm sorry."

I had a full shock of dark hair and long legs like the rest of the women on Freddie's side of the family, but no one noticed these things. No one saw anything but the wings, which were heart-shaped, crinkled like a paper fan. They were smaller than Freddie's palm, slick with primordial ooze, compressed accordion-style against my back. The doctor whispered, "Some kind of birth defect." *Defect.* "How some kids are born with tails and others with cleft palates." He mopped his brow. "But I've never seen anything like this."

My birth was not particularly pleasant. As a matter of fact, I think that as a fetus and then a baby and then a human being, I came between my parents. Before I emerged, Freddie and Veronica were in love, and they might've remained that way if it weren't for me. But it's not my fault that they had unprotected sex. It's not my fault or my doing that they mixed this mad concoction that produced a Prudence Eleanor Vilkas. My father chose the first two names. Vilkas is my surname, my Lithuanian birthright, the name I share with the Old Man. This story is as much about him as it is about me. We are mixed up, tied together by twine and twig, the stuff of nests.

Freddie said, "Little bird. Our Prudence is a little bird." If I'd been a boy, I was to be Paul or John. He wasn't sure. He hadn't wanted to choose between them: Paul McCartney and John Lennon. He'd wanted a girl, and here I was. He was smitten even while I was slimy with bird wings and birthing. He loved me. Like a male bird, he had a maternal reaction. He loved me more than he'd ever loved anyone. I was from his loins, from his high-functioning sperm. He was in awe of what he had wrought. I'd been caged inside my mother's womb and now I was let loose upon the world. Upon him.

On the day I was born, I usurped my mother's importance. These things happen. Freddie wasn't letting me out of his sight. He insisted on helping the nurse clean me up. "Just look at that," he said. "She's amazing."

"This is highly unorthodox," the nurse informed him.

"Leave him alone," the doctor scowled. "The poor bastard has a bird for a daughter."

My father's Caribbean-blue eyes were probably my first clear image outside the womb. Freddie was a looker, which is one of the reasons he and Veronica got together. He's the kind of man that women know they should stay clear of, but they never do. He isn't a bad guy, just his own man with his own dreams, so monumental that they supersede the rest of the world, including any woman. Not me. I wasn't a woman. I was part of the dream, part of him, a contributor to his life's accomplishments.

As the nurse tried to discern my Apgar score, Freddie cooed. The nursing staff would've never allowed him to participate in this initial examination, no matter what the doctor said, but they were alarmed, taken aback by my wings. *Do the wings*, they must've wondered, *give her a zero score for appearance? Do they affect her respiration? They're seemingly close to the lungs. There should be a battery of tests. Someone should telephone* Ripley's Believe It or Not!

I was swaddled and my Apgar score recorded at one minute and again at five minutes, both times as six out of ten, due to my appearance and a general concern for my future ability to breathe. Freddie followed me to the nursery, where he remained, making faces at the glass. Hours later, he held me in the recovery room. The doctor returned smelling of vodka. Veronica was being administered drugs for the episiotomy and follow-up stitches. She was not going to nurse because "there's something wrong with it." She meant *me*. She didn't want to hold me either. I don't blame her. Not really. Freddie said, "What's wrong with you? This is our baby." Veronica was twenty years old, with no clue that there are sometimes babies born with wings. Freddie gave me my first bottle of formula. If he'd had mammary glands, he would've nursed me. The doctor said, "There will be no tests." Having overheard the nurses, he added, "No one is calling *Ripley*." He cleared his throat. "It's not a big deal. We'll incise the bifurcated protrusions when she's a little older."

From then on, they were bifurcated protrusions and not wings, to everyone but Freddie. And me. And later Wheaton and the Old Man.

Freddie didn't know that our family birthed birds. The Old Man, Freddie's father, my grandfather, had never told him, or if he had told him, my father hadn't listened.

The doctor told my parents, "If there are no emergencies in the meantime"—I guess an emergency would've been if I'd started flying around the house—"we'll operate when she's five months old. I'll take some X-rays."

"The sooner the better," Veronica said.

On September 10, 1973, my wings were surgically removed. They weren't biopsied, stored in formaldehyde, or shipped to a freak show. They were discarded as medical waste.

For the next seven years, I lived wingless in Nashville. I was a good kid, or at least a caring one. I tried to resuscitate road kill. I had a first-aid kit and pretended to be a veterinarian and sometimes Florence Nightingale. I wore a white handkerchief over my dark hair. Taking care of baby birds, feral kittens, and squirrels fallen from their nests, I got cat scratch fever twice and had to take a monthlong course of antibiotics both times. I kept toads, turtles, and Japanese beetles for pets. I liked getting along. I didn't want to upset anyone, not Freddie or Veronica. I always had this feeling like I was standing on a precipice and if I did something wrong, we'd all topple over. Because I was in the middle, I was the glue holding us together. I was grateful for the smallest things, even the starlings who, unable to nest in my hair, defecated there instead. Freddie called me little bird, even though there were no wings, just scars. He played acoustic guitar and sang, "The sun is up, the sky is blue, it's beautiful and so are you." There were instruments strewn and stacked throughout the house. Freddie played whatever was closest.

Those first seven years were good. In fact, compared to the next seven, they were downright stellar. I remember watching Saturday morning cartoons, Freddie still half-asleep, drinking coffee and tickling me. Veronica liked Bugs Bunny. On Saturdays, when we were all home at the same time, we did what I'd later consider normal family activities. We played kickball in the front yard. If it rained or there were too many mosquitoes, we piled on the couch and watched an old movie, whatever was on TV. In the evening, Freddie made homemade pizza or chili. He and Veronica kissed a lot and said how much they loved each other. After I'd gone to bed, Freddie left the house to play music. But before I went to sleep, when they were both in my room, Veronica or Freddie reading to me (they took turns), I pretended Freddie wasn't leaving to play music. I pretended that every night would be like this, the three of us together. Then, just as I'd doze off, I'd hear the car door squeak open and shut. I was happy. I was just a kid.

I attended kindergarten through half of second grade in Nashville. Freddie played his music, and Veronica worked thirty-eight hours, just shy of the forty-hour week that would've gotten her health insurance, at the Piggly Wiggly. Punching a clock, she rang up pork chops and potato chips. I don't know if things would've ended like they did if John Lennon hadn't been shot and killed. It was not only the end of a man's life but the end of my parents' love song. I wonder how many other relationships came to an end on December 8, 1980.

Already, even though it was four months off, I was looking forward to my birthday. We were going to rent a trampoline. I was inviting six girls to my party. Freddie had *Monday Night Football* on the TV. Mostly, he just listened to the games and tinkered with his instruments. On this particular night, the sports announcer, Howard Cosell, interrupted the game. He said, "John Lennon was shot; John Lennon was pronounced 'dead on arrival' at Roosevelt Hospital."

December eighth was the end. Seeing Freddie bereft, on his knees riffling through albums and crying, convinced Veronica that she'd made a mistake. In Freddie, she suddenly saw her own father, a man obsessed with form and scales, a piano teacher puzzled by emotions. Not that Freddie was cold. But he loved music more than he loved her, and she was tired of competing when there was no chance of winning. That night, she packed our possessions more carefully and far more slowly than she'd packed the night she ran off with Freddie. She was still debating what to do, folding T-shirts, flipping through our only photo album, and eavesdropping on Freddie in the living room. I don't think she wanted to leave. I think she wanted to get his attention, but sometimes when you start something, you end up following through with it no matter your intentions and the repercussions. I think that this is what happened to Veronica, and by extension, to me.

The next morning, the three of us stood in the driveway. Freddie and Veronica smoked cigarettes. "What are you doing?" he asked. His face was red from crying all night, not because of us leaving, but because John Lennon was dead. He said, "Don't go, Veronica. Come on. What the hell are you doing? Seriously?" I think that if he had said, "Don't go," and "I love you," and left it at that, she might've stayed. *We* might've stayed, but he said the wrong thing, and she responded, "I can't do this anymore." She held back tears as I held out hope that we wouldn't leave. In 1980, she was beautiful in that good simple way: sunny blond with brown eyes, like the state of California.

"Tell me what you want," Freddie said. "Tell me what I can do."

She didn't say anything, but even at seven years old, I knew what she wanted. She wanted *The Brady Bunch*, *Father Knows Best*, and *Leave It to Beaver*. She wanted a husband who worked nine to five, who came home for dinner, who took his wife out to the movies and dancing, who had time to do what other families were supposedly doing: bowling and camping. Those normal family activities. But thinking back, half of my friends' parents were divorced in 1980. I don't think anyone had it as good as what Veronica imagined it was supposed to be. After Veronica got in the car and started the engine, I was still standing in the dirt. "You need to go with your mom," Freddie said.

"I don't want to go."

"You better go." Freddie reached into his jeans and pulled out his pocket watch. "Keep this for me." Holding it, I could see my reflection in the polished gold. At seven years old, I didn't know that a watch could tell not just time but a family's history. I didn't know the significance of the gold timepiece my father nightly set by his bed. I slipped it into my pocket, thinking it was a stupid gesture. He might as well have given me a mint. I wanted my dad, not some piece of men's jewelry. On that cool December morning, I thought we'd be gone for a day or two. At most, a week. I had no concept that my life was changing forever.

Two days ago, my Oma telephoned to tell me that the Old Man had been hospitalized. She said, "He doesn't have much time, Prudence."

The last time I saw him was six months ago. He'd looked slight, half his former self, his beard scraggly, his face jaundiced. His blue eyes had lost their luster. When I asked him how he was feeling, he said, "Fit as a fiddle." We sat together in his study, and he lit a cigar.

"You shouldn't be smoking," I told him.

"Don't lecture me!" He pulled on his cigar. "Are you up to no good?" he asked. "What good do you know? Are you teaching the kids birds? What do you do this month?"

Interpreted, he meant, "Do you still have a job as a teacher of ornithology?"

I teach budding zoologists at the Eastern Coastal Aquarium. I run the aviary, lecturing students from middle-school to college-age about birds: mating, roosting and nesting, diets and migration. I teach my students about environmental impacts; why some birds are louder than others. Why some birds don't mate forever but find a new mate every couple of years. I love my job. The Old Man thinks it's peculiar that birds have their own science. He thinks birds have more to do with art than science. He's a smart man.

I know that old people die, but the Old Man has been old since I met him. He's not supposed to die. We used to talk a lot about history, about the notion that life loops over and eventually you'll catch up with your younger self. Things repeat. Life keeps happening. Maybe that's what's happening now, maybe the Old Man is slowing down to catch up, and he'll leave the hospital a younger Old Man. All better.

He used to say that the observers, people like us who like to watch the birds, are far wiser than the TV watchers. We learn more from the birds, including how to nurture, how to sing, and how to adapt and change. You don't learn anything watching wars play out on the evening news.

When we take the boats out to tag migratory birds on their way to warmer climates, I always think about my first visit to Lithuania with the Old Man. He was amazed that I knew the names of so many birds. His mother was loony for vast-winged birds like gooneys, big birds that can traverse a whole ocean. The Old Man didn't know that I'd been studying coastal birds since I was eight. On the phone, I asked Oma, "What's wrong with him?"

"He's old, Prudence."

It's June 1, 2005, so he is eighty-four. When I met him, he was sixty-eight.

"He should live to be one hundred."

Oma sighed deeply.

"I don't want him to die," I said. That's not how the Vilkas family rolls. We don't lie down in some hospital bed. We take a bullet to the brain.

Oma sighed again. I knew I was being ridiculous. She's spent her life with the Old Man. If anyone has a right to be upset, it's her.

"If you're going to come," she said, "you should come soon."

2

Prudence

*T*here's this quickening and breathlessness at night that calls to mind the baby birds we've rescued. The insides of their mouths are pink, nearly the color of the setting sun. They are the most vulnerable creatures in the world, which is how I feel now. Exposed, ravenous for life, for one more trip to Lithuania, one more adventure with the Old Man.

I called Oma this morning. "How's he doing?"

"Not good, Prudence." Her voice broke. "Are you coming?"

"Of course I am."

When I met the Old Man, I was sixteen, rubbing my scars like pieces of flint, praying for a spark. As it turns out, I come from a long line of leggy bird women, women to whom I am allied by blood and birthright. The Old Man knew our history. When we finally met, he told me about the birds.

The first one we know about was named Aušrinė. She was the Old Man's grandmother. Her name is Lithuanian for the morning Venus, the Sun's daughter. According to the Old Man, she was a girl hiding beneath the thick Lithuanian forest, her own wings bound by strips of cloth. She was an only child, always within reach of her parents, living under brush and pine, in trenches, battling Czar Alexander II's Cossacks in the darkest night, hand to hand, knife to knife. Aušrinė crouched beneath her

mother's skirts, three of them—khaki, dirt brown, and potato-colored—
sometimes all worn at once. Every few days, Aušrinė's mother washed
one of the skirts in a stream and beat it against a rock, and then she wore
two. Once that skirt had dried, Aušrinė's mother made it the top skirt,
and Aušrinė's worldview alternated from khaki to dirt brown to potato.
After midnight, nearby villagers, supporters of the freedom fighters,
ventured toward the forest and left baskets of food, but it was never
enough.

In January, the fresh skirt froze along with Aušrinė's mother's hands
so that none of the skirts was particularly clean or warm. Within this
frozen cocoon, Aušrinė held fast to the heat of her mother's thigh.

The Old Man heard these stories from his mother, who heard them
from Aušrinė. These stories are as much a part of me as my own life experiences. When I feel the warmth of an injured dove in my hands, its
tiny heart pounding, I think of Aušrinė, vulnerable, terrified, holding
fast to her mother's thigh.

According to the Old Man, the trees came to life back then, shaking
black dirt from their roots. They marched forward, a brave effort to
bolster the freedom fighters; their tall piney boughs turning into knobby
arms, they tossed the Russian soldiers from their midst. The pines meant
to protect their people, the Lithuanian freedom fighters, but it was not
hard to light a match or follow a trail of boots to a hole where a man,
woman, and little girl hid. Eventually, all the freedom fighters would be
shot or rounded up. Aušrinė's parents were killed because they wanted
to be Lithuanian and not part of Western Russia. Aušrinė would be
dragged from the forest. Her body was limp. Her parents were dead.
Her head was shorn to protect her from lice and rape. It was January
1864, and she was walking beside other orphaned girls, girls pretending
to be boys, their faces smudged with dirt. She was taken to her grandparents, who were already walking away from Lithuania. She would now
walk with them. No one told the exiles where they were going, only
that they were going.

Day and night, men and women begged the Russian soldiers to go home. They were shot and fell to the snow. There are tales passed down from one generation to the next that recount how the snow remained white, that no one bled, but these are stories, fantastical rememberings, or if fact, maybe the men and women were too frozen to bleed.

Aušrinė walked in her mother's shoes, much too big for her, her wings itching under a wool tunic that was cinched beneath a man's coat. It dragged the ice.

As she walked, Aušrinė remembered the Lithuanian music her parents and grandparents had taught her. She pictured the scales and notes, their ascent and descent. She was thirsty, licking her lips until they were twice their size, blistered and numb, the skin flaking black. She remembered her mother on violin before the great uprising, before they fled to the forest. The year was 1863. Her parents had explained to Aušrinė that as they were born on Lithuanian soil, so too they would die on Lithuanian soil. They would not abandon their country. Aušrinė thought that she was not as fortunate as her parents. She was forcibly leaving the Lithuanian soil they so loved.

Her grandparents were nervous and old. Aušrinė thought that they would all succumb to the snow and die in some no-man's-land between Lithuania and nowhere, but her grandfather kept patting the wool cap on her head, assuring her, "We will walk home again. Do not worry, little bird." He didn't mean him, that he'd walk home again. He was going to die of exhaustion and frostbite in a foreign land. He meant Lithuania would walk home again. He meant Aušrinė.

When I met the Old Man in 1989, he told me that I should be proud of my Lithuanian heritage. "We Lithuanians are not shirkers." The Old Man was lively, smacking his fist in his palm. "We are fighters, Prudence Vilkas." He pointed his cigar at me. "You are a fighter." Up until the day the Old Man first telephoned me, I had no idea that I was Lithuanian, that other girls had been born with wings, or that I was born a fighter.

When Aušrinė's grandfather fell to the ice and could not rise, he pressed the gold pocket watch, the same watch my father passed on to me, into Aušrinė's palm. She slipped it in her coat pocket. The watch was real gold, and all that was left of their estate. Aušrinė concealed it as carefully as she hid her wings, telling herself that she carried nothing, not wings, not watches, not dreams. When her grandmother disappeared in an icy mist, Aušrinė considered falling to the ground. It would be easy to sleep; she could join her mother and father in Heaven. But then she felt a gloved hand from this world, the cold desolate one, squeeze hers. Nearly frozen, she squeezed back. It was all she could do. She had lost her voice.

During the day, Aušrinė walked without resting, and at night, the soldiers herded her and the other exiles into makeshift jails. All the while, the gloved hand that belonged to a boy two years her senior reached out to hold hers. This boy's parents were also gone, fallen victim to starvation. They had given their last bits of food to him. His name was Steponas, and every time Aušrinė dropped, because she wanted to give up, he pulled her to her feet. He wasn't letting go. At times, he held her from behind, feeling her shrunken wings against his chest, his hands clenched in a fist, to keep her from falling down.

Their caravan of sleighs broke down on the steppes of modern-day Kazakhstan. The exiles were told repeatedly that they would never return to Lithuania and so they worked to make a new home. Lithuania was a memory in their muscles and bones. Lithuania survived in the sweat on their brows as they shaped bricks from hay and mud to build houses before the next winter arrived. Steponas and the other boys erected a cross. As the Old Man explained to me, "They made a small Lithuania away from their Lithuania. They made it their own. In secret, they sang and danced and recounted their Lithuanian history."

Over many years, the exiles built farms and schools where they spoke Lithuanian. Outside their homes, they spoke Russian, but behind closed doors, always Lithuanian. They lived this way, reaping what they'd sown, making babies, building fences to keep thieves at bay. In 1874, Steponas married Aušrinė. She gave birth to two sons. Their younger son, Petras, was the Old Man's father. Their older son was called Juozas, but later he would Americanize it to Joseph.

Fifty-four years passed. In between, one generation died and one was born.

As the First World War neared its end, Aušrinė's husband, Steponas, and their two sons, Juozas and Petras, made plans for their return to Lithuania. Petras had dark hair and blue eyes. Like the Old Man. Like Freddie. I am tied to all these people by more than wings and watches. If I ever think to forget where I come from, my scars itch and my breathing quickens.

The Old Man said that as an old woman, Aušrinė stopped concealing her wings. Instead, they bulged and quivered beneath whatever shift she wore. The townspeople in the village in Kazakhstan called her Paukštis, *bird*. Their village thrived. The farms produced crops. Not everyone was making plans to walk back to Lithuania. For many, too many years had passed. It was too risky to leave. For some, they were too old for the long journey, and for others, they couldn't find proof of their Lithuanian identity. The children and grandchildren of the exiled knew Lithuania only through stories and music. Aušrinė and her husband hadn't seen Lithuania in more than half a century. Petras had never seen it. Papers had to be drawn. It was a difficult undertaking, but they all agreed that they must return. Aušrinė and Steponas and their children, Juozas and Petras, and Petras's wife, Aleksandra (the Old Man's mother), gathered all the possessions they could stow in two wagons and began the year-long trek back to Lithuania. Aušrinė and Steponas never doubted returning to a land they knew from distant memory kept close in the bone because the land itself, the rich soil, belonged to them. Lithuania was their birthright.

Aušrinė's grandfather's gold watch was hidden inside a mattress along with what valuables the family had acquired over five decades. The mattress, piled with a chest, carpets, and bedding, was in the bottom of a camel-drawn wagon. According to the Old Man, when they first saw the ancient Lithuanian forest, Aušrinė's wings expanded, slicing through her wool shawl. The group wept at the sight, not of Aušrinė's wings, but of something even more spectacular: their homeland.

In 1918, when Aušrinė sat on Lithuanian soil, drawing lines in the dirt she remembered so well, she was sixty-four, the same age as her grandfather when he died in the snow. As predicted, she had walked home again.

In the 1920s, Petras, who taught music at the university, and his brother, a tailor, purchased a plot of land. The earth was thirsty for Lithuanian sweat. Everything Petras planted grew as if fertility spells had been cast. The Old Man told me, "Nothing died, Prudence. I whacked a stick at the flowers, because I was a stupid boy, but nothing died. The stalks grew to spite me. The gardens were lush with vegetation. The ladybugs like jewels." According to the Old Man, it was a magical place.

Last night, I tagged white pelicans, the first I've seen this year. Later, I called Veronica to ask if she knew about the Old Man.

"Your father told me a few days ago."

"What do you mean? Why didn't you call me?"

"I figured you knew more than I did. I figured you'd call me when you were ready."

Although the Old Man still refers to her as the "woman who is not Lithuanian and not German," Veronica likes him. It's hard not to like him. Last night when I put a band on a toddler pelican, it flopped around in the nest and the female and male pelicans shielded it with their feathers. There are fewer toddlers this year. Usually, we see three per nest, but this year, there are only one or two in each nest. We don't know if there is a new predator or if the pelicans are laying fewer eggs. On the phone, Veronica said, "Are you going to fly up and see him?"

"Of course."

"I can fly up with you. I can drive your way and we can fly up together." When I didn't respond, she took my silence to mean yes. I know that she is trying to be nice, but this sadness feels like my own, not something to be shared.

Next week, I have a group that's supposed to take a charter boat to see the purple martins flock in the tens of thousands to roost under

Mariner's Bridge, one of their many stops, en route to South America. I won't be able to go this year because I need to get online and buy a plane ticket. I have to find a replacement to tell the students and visitors about the importance of building and protecting the man-made structures that the purple martins call home. Their homes are no less important than anyone else's.

I know logically that I met the Old Man in 1989 when I was sixteen, but it doesn't feel that way. It feels like we've always known each other, like we're spokes on the same bicycle wheel. We've been part of this vehicle for as long as Lithuania has been a nation, since our homeland was a grand duchy, the wealthiest land in Europe. At the wheel's center are Aušrinė and all the other Vilkas birds who blurred the line between grounded and free, between imprisonment and flight. In that way, the Old Man is also a bird. We are Lithuanian freedom fighters, and now is the time to stay and fight.

When I see the Old Man, I will remind him of this.

3

Prudence

*I*n 1980, Veronica and I went away. We migrated like geese, except that they have a destination, and we did not.

Veronica did not understand that leaving Freddie would be irreversible, that the farther she drove from his guitarist's hands, the harder it would be to go back. We drove south past McDonald's, Howard Johnsons, Holiday Inns, and Motel 6s. I remember that the roads, the rooms, and the fast food tasted the same—how gray would taste if you could eat it. Even though it was December, there would be no Santa photographs, no tree trimming, no presents.

At first, Veronica planned to stop in Chattanooga. It was a decent-sized city, but then she figured that if she was leaving Nashville, she ought to at least leave the state of Tennessee. Next, she decided on Atlanta, Georgia, but approaching the city, there were too many highways with too many lanes; too many billboards and too many cars. She kept driving through the small town of Cordele, where she thought about heading due east to Savannah but couldn't make up her mind. While I pretended to sleep, Veronica pulled off the side of the road. She turned on the overhead light and opened her map to choose a destination. All the while, I kept my mouth shut, just praying that we'd go back. Moving her finger circularly above the map, she landed on Jacksonville, Florida, and folding the map willy-nilly, tossed it to the passenger's seat.

We got a room with a stained burgundy carpet and a dead-bolt chain hanging from one screw. Veronica told me that her father had never loved her, that it was no surprise that Freddie never loved her. I was only seven, so I wasn't going to convince her otherwise.

Veronica was A plus number one at feeling sorry for herself. She had somehow forgotten that *she* had made this decision, no one else but her. We stayed in this room off Interstate I-95 for three days until Veronica's eyes nearly swelled shut from drinking and crying. Then two child abductions were reported on the local news, and that was it. She was done. Jacksonville was not for us. She stuffed our clothes in a paper bag and we were once again in the car, directionless. In 1980, the last thing I wanted to do was run. I sang along to the radio, Stevie Nicks, "When you build your house, well then call me home." It was like Stevie Nicks was speaking to me. Home didn't seem like a tall order, but it was.

I listened to Veronica lament how she met Freddie in this juke joint in Troutville. He was playing country standards, and right away, she thought he was the man for her. She liked the looks of him, but there was something else too: his passion for music. When Freddie played "Long Black Veil," Veronica got onstage and took the microphone. She imagined herself a siren and Freddie her sailor. She bewitched him. I didn't doubt that they loved each other, but even at seven, it seemed to me that they were too selfish to be together.

There were no cell phones back then, no GPS, no way to track anyone down. Who knows what my father was doing that December? Waiting for us to return? Playing tributes to John Lennon? A little of both?

Veronica was reminiscing, talking about their first night together, how they split a beer and had sex with her head sandwiched between a banjo and an amplifier. All the while, I was thinking that maybe she was talking herself into turning around, but unfortunately, she wasn't and we weren't.

This was the beginning of the end. It's sad how things devolve, how if you hear just the early part of Freddie and Veronica's story, this romantic romp between a blue-eyed guitarist and knobby-knuckled songstress, you imagine they'll go on forever.

Veronica had tied her line to Freddie's. That's how she put it. I know all about ties, lines, rope, grass, cords, glue, paste, knots, yarn, floss, the stuff of nests stringing us together. I understand. I think I've always understood. I even understand why Veronica had to sever her line to Freddie and strike out on her own. I just didn't like it.

My mother grew up in Troutville. Freddie was the bigger fish she'd been looking to fry. One trip, headfirst, through her darkened bedroom window while her father slept, and she was ready to go, to leave forever, squeezing my dad's hand, pretending that she had to sneak off, when in reality she could've traipsed through her father's front door, and he would have gladly let her go. Veronica was pulling anchor, setting course, and reeling in this fine-looking out-of-town musician. She was pretending that her father would care that she was leaving. She was pretending that her mother hadn't left when Veronica was three. She was pretending that she knew how to be loved, that somebody had loved her before. Veronica was great at pretending.

After my parents were married, they got a room at the Moby Dick Motel, where they admired their adjustable bubble-gum wedding bands. Freddie never did buy her a real wedding ring.

I remember our destinationless trek, listening to Veronica's stories, kneading the hem on my T-shirt, craving clean clothes and a hot bath, real food: steak and mashed potatoes, something homey, but Veronica kept driving. We only stopped when the road ended, when we were face-to-face with the Atlantic. I remember squinting in the light that glinted off the water. We weren't the first homeless people to drive until the road ended. Los Vientos, Florida, was a township for the troubled. Whether you'd run out of luck or out of love, you eventually ran out of road. If they'd had a billboard for Los Vientos, it would've said, "Where the uprooted and downtrodden hide between sand and surf." Nothing concrete, nothing stable. We sat Indian-style on the beach, watching seagulls skim the surf. I knew there were worse places to be.

* * *

Within two weeks, Veronica got a job assisting an uppity Realtor. She thought it was a far cry better than working at the Piggly Wiggly. Next, she found us a home, a rental property in a dilapidated section of Los Vientos where the houses were squat with tar paper roofs, the doors hidden behind crumbling latticework.

Most of Los Vientos was dilapidated. There were a few nice homes, but the majority of the money was across the causeway in Saint Mark's. We got the keys to our clapboard shack on January 20, 1981. Our suitcases were piled largest to smallest like a fancy cake on the front lawn. Veronica was on the back stoop smoking and hiding, stifling cries that intermingled with the squeaks and squawks of grackles preening in the yard. This was the same afternoon that I met my best friend, Wheaton Jones. Veronica and I had been at our new house less than two hours when Wheaton walked up our cracked sidewalk. His right sneaker was torn around the rubber sole, and there were sandspurs on his tube socks. His curly hair was long, swooped at his shoulders. He said, "I'm Wheaton Jones. I live across the street." He brushed the curls from his eyes, which were white like bowls of milk, like you could fall into them.

He said, "I'm glad you're here."

"What's wrong with your eyes?" I asked. Needless to say, he was peculiar.

He shrugged. His eyes had turned an iridescent green. Even now, twenty-four years later, I remember every detail of that first meeting. I asked him his age and he asked mine. We were both seven. My birthday was March twenty-ninth and his was April fourth. Using the concrete walk, he pulled back the torn rubber sole of his shoe and I could see a hole in his sock. "Are you a Girl Scout or a Brownie? Do you know how to darn a sock?"

"I don't sew."

"Where's your dad?"

"In the country music capital of the world." It sounded better than saying Nashville. Then we were quiet, in our own ways equally defeated that there was nothing else to say.

Wheaton and I sat side by side on the front stoop. Seagulls squawked. Occasionally we'd hear Veronica take a deep breath. The suitcases remained, like a statue, on our prickly lawn. For lack of anything better to say, I confessed to Wheaton, "My mother thinks my father never loved her."

"Did he?"

"I think so."

"That's good." He fingered the hole in his shoe. "I think my mother is in love with Mr. Doddy."

"Who's that?"

"Just this man who lives down the street."

"I might be able to darn a sock. I've never tried."

"You have pretty hair," he said.

"Thanks. My mother calls it unruly." *Unruly* was a good word to use.

Wheaton said, "I'm generally unruly." I liked how he picked up my good word.

"Tell me more."

He said, "People don't like me."

"Why?"

"I can see things that other people can't see."

I didn't believe him. Of course I didn't believe him. "What are you talking about?" I said. "Can you see God or something? I knew a girl in Nashville who said she could see God."

"What did he look like?"

"Same old, same old, like an old man with a white beard, which is why I never believed her."

Wheaton said, "I don't see God. I don't even know if I believe in him."

"What do you see?"

"You used to have wings like a fairy or a bird or a butterfly, or like a mythical creature."

Immediately, I was terrified, more scared and more uncertain than I'd been since leaving Nashville. How could this boy, this nobody with ripped-up shoes and milky eyes, know about my wings? Dropping my head between my knees, I threw up the Fruity Pebbles I'd had for breakfast.

Wheaton said, "Are you all right?"

I was staring at the bright oranges and pinks of upchucked cereal. "I'm all right." I reached back to feel the two seams that were my scars. I didn't want Veronica to know what Wheaton had said. I didn't want her to know that I'd thrown up.

"I can see stuff," he said. "That's all." We were quiet for a minute. "I didn't mean to upset you."

"You didn't upset me." I lied. His right knee touched my left. I was pretending that I hadn't thrown up. I was pretending that everything was going to be okay. I was pretending that Wheaton couldn't see things no one else could see. I guess I was a lot like Veronica—good at pretending things were okay when they weren't. Wheaton and I, in our different ways, were painfully old for seven.

If I knew where Wheaton was, I'd call him and tell him that the Old Man is in the hospital, but I don't know where he is. I haven't known for years.

"What do my wings look like?" I whispered, tugging at my shirt to show Wheaton my scars. "They thought I had a birth defect."

He said, "It seems like the scars should be bigger."

"They cut them off when I was a baby."

He ran his fingertip along one seam. His hand was moist from a habit of pulling on his fingers, thumb to pinky, counting noises, birdcalls, and syllables. It was a habit I eventually tried to break, the pulling on his fingers. Now it seems stupid that I cared so much about a boy trying to decipher the universe. All he was doing was counting, trying to line things up. It was one of the few things that kept him sane.

He said, "I don't usually tell people what I see or hear. It's dangerous." His fingers were still pressed to my scars. When he was five, the year he started kindergarten, his parents placed him in Magnolia Gardens, an institution designed to fix problem children before they became adolescents. The Gardens, as they were called by Wheaton, had killed the voices and visions, but only temporarily, and only by using a low dose of lithium. The drug had not only quieted the visions but had dulled Wheaton. He couldn't think, and when he tried to talk, his words were garbled. He also got confused about time: days of the week and the order in which things happened. His dreams and his waking life were one and the same.

Before the Gardens, Wheaton had been close with his mother. This closeness was one of the reasons he was *placed* in the Gardens. He always used that verb *placed*. He never said "locked away" or "institutionalized." His mother's name was Lily.

When Wheaton heard the voices, Lily had quieted them. She taught him to sing and count sheep. When he saw people no one else could see, Lily called them "imaginary friends." She did everything she could to normalize Wheaton's experiences, but then he started school, and Lily wasn't there to reassure him. Rather, the guidance counselors thought he needed professional help. At home, his father tended to agree with them. It wasn't normal for a boy to be so attached to his mother. Like a skipping record, Wheaton heard his father say, "There is something wrong with him." Seven syllables, thumb to pinky, ending on the pointer finger. Thumb to pinky is the only way to count.

Lily chain-smoked as she drove Wheaton to Magnolia Gardens. Wheaton's father, who aspired to be a great American novelist, sat in the passenger's seat reading lines of dialogue aloud. He was oblivious to Wheaton's nervous finger pulling. *I don't want to go away.* Seven syllables, thumb to pinky, ending on the pointer finger. *Pointer finger.* Four syllables ending on the ring finger.

Wheaton had curly blond hair and big eyes, usually green, but when he had visions, they rolled up white in the back of his head. Years later, when I was in my twenties, I'd see junkies on the bus, their eyes doing the same thing, spittle in the corners of their mouths. Wheaton was never a junkie, and the only time he'd drooled was when he was pre-scribed lithium. If you ask a psychologist or psychiatrist or even a general practitioner about administering lithium to a five-year-old, they'll tell you it's a bad idea, a last resort. Aside from his eyes and the peculiar things he said, Wheaton was attractive, *a looker* like my dad, and from the finger pulling to the visions, he was special. Unique. He liked to draw and carried a small brown notebook, an old recipe book, in which he doodled, sketching whatever I requested, from dragons to birds. Wheaton was my best friend, my confidant, my comrade, my compadre.

We were as close as two people could be, or so I thought, but Wheaton had secrets—his own treasures. Perhaps if I'd paid closer attention, I wouldn't have lost him.

Veronica is on her way here. We're flying together. Arrangements have been made. I am trying to get my Oma on the phone, to let her know our plans, but her friend Rhonda answers. "Your Oma is at the hospital."

"What's the room number, Rhonda? I don't have it."

"Ten-three-seven. Ingeburg thought you'd already be on your way." She hesitates. "She thought you'd have left by now."

I do not particularly like Rhonda. "I'll be there tomorrow. Do you know if my grandfather is conscious?"

"Ingeburg says that his oxygen levels are low. He doesn't have much time."

There it is again—time. It's two in the afternoon. June 3, 2005. Friday.

I picture the Old Man smoking his cigar and pointing with it, telling Rhonda to shut her mouth. It's an extension of his hand. Sometimes I thought he was going to poke Freddie in the face with it, but he never did. Rhonda is frustrated with me. I think I might've accidentally told her to shut her mouth. She's hung up.

If the Old Man is unconscious, I hope he's dreaming, and if he's dreaming, I hope there are big birds, black bears, and long-limbed pines. I hope that the birds are frenzied, muting the drone of hospital noises, like the spongy squish of rubber soles on vinyl flooring and the hum and blip of man-made machines. I hope the bears are fierce, protecting him from needle pricks, and the boughs are bendy, embracing him. Perhaps his mother is there, and she's singing opera. Tomorrow, I will be there, and I will try not to be afraid. Tonight, I will try and dream of the Old Man. In my dreams, he is never old.

4

Prudence

The plane is crowded. Veronica and I couldn't get two seats together, so I'm back near the bathroom beside a man who, from the smell of it, is drinking scotch. He has blond curls like Wheaton's. Candy hair, I used to call it, the kind of hair that loops around your fingers.

The plane is rumbling down the tarmac. My stomach drops. Please let the Old Man know me. Please let him hold my hand and sit up. "Where's my cigar?" he'll ask, tossing whatever blanket they've draped over him to the side. He'll tell my Oma that they've made a big fuss over nothing. Already, I've lost Wheaton. I can't lose the Old Man.

I am thirty-two years old. Wheaton would explain this as sixteen times two, as four squared times two. As one year younger than Jesus when he was crucified. As four times eight or eight times four or two digits or fingers away from making sense. When I was half the age that I am now or take away four squared plus one, my life changed for the better. It began with one of Wheaton's visions and culminated in honest-to-God revelations. Big stuff.

Like so many good stories, it begins with an apparition, a ghostly girl—but not just any ghost. This ghost had wings. Wheaton saw her on the pier and for a few seconds mistook her for me. Our pier in Los Vientos was concrete, *not* how a pier should be—slatted wood creaking with the ocean dizzily underfoot—but hard, the kind to crack, not splinter. If we lay down, we didn't even feel the sway of the Atlantic beneath us, but we could watch the clouds pass overhead. Because of the winds, they passed quickly, but like all piers, our pier had an end where ocean met sky. This was where the ghost of the girl appeared, and because she had wings, it seemed only right that I should be able to see her too. Wheaton and I went out together to look for her, a spring squall blowing, our local brown baggers fishing for their night's supper. Like most of Los Vientos's population, these men and women had gone as far as they could, and without wings or fins, had to stop.

"I don't see her," I said, frustrated. Of course I couldn't see her. I didn't have the sight like Wheaton, but we both suspected her appearance had to have something to do with me. Wheaton saw her "plain as day," and told me she was staring at the sea. I reached out to try and touch her but felt nothing. Just the same, I was hopeful.

Lightning flashed in the distance.

Wheaton told me that her wings were enormous. Big and white, rounded above her shoulders and pointed at her feet. "She looks like you," he said. There was another flash of lightning. Waves splashed against the concrete beams, the clouds swelling magenta. We were on the verge of something. We both knew it—anticipation was buzzing like electricity. And then Wheaton said the ghostly girl was gone. Vanished.

There were storm clouds in his eyes, and the sky spit rain. Later, he drew her picture. Like the ghost herself, the picture was murky, Wheaton's charcoal smudged, making it difficult to discern the shape of the face or the bend in the wing.

My scotch drinker is a pilot who flies private jets. I don't know exactly what that means, so he explains: "I fly airplanes for people who are rich and own planes but don't fly them. It's a living, and I get to travel." His name is Sam Kirk. We shake hands. His fingers are swollen. There's a tan line where a wedding band is missing. I order a vodka and cranberry and we clink glasses. This is better than sitting beside Veronica. I can be alone with my thoughts, holding fast to the Old Man. I met him the same year that our ghost appeared.

Wheaton and I knew that 1989 was an important year. The sky was bluer. The moon brighter. The tides higher. The sun warmer. Food tasted better. So did cigarettes. We eagerly but somewhat anxiously anticipated whatever was coming our way, the waves smacking the pier's concrete pilings, spitting foam like beer; fish jumping out of the water, pelicans diving swoosh into the blue, our world like boiling stew.

In March of that year, I went alone to the Saint Mark's Nature Reserve. I was a regular there. The volunteers and researchers knew me by name. It was a Sunday, and I expected to see more tourists, but the place was empty. In search of darkness and air conditioning, I went into the audiovisual room. There was a film about birds looping continuously. The narrator said, "Bird nests are works of art, each singular. Even today, as birds struggle to adjust to a loss of natural habitat, they succeed by incorporating Styrofoam and plastic into the construction of a suitable nest. In cities where noise pollution from traffic and construction has increased, many species of birds have developed a louder call to attract a mate. For most of the nine thousand species of birds, the male constructs the nest, building and rebuilding until the female is content. The nest has to be sturdy and safe from predators. It also has to be exactly what the female wants. If it's not good enough, she'll leave."

In the video, a baby osprey was born, cracking its shell, squirming and kicking, the head poking through, the wings pulsing, eventually unfurling. Later, the video showed the baby's downy feathers. The mama bird circled the nest.

An announcement came over the loudspeaker: "Five minutes until we close." My shoulders and back itched. The low volume on the videotape started buzzing. I was born in the wrong nest to the wrong parents. I stood up but sat back down. Something hurt. I got to my knees on the institutional carpeting. The movie screen was close enough to touch, a blur of red and pink, orange and white. A baby bird's mouth opening.

My back burned. *It is the male bird's job to attract the female with flashy colors and calls.* On my knees, I said, "Wheaton." I felt them, the tips of them, slicing through my back. It hurt. I rocked forward. A mama bird was squawking. I reached for the screen. The light was magnified. The room glowed, and it seemed to shine for me. *Many birds mate for life, while some females tire of one mate, abandoning the nest for another male's colors and call.* There was a buzzing in my ears, a weightlessness, the floor disappearing. I was compressed and filled. *The male protects the baby bird, calling to the female if a predator approaches.* The wings unfurled. *My* wings. I was crying. Brilliant. They were as wide as I was tall and grazed the carpeted walls of the small room. The intercom crackled, "Two minutes until closing." I was born with wings. Rocking back and forth, seeing the reflection of my wings bathed in the red film light of two cardinals zipping tree to tree. This is how I was born. The light switched on. It was Dr. Neal Carl, one of the researchers. "Why are you on the floor, Prudence?"

"Look at me," I said.

"We're closed," he said.

"Look at me!" The wings were as real as my legs.

"I'm looking."

"Can't you see them?"

"See what?" He looked at his watch. "It's time to go. I'm making dinner tonight. We're having tacos. Time to vamoose, Prudence."

I rose slowly for fear of hurting them. I could see their magnificence reflected over the rolling credits. I thought that Dr. Carl was blind. He said, "Are you all right?"

"I'm incredible."

I reached for my messenger bag but was afraid to bend down.

"Are you sure you're all right?" Dr. Carl handed me the bag, which I held at arm's length. I didn't want to damage my wings.

I couldn't take the bus, not when my wings had emerged. I had to show Wheaton.

I will never, as long as I live, forget the wonder of that day. I had never experienced anything miraculous. I walked past my own house.

Veronica was on the front stoop, smoking a cigarette. She said, "Where are you going? Where have you been?" I rolled my eyes.

I traversed Wheaton's yard and pushed the front door open. He bumped his chest against mine like we were on the same sports team and I'd just made the winning score. He knew. His eyes were the color of malachite. He grasped my hands the same way I sometimes held his, to quiet them.

"Can you see them?" I asked. "Can you see them right now?"

"I've always seen them." He smiled. "Please don't fly away."

"What? What are you talking about?"

"Don't leave me."

I wasn't going anywhere. I remember thinking that he was being silly, but in actuality, he was being ironic because he's the one who flew away. Not me.

I hook my thumbs together and make wings with my hands, a bird inside a plane. I can't see my mother from my seat, only the slushy pilot to my right and on my left, the polyester skirt and nylon ankles of the flight attendant wheeling a cart of pretzels and soda cans. In 1992, the year Wheaton went away, the Old Man took me to Coney Island. I was nineteen, perplexed and sad, but we laughed about the deadbeats operating the rides. "Shiftless," the Old Man called them. "Who can afford to be drifting in this world? Time is short." We rode the Ferris wheel, and I remember him telling me, "Sometimes life is like this Ferris wheel. Even when everything seems wrong, the sky is black, it's starting to rain, and some lady throws up on you, the wheel will keep right on turning to spite you." Wheaton was gone, but the wheel was going to keep turning.

Last year, the purple martins turned the sky black. This year, I'm missing it, missing them. The sky outside my window is as white and clean as Wheaton's eyes after they capsized. I want to save the Old Man. I know that I'm selfish, but I need him to stick around. I am counting on yet another miracle. There have been so many in my life. Why not one more?

PART TWO

Yes I would say Here I am I am tired I am tired of running of having to carry my life like it was a basket of eggs.

—Joe Christmas from *Light in August* by William Faulkner

5

1989

*I*n Bay Ridge, Brooklyn, the Old Man swallowed his high-blood-pressure tablet, and like he did every morning, complained about this spoiled generation: "Nobody saves a penny." When his pie-faced, German-born wife, Inge, asked if he'd heard from their son, the Old Man grimaced. "That boy's got no sense. What's he doing with his life?" The Old Man lit a cigar and rocked back in his easy chair. "You do for your children and they do nothing for you. Get me a beer, will you, Inge?"

"I have nothing better to do with my time?"

The Old Man opened the newspaper, and before Inge had delivered his Black Label beer, he fell asleep. Inge stubbed his cigar.

Later that evening when she tried to wake him, he brushed her aside. "Leave me alone."

"Come to bed."

He didn't answer, and she left him in his easy chair.

With his beard on one shoulder, the Old Man dreamed. For the first time in at least a decade, he dreamed about his sisters. In the dream, the three girls held hands.

Before the war, the Old Man was called Frederick.

In his dream, Frederick was young, and he was shouting, screaming, warning his sisters about what was coming. "Audra, Danutė, Daina! Listen to me. Run! Get out of there," and even though they could see him in his dream, they could not hear him. Their names meant Storm, Gift from God, and Song. Daina was the baby. She was their little songbird. Everybody's favorite, and no one made it a secret. He was shouting at the three of them, but there was no sound, even as his voice strained. In the dream, he touched his throat. His sisters waved like nothing was wrong. Groundless, nowhere to stand, the Old Man kept screaming. "Get out of there!"

When he woke in a sweat, he went to the kitchen for a glass of water and steadied himself against the counter.

His sisters had been real in the dream, and just like in real life, he hadn't managed to save them.

In Bay Ridge, the Old Man finished his water and went upstairs to his wife. She looked like a girl when she slept. Her brow was unwrinkled and her mouth was pleasant, not turned down, like when he saw her at breakfast or at lunch or at dinner. Like when he saw her tidying, walking to and fro, through rooms where he wanted to sit in peace and listen to his music. Since he'd retired, she drove him crazy, talking on the phone and watching the blasted television. "Turn it down," he complained.

"But I can't hear it then."

"Because you're deaf. See a doctor."

But tonight, the clock radio showing two a.m., the Old Man felt more like Frederick than an old man. He took two Benadryl to help him sleep without dreaming, and feeling scared for the first time in many years—the past too close, his sisters too close—he climbed into bed, nuzzling Ingeburg. His chest against her back. When she startled awake, asking, "Is everything all right?" he said, "Everything's fine. Go back to sleep."

He would never tell her that he was scared. It was enough that she was there looking like her young self. *Why can't my sisters hear me? It's my dream.* Then he closed his eyes and fell dreamlessly to sleep. You'd think that in forty-eight years, a man would stop grieving his family, but life doesn't work that way. Life speeds by until forty-eight years seems like one bar in one song, like one scene in one act in one opera. Like one stroke of paint on the *Mona Lisa*.

The next morning, the Old Man was nearly himself again. He shoveled eggs and fried potatoes into his mouth, sopping his plate with day-old bread, but after swallowing, he brightened and raised a finger. Ingeburg knew him well enough to know that he was going to make some point, and however trivial it might seem to her, she should feign interest, for the Old Man's benefit.

"Yes, Frederick?" she said, taking a seat at the table. Was this going to be some recounting of a story she'd already read in the newspaper? Was he going to critique *The Harvard Dictionary of Music*, as he'd done last night at dinner? Ingeburg smiled and waited.

"We have a granddaughter."

"Yes, we do." This was no great revelation.

"We should meet her." His pointer finger was yellowed from cigar smoke.

Inge said, "What? We do not know her, and she is nearly grown. I wanted to go and meet her when she was born. She is not a baby, Old Man."

"We should know her."

"I don't even know how old she is." Inge rose and untied her apron. "You're crazy."

"She is the same age my sister Daina was the last time I see her. I think she has a birthday on March twenty-ninth. She is sixteen."

Ingeburg sighed. "Freddie's daughter is not your sister."

"She's my granddaughter."

"She's our granddaughter."

"I am dreaming," he said. "Last night."

"What were you dreaming about?"

"What do you think, Inge?"

"I don't know."

"Of my sisters."

She pointed her spatula at him. "How am I supposed to know what goes on in that head of yours?"

The Old Man said, "I want to meet the girl. I wonder if she looks like my mother or my sisters."

Inge said, "The girl's name is Prudence. We have pictures from Freddie."

"Does she look like Daina?"

"How do I know what Daina looks like? You have one old photograph. I can't tell who's who in that picture."

"What kind of name is Prudence?"

"From the Latin, I guess. 'Cautious.' American now."

"Nothing is American but the Indians, and they are dead. You'd think our son would care about his heritage, but he doesn't care. No one cares anymore."

Ingeburg rolled her eyes. "That's not true."

"We will meet the girl," he said. "Before I die, I want to meet her."

"Are you dying soon?"

"Sit down now, Inge, and let me talk at you. And you try to listen for once."

Ingeburg rolled her eyes and, sitting down, folded her hands on her lap.

"Family is important," the Old Man began. "Most important. After family, land is most important. In 1918, with Lithuanian independence, we had our land back. Father was so happy to have his grandfather's land back for the Vilkas family, but father's brother, Joseph, cared more for money than for land or family. You know this."

"I know this story," Inge said.

"Listen, woman. You don't know everything how you always think you do."

Inge rolled her eyes.

"And don't go to sleep on me."

"I better make a strong pot of coffee."

"You're a funny woman, Ingeburg." The Old Man cleared his throat while Inge put water on to boil. "So my uncle Joseph sold his half of the estate to not one but four separate families." At this, the Old Man held up four fingers. "They were Lithuanian families, but like us, exiled from the country since the great uprising. They were good people. They later became our friends, but Father never forgave his brother for dividing the land into parcels. Father's brother, useless Joseph," at this the Old Man made the sign of the cross, "and his wife, Lina, take a boat to America, where Joseph is going to sell men's clothes and work as a tailor. I remember Father spitting on the dirt and saying, 'Juozas is dead to me,' and so Uncle Joseph was dead to all of us, and then came 1940 when the Red Army is occupying Lithuania, and then came 1941, when we are all doomed to die, and don't think we didn't have suspicion all the time that the Red Army was going to do something evil. What is wrong with people? In 1918, Lithuania was independent. But when the Red Army marched into our country, no one did anything. Not even us because the lying Soviets said that we wanted them there to protect us from Hitler. No one, except for maybe some Jews, wanted the Russians there. My neighbors, the ones who saved me, were Jewish. Did I tell you that?"

"You told me," Inge said. *A million times!*

"The Soviets told lie after lie—that we need them to protect us from Hitler, that there will be another war, and they will keep us safe. They said that we voted and decided to become part of the Soviet Union. They were liars. All the while, they'd signed a secret pact with Germany, saying that Stalin could have Lithuania, Estonia, Latvia, and half of Poland. In exchange, the Soviets would leave Germany alone, stay out of Hitler's business, and let him have the rest of the world. When liars make contracts, no one is to be trusted. Everywhere, we see the tanks and the red stars. Everywhere, they wave their flags and banners. Everywhere, is the face of Joseph Stalin. There were two sides: evil and more evil. Even as a young boy, I remember hearing mother cry about Holodomor in Ukraine. I was eleven or twelve and Mother was telling Father that the Soviets are shooting children in wheat fields. We were never not afraid of Russians. She had read about it in the newspaper. A whole nation starving to death. Father is saying, 'Don't worry, Aleksandra. We are not in Ukraine.'

"But then the Soviets are in Lithuania, and there was plenty of time for Father to telegraph or telephone Joseph in America and ask for his help. There were planes flying overhead and tanks rolling through town, and we hear about the nationalizing of the stores. We hear about the men and women disappearing in the night. We see the men in black coats. Mother said to Father, 'We can visit Joseph and Lina in America. We should go.' Father put his hands over his ears and shook his head at Mother like she was too loony for her own good. 'This is our home,' he told her. 'This is our soil.' He kneeled down and ran his fingers along the dirt. 'We don't run, Aleksandra.'

" 'But the girls,' Mother said. 'And Frederick. I am sick with worry.' Mother was always worried about us. She wanted to protect us no matter what. She didn't even want us to know that war was coming, but we knew. You couldn't help but know.

"Father said, 'Frederick and the girls will be fine. You worry too much.'

"I listened to everything they said. I don't think Father was stupid, just too optimistic. I don't know.

"Three months later in June, 1941, everyone was gone. Our house is filled with the men in black coats. The front doors are ajar. The furniture stands on the front lawn with no one sitting or playing piano. There were trucks and wagons. Our house is nationalized and then the land will be collectivized and the family is no more.

"My neighbors are alive. They are one of the families that had returned to Lithuania twenty years earlier and the men in the black coats didn't bother them like they did us. They did not own enough. Or maybe their house was not big enough. Or their land wasn't rich. Or their chickens didn't lay golden eggs. Or maybe they keep to themselves. Stalin killed randomly. They might've had a magic beanstalk. You see, Inge, it was always with no reason. You know that."

"I know," Inge said. "You say this every day, Old Man. As if I don't know from Stalin."

"Mother's name was Aleksandra."

"I know, Old Man."

"We never say it. We always say Mother."

"Who is we?"

"Me, Father, and my sisters. She was Mother, but she had a name."

"Of course she had a name." Inge yawned and filled two cups with black coffee.

"I hid in the darkness, eating the neighbor's leftovers. They were Jewish. Did I tell you that?"

Inge pulled a skein of yarn from her basket. She had to keep her hands busy even while her mind was idle.

"All the while, I was hearing the Red Army fire guns in the air. I got on my knees and prayed for my dead. Father, I knew for certain because I'd seen him die, but Nelly, my neighbor, said that my sisters' bodies were carried from the house. I asked her, 'All three?' and she said, 'Do you think they would spare one?'

"'And Mother?' I asked. 'Are you sure about Mother?'

"Nelly said, 'They took her right after your father. I saw your sister Daina. She was crying, coming back from the train station. They forced your mother onto a cattle car bound for Siberia. Your sisters were going inside to pack.'

"'Did you see them?' I asked Nelly. 'Did you see my sisters?'

"'After they brought out Audra, I couldn't look,' she told me."

The Old Man covered his eyes. "For a while, Inge, I really had some hope. I told you."

"You have told me," Ingeburg said. "You've been telling me since 1942."

"Just listen, woman!" The Old Man banged his fist on the table. "I thought that maybe Daina and Danutė had survived, but as the days passed and there was no sign, no word, I knew that I was being naïve. I prayed and even as I prayed, I doubted God."

"Stop, now, Frederick," Inge said. "This is ancient history. All of it. No more talk and no more dreams."

"It doesn't seem so ancient, Inge."

"Just stop it, Old Man! Our son is right about one thing: you live in the past."

"But I have a point."

"Then get to it! Will you?"

"Our granddaughter. She is not in the past. We are going to witness her."

"But how? What if she doesn't want to see us?"

"We will fly to where she lives. I will call Freddie and find out where."

"I'm not getting on an airplane."

"It's too far a walk for you, Ingeburg. You're old."

"Very funny. Don't call me old." Inge sipped her coffee. "Why now, Frederick?"

"Why any time, Inge?" He puffed on his cigar. "We don't know. Only God knows."

The Old Man wasn't feeling so old, not since his dream. The past had caught up and kicked him in the rear. He was hopeful. What if his granddaughter resembled his mother or one of his sisters? He was hell-bent on knowing her. He stifled a smile and folded his hands in his lap. He loved his Ingeburg, but sometimes she did not understand the world as good as he did.

6

Ingeburg Rosemarie Kischel

*W*hile the Old Man is always talking about his Lithuania, I keep quiet. But I have a history. I am a person, a girl, a daughter, a woman, a wife, a mother, and now a grandmother. I am no less important, nor is my history.

My mother was named Emilie Vogel and my father was called Alfons Kischel. I was born in a hospital bed, my mother unconscious, a nurse pressing down on her stomach and a physician between her legs, his forceps gripping my jaw. The year was 1925.

Like my parents, I was intelligent, but I didn't care about studies. I was more concerned with making everyone laugh. I had a happy, well-to-do childhood with my older brother, Francis, two years my senior, but like anyone growing up in a country bent on war, we felt our happiness unraveling. As early as 1936, when I was eleven, we knew that things were not good. We were not blind, but everyone wanted to feign ignorance and believe in the nation. We were safe. No one was hungry. Father had friends, veterans of the First World War, who'd lost their citizenship because they were Jewish, but no one wanted to acknowledge what was really happening. Some of my mother's friends earned medals for having more than four children. We would laugh about it, how they deserved those medals because their children were rotten.

For forty years, I have listened to the Old Man's family history, hearing over and over about his shame at having to petition his uncle Joseph in New York for sponsorship to the United States. "Inge," he said, "I did it for you. We had to get out of there." But it was never for me. It was for us. Putting the weight on me lessened his shame.

There is no such thing as ancient history. I know it, but I try not to dwell on what I cannot change.

I met Frederick early during the war. Inside, he might've already become the Old Man, but on the outside, he was Frederick, handsome and fit. He was a sort of postal carrier, carrying documents, correspondence, and packages back and forth to Berlin. I was a nursing student, a practical joker. Tall, with dark hair and good teeth, my friends teased that I'd make a better actress than nurse. "Ingeburg is so dramatic," they said. "She'll be the next great film star. Her smile is over the top."

I met Frederick in a beer garden in the summer of 1942. He was there delivering a package to an albino wearing a brown leather eye patch. Immediately, I was intrigued. As I said, he was handsome, with sweeping dark-brown hair and blue eyes. I watched him. After he handed a paper to the albino, the man slipped it inside his jacket and remained at the bar.

"Stare much?" my friends asked.

"He's cute, isn't he?"

"Which one?"

"Stop it," I said. I was proud of my smile, and I didn't shy away from showing it off.

The albino man left through a flowering archway that led out to the street, where there was a parade in progress. The sun was bright. Women and children, dressed in traditional lederhosen, tossed flowers at the marching soldiers. There was music, laughter, and cheering.

In the beer garden, I rested my chin in my hands and stared at Frederick. Because of the festival, our nursing instructor had dismissed class early. There were five of us out enjoying the weather in our blue starched uniforms.

Frederick turned around and saw me watching him. After finishing his pint and ordering another, he approached our table. It's funny to me now, how he was so young and full of potential. His black cap was under his arm. His cheeks were rosy. We had yet to share our war stories.

I was laughing. "He's coming over here!"

"That's what you get!"

He was foreign, but his German was good. "May I sit down?" he asked.

Despite his bright complexion, right away I detected his sadness and was drawn to it. Sadness was something I understood. I think it was why I was always trying to make everyone laugh. Shielding my eyes from the sun, I said, "Where are you from?"

He'd come to Germany after the army had "liberated" (according to the Germans) Lithuania, and he knew how to behave. Like the rest of us, he knew to say "Heil Hitler."

When I asked about his family, he told me, "They're not around." My brother and father weren't around either, so I thought that I understood. They were both fighting in the war.

I was flustered, but I wrote my address on a corner of my class notes and tore the paper. Frederick pressed it to his lips. In Berlin in 1942, apart from Hitler's speeches, it was hard to detect that there was a war going on. There were parties and parades. Everyone swelled with pride. There was nothing the Germans couldn't do. As a nation and as a people, we were truly better than the rest of the world. It was tangible.

In the garden, Frederick kissed my hand. I smiled for him. My friends exploded in laughter. After he'd gone, they teased, "You only like that boy because he's sullen. You like the quiet ones."

I rolled my eyes, but it was true. On that first sunny day, I had this sense that he understood the war how I did. Like maybe we could confide in one another. We were pawns, victims of circumstance, pretending we weren't caught in someone else's chess match. Pretending that the butchers weren't sharpening their knives.

A few months later, Frederick told me about his family, how he'd marched across Poland and been assigned a bicycle. He'd taken an oath and sworn allegiance to Hitler and Germany. They gave him a black cap and an armband. He slept in the homes of strangers, traveling back and forth to Berlin, delivering papers and packages to men and women he didn't know, fearing for his life.

He was quick on his bicycle, and he was quiet. He didn't know what he was delivering, and he was never to ask or to look.

Ten years after the war, Frederick learned of his missions. He'd been delivering details of the Final Solution, the answer to the Jewish question, from Western Poland to Berlin. On more than one occasion, he'd unwittingly received papers from SS chief Heinrich Himmler—in charge of the systematic annihilation of European Jews. In Lithuania, he'd known a girl named Nelly. Her family had hidden him after his own family was murdered. She and her family had been part of this terrible solution.

Riding his bicycle across Germany, Frederick carried details about the first three designated killing centers in Poland. Later, he carried information about the success of mobile gas vans, paneled trucks that pumped carbon monoxide into their locked confines. He delivered recorded numbers of dead, details on the evolution of murder from bullets to gas chambers. All the while, never daring to look.

To the Germans and to the world, he was a nobody, a patsy. He was a Lithuanian boy riding a lent bicycle across Germany. It was too dangerous to convey details of the Final Solution via wire communication. What if the plan was discovered and broadcast? How would the average German react? How would the rest of the world react? Hitler couldn't afford a changing tide. Already, the top SS chiefs knew that it was too psychologically taxing for an average man to shoot a woman or child at close range. That's where they'd started: copying Stalin's methods. But they'd evolved. They'd industrialized killing to odorless gas. They were doing the world a favor—exterminating the undesirables. Frederick was part of this master plan because he was nobody. He had nothing. When I think about how meaningless we were to the greater schemes, plans, and solutions, I cross myself and thank God for my son, who brought hope to my world.

Poor Frederick, though. I don't know sometimes how he has survived day to day with so much regret. For all the years I have known him, he's carried a sense of worthlessness and guilt. It pained him that he'd been afraid to look at what he was delivering.

Frederick was good to me. He was better than good. Two weeks after we met, my mother and I found out that my father had been killed in Tunisia. Two months later, my brother died in France. Frederick was the confidant I'd anticipated on that sunny June day. He took care of my mother, reassuring her, telling her that everything would be all right. He never believed it, I don't think, but he was good to my mother.

Sometimes we went to the cinema. My mother was bereft, inundated with medals and letters of gratitude, when all she wanted were her men back. She loved my father and brother so dearly. Frederick could never take their place, but he took my mother to the cinema with us. He patted her hand and said she was beautiful. He praised her garden that she loved.

The neighbor with the four kids was no longer something to laugh about. Her boys were sent to war, her husband wounded. As much as I sensed doom, I didn't understand what was coming, how things could get even worse. I stayed in school, anxious to treat the injured coming home. At least at the hospital I could do something helpful.

A month before the war's end, I was inducted into the army. We all were, I think. I was twenty. I remember that I shot a cow. My rifle just went off. "Give a girl a gun," I told everyone, "who's looking for a thermometer, and see what you get. I think I shot the beast right where I'd have stuck that thermometer." I was still using comedy to hide my grief. I had to be strong for Mother.

No one laughed. Nothing was funny anymore.

At night during the blackouts with sirens screaming, Mother tended her roses. She had so many varieties: sweetbriar, tea, and dog roses; the heavy smell of apples from the sweetbriars wafted through the air. In the darkness, Mother pruned and removed the slugs and beetles she could see. These flowers were something bright, something of beauty, something to covet in a world gone mad.

After the war, Berlin was divided among the four Allies: the United States, the United Kingdom, France, and the Soviet Union. Unfortunately, Mother and I lived in the Soviet-occupied zone, and even though some of our neighbors had left their homes to stay with friends in the other occupied quadrants, my mother wasn't going anywhere. "Who's going to tend the roses?"

Then, with the war over and Germany defeated, everything went from bad to worse. I hadn't thought this possible. Already, I'd lost my brother and father, but then I came home from working at the hospital to find the lock on our front door busted.

"Mother," I called hesitantly, and heard men laughing. I thought about going for help, but there was nowhere to go. The street was abandoned. Entering our formal living room, I saw Mother. She wore a slip, bloody around her unmentionables. I can't tell anymore about this part, except that one of the soldiers pointed at me. They were going to have their fun with me next.

My mother told me to go. "Get out of here," she said. "Go now!" She had brown-cow eyes. Big saucers.

"*Mutter!*" *Mother!* She was all I had left in the world. I didn't want to go.

"*Du laufe!*" *Run!* she said.

But I couldn't move. Even knowing the soldiers meant to take me next, I couldn't leave my mother.

"*Du laufe, Inge!*"

"*Mutter!*" I tucked my hands into the pleats of my uniform.

One of the soldiers came toward me. He was eating a slab of some kind of meat.

"Jetzt! Du laufe, Jetzt!" Now! Run, now!

I dodged him. Then another soldier, who'd been sitting on the floor cleaning his fingernails with a knife, crawled toward me. They both spoke to me in Russian. I looked for a way to take Mother with me, but she was not moving. I couldn't understand the men, but I understood their tone well enough. I knew that I had to go. *Fight or flight* is something that's since been explained to me. I flew, and I'm not supposed to feel guilty for it.

Who, I ask, is guiltless?

Instead of heading for the front door, as the soldiers expected, I ran toward the back of the house, through the kitchen, and across the yard. It was pocked with recently dug holes, men searching for valuables, my mother's roses trampled.

I was being chased and so I ran without thinking. Frenzied, I fell, knocking my lip against the wrought-iron gate; a metallic taste of salt and blood filled my mouth, but I never stopped. I didn't look back. I didn't think on it then, but I lost my pretty smile. My tooth was chipped and my lip split. I still have the scar.

It was nearly a mile to the American camp where Frederick sat eating canned meat and crackers. He'd already made efforts to find his Uncle Joseph, to emigrate to America.

"Mutter!" I told him. I kept repeating *Mutter* and then I added "Russians" and "help."

Frederick held me tighter than anyone ever had. I remember that I bled on his shirt.

"You're safe." He kissed my forehead and cheeks. My front tooth had broken on the wrought iron fence where I'd fallen. He got a cool cloth and pressed it to my mouth. I yanked it away. "We have to do something!" I pulled away from him and, using my best English, begged the American soldiers to help me.

Frederick urged me to stop. "We'll get your mother," he said, "but it might take time." He was relieved that we'd be able to leave Europe and sail to America. His Uncle Joseph would sponsor us. I cared about nothing save my mother. Every time he tried to hold me, I fought him. I followed the American soldiers, who seemed to be standing around, doing nothing, except avoiding me. "No," they said, under no circumstance could they enter a Soviet-occupied zone.

I would not give up. All around, there were women setting up makeshift beds, men playing cards, children shooting marbles in the dirt. I remember the smell of boiling cabbage. "What if it was your mother?" I demanded of each soldier.

"Your mother . . ."

By the next morning, two soldiers were willing to help. One of them was a Russian translator. He had bribed Soviet guards with cigarettes and Wonder Bread before. He would help me. The other soldier loved and missed his mother. That was his singular motivation. Crossing into the Soviet zone, the American soldiers were understandably antsy. We all were. Thinking back, we were just kids. The Russians who accompanied us to my mother's house were also antsy because they weren't taking orders from anyone and they hadn't been for weeks. Their chain of command, whatever chain there'd been, had broken down. Anarchy reigned, and while it lasted, the Russian soldiers were pilfering money and food and whatever they could find of worth.

Entering my home, I immediately felt the emptiness of the place. I knew Mother was gone. Our family photographs had been smashed, glass littered the foyer. Our pantry door was open, the little food we'd had, gone. The sideboard drawers had been pulled out, piled by the steps. There were bloodstains on the duvet where I'd last seen my mother.

An American translator said something to the Russians, who shrugged. They had no idea. It must've been some Germans or maybe the Poles who'd done this. Probably the Poles. It would do no good to insist that my mother's murderers spoke Russian.

We found my mother, Emilie Vogel Kischel, in the bathtub. Even though her wrists were slashed, and my father's razor blade was in her grip, her hand resting on the porcelain ledge, I refused to think that she'd taken her life. I still don't believe it.

That afternoon, amid the shallow holes pocking our backyard, the two American soldiers and Frederick dug a grave. Hours must've passed, but I remember nothing of time, of the sun dropping lower in the sky. The one thing that has always stood out in my memory is the little girl who pushed open our wrought-iron gate just as the last shovelful of dirt was tossed aside. The men were breathing heavily, leaning against their shovels. The little girl came up and pulled at my skirt. "My mother said to bring you this." She placed a gold foil–wrapped marzipan chocolate in my palm. A cold wind lifted the hem of her soiled dress. As she turned to go, I said, "Thank you," noticing the grayness of her socks that drooped over untied laces. My mother was dead and my country in ruin.

"Who was that?" Frederick asked. The Americans propped their shovels in the dirt and motioned for Frederick to help them lift my mother's body. She was wrapped in a quilt that had been her mother's.

I shook my head that I didn't know the girl whose dirt-smudged face matched my mother's grave. Instead, I slowly unwrapped the chocolate, folding the foil into a tiny square, and as my mother was lowered into the grave, I sucked the marzipan from its chocolate shell.

I remember that I wanted to believe that the little girl was sending me a message from wherever the spirit goes when it departs this world. I wanted so badly to believe. All my life, I've tried to believe it. I've tried to believe in the goodness of life. The marzipan was flavored with sweetbriar roses, just like the ones Mother had grown. I could taste the flowers. Licking my fingers, I cried soundlessly as dirt rained down on her body. The marzipan melted on my tongue. Frederick squeezed my hand.

He is sixty-eight years old this year, and he is a good man.

The year is 1989.

I am going to meet my granddaughter.

7

Prudence, 2005

*L*ast month, two of my colleagues and I were walking home from an early dinner when I spotted a baby house finch, a downy thing with pinkish feathers, teetering on the pavement. As its mother squawked, the little bird attempted to camouflage itself beneath a pile of twigs. I looked around, but I couldn't spot the nest.

"Someone is going to step on it,"Whitney informed me. She teaches basic zoology.

Her girlfriend, Lenora, added, "That bird's going to get eaten by a snake or a cat. It's a goner."The sun had barely set, and the night had all the makings of a gruesome fairy tale. Being the bird girl, I was supposed to be the savior, but I had a very strong sense that this little finch was not injured, more likely a fledgling fallen from the nest. If I removed it from the twigs, it would never see its mother again.

As the sky darkened, melding from orange to pink, I explained with little confidence to Lenora and Whitney that this fledgling house finch did not need saving. He would fly by morning. They weren't so sure. As they walked to their car, I took a seat on the winding trail. I planned to keep watch. I was feeling then as I'm feeling now that we're each as vulnerable as that baby finch, little more than the gnash of beak and crunch of bone, in desperate need of someone to watch over us.

✳ ✳ ✳

In 1989, the Old Man called and made the most innocent proclamation. "I am telephoning to speak to my granddaughter, Prudence Vilkas. Do you know her? She is my family."

I knew her. "Yes, I know her. Yes . . . This is she. I am Prudence Vilkas."

"I am your grandfather. You are Lithuanian."

I don't know what my parents said to one another about this initial revelation. It didn't matter. It still doesn't. I knew that I had been found. Finally, there was someone to watch over me—not that my father had been *entirely* absent. Not that Veronica hadn't tried. She occasionally took me for a pedicure and a fancy green salad. I hate to have my feet touched and I don't like rabbit food, but I never said anything.

Freddie sent guitar picks and funny postcards. He came to visit once a year, typically when he was nearby, touring with some band. Veronica would drive me to a Ruby Tuesday or some other strip-mall restaurant and wait outside while my father bought me a hamburger and tried to catch up on the past year of my life.

Mostly, I talked about Wheaton. I didn't have a whole lot else to say. I was a good student and a bird watcher. My father took note, buying me a pair of high-dollar binoculars.

The fledgling cried out in the night, stirring the twigs. I was worried about a hawk swooping down. If I housed the little finch, he'd be safe for sure, but his mother hadn't abandoned him. If I removed the bird, she might.

My neighbor Carlos came out to see what I was doing, why I was sitting on the pathway, night falling. I indicated the bird. "But what are *you* doing, señorita?" he wanted to know.

"Keeping watch."

Throughout the night, the fledgling's mother flew down to feed. The baby bird tucked his beak into his breast to keep warm while the mother sang to him.

At first light, the fledgling burst free of the twigs. He kicked his feet like a runner at a starting line, flapped his wings, his head low to the ground, and after three wobbly attempts, my little house finch took flight. I watched his mother and then his father trail his course. I was eaten up with mosquitoes but I didn't care. I cried. At six a.m., I called Whitney to tell her the news. When I see the Old Man in the hospital, I'll tell him this story. The Old Man likes a good story.

We've been on the plane for forty-five minutes. The scotch has made my pilot neighbor loquacious. He doesn't like flying planes for rich people. He'd like to be rich. He'd like to have his own plane. I understand. I'd like to have my own boat, but I don't see it happening any time soon. I had wanted silence. I didn't want anyone telling me their problems. I have my own. But Sam Kirk is better than sitting beside Veronica. Like I said, his hair reminds me of Wheaton's.

8

Freddie

As a boy, Freddie Vilkas did not understand what his father knew implicitly, with every breath, with every pull on his cigar: that "family is most important." Freddie was a dreamer, and despite his father's tales of murder and mass graves at the hands of Joseph Stalin and his Cossacks, Freddie was an optimist.

In the 1960s, Freddie tried to tell his father, "The times, they are a-changing," and the Old Man laughed at him. "You're a fool, son. Nothing is changing until I can breathe in a free Lithuania. Stop being a hippie."

Born in 1951, Freddie could've been a hippie, but not in his father's house.

The Old Man pointed his finger, yellow from cigar smoke, at his only son. "I was born Frederick. My mother was loony-gooney because she was crazy about big birds, birds she read about in books. Birds that can fly for thousands of miles." The Old Man showed Freddie the sole remaining photograph of his family.

The picture had been taken two months before his family's demise, when his sisters were sixteen, seventeen, and eighteen. Daina was untamed with a penchant for tree climbing. The older girls were more serious, bookworms, studying medicine, playing bass and flute. All three were headstrong. The Old Man remembered his former self as protective of his sisters and his mother. When his father traveled, he was the man of the house. "It is not easy to be a survivor," he often said, "to be the one left behind."

Music was as much a part of the Old Man's childhood as his nightly meal. Music was a language kept and cherished. In music, there was history and joy. He could hold back tears. He could press his palms to his eyes and pretend he was blind and that the world was less ugly. In music, he could put aside the worst of the horror and eke out something beautiful, remember his youngest sister's face as she played violin, the concentrated gaze of a not-so-serious girl. Her name, Daina, meant song.

The Old Man hadn't protected anyone like he should have, but he could save the music. He tried to do this with his son. Freddie was born with a violin lodged between his chin and collarbone, made to practice two hours a day, the Old Man's wrist gliding the air like a maestro.

Brought up in the Catholic Church, Freddie suffered through public high school in high-water denim, his hair shorter than everyone else's. The girls laughed at his musty, ill-fitting jackets, his white tube socks and scuffed loafers. The Old Man told his son, "You complain about being bullied? You don't know what it is to be bullied. You know nothing. You understand nothing."

Freddie's mother tried to temper the Old Man's jabs: "How can he know what he did not live?" But no one could protect Freddie from the wrath of his community. When he was twelve years old, Freddie grumbled in church. The service had ended, and the parishioners were milling about, waiting to thank the priest. The entire congregation, and those who didn't hear, were later told, "Freddie Vilkas said, 'Lithuania wasn't even a country for very long. Nobody's ever heard of it.'" A collective gasp rose to the rafters.

The Old Man walked over to Freddie and smacked him. He pointed his finger. "You ungrateful, you. You keep your mouth shut forever." The collective gasp evolved into a collective but silent cheer. Freddie had it coming! How dare he disrespect his homeland? Even the priest comforted the Old Man: "One day, he will understand." The Old Man was ashamed of his son. Freddie was humiliated.

As long as Freddie lived in Bay Ridge, Brooklyn, he was Lithuanian. He would speak it, write it, and play its music. To do otherwise was unacceptable.

He tried.

When the Old Man was at work, Freddie sometimes handled the singular photograph, imagining his father's family as they might've been before Stalin killed them. Trying to imagine what his father and the other Lithuanians felt. But he couldn't, and it wasn't fair that he should suffer because of the past. Freddie was still under the illusion that the past is past, that it doesn't repeat itself, catch up with itself, loop over and over, unstoppable.

When Freddie was just a boy, he eyed the photograph with suspicion. Maybe the Old Man exaggerated the past. Maybe he couldn't think straight because he was old or because he'd survived a war. The Old Man was always old. Freddie was sick to death of him and his death stories. Freddie couldn't conceive of a world where grown men murdered girls.

The photograph's border was frayed by Freddie's eager hands. He wanted to know the truth. It was hard to tell what anyone looked like, but according to the Old Man, his mother was blond with a pert nose like a finch's beak. His father was tall with hair like his own, how the Old Man's hair used to be before he went gray. All three men had blue eyes, swirly ocean marbles. Daina had starburst eyes, hazel with an orange sun. Danutė and Audra had gray eyes, alternating hues of soft blues. They were both blond like their mother, Aleksandra, while Daina was brunette. The Old Man's father was named Petras. In the picture, Petras was supposed to look stoic, but a smile broke through. According to the Old Man, he was a jovial father when he should've been more serious.

At night, Freddie dreamed his grandfather Petras to life, but instead of a mass grave, Petras was blindfolded like in the movies. His last request was a cigarette, and a Russian general hurried to give it to him. In Freddie's subconscious, there was romance in everything. The Russian general flicked open his lighter, shielding it from the wind. Petras inhaled. With his hands tied loosely behind his back, the cigarette dangled above his handlebar moustache. Until the end, Petras wiggled his fingers, keeping time with some song. He was smiling and smirking, arrogant as hell—as heroes have license to be—when the bullet reached his brain.

Freddie lived between his dreams, between mythical dark pines coming to life and the Old Man's horror stories: "No one escaped! My sisters were butchered."

Freddie needed an ally: someone, anyone, who'd understand him. He managed to find this savior in an Italian kid named Marco. Marco's parents had suffered the wrath of Mussolini. They carried their own horror stories to the United States. Together, Marco and Freddie formed an alliance dedicated to living in the now. All things contemporary. Movies, comic books, girls, and music. In 1967, Freddie thought he'd move west when he graduated—find his place among the much-maligned hippies. Play in a band or something. There was no doubt he could play anything with strings. Even the Old Man had to admit, "I taught him well."

The day that Freddie left Brooklyn, the Old Man stood on the front stoop of their brownstone. He puffed and pointed a cigar. "You'll be back with your legs between your tail." He tended to reverse idioms. "You don't know nothing!" And speak in double negatives. "The world will eat you up."

Ingeburg watched from the window. She'd already said her good-byes. She'd given Freddie sixty dollars and a dozen Spam sandwiches.

The Old Man narrowed his gaze.

Ingeburg's palms itched and she broke out in a sweat. She banged on the wavy glass of the living room window—"Wait!"—and hurried onto the porch. "You have something for him! Don't you have something for him?" Her expression pained, she added, "Don't be not smart, Old Man. Don't be that way."

Freddie looked to his doting mother. "I don't want anything from *him*. I've had enough."

Ingeburg stared pleadingly at the Old Man, who dug into the left pocket of his high-waisted trousers. "Come here now!"

Freddie rolled his eyes but climbed the steps. Ingeburg's heart broke—seeing them together, so much alike, yet so different—seeing them part.

"Put your hand out, boy," the Old Man said.

"I'm not a boy."

"Do it."

Freddie held out his palm. He expected money, but he'd turn it down. He didn't want anything from his father. But then the Old Man did something unexpected. He pressed his father's gold timepiece into Freddie's palm, and cupping both hands around his son's, he said, "You can come home when you're ready."

Freddie looked at the watch. He was confused. *Why are you giving this to me?* He wanted the Old Man to say something kind, something apologetic, something meaningful about Freddie's ancestors and the timepiece. Unfortunately, the Old Man wasn't like that. He turned to Inge, flicking his cigar ash, and said, "I gave it to him. Are you happy?"

Freddie slipped the watch in his pocket. "Thanks." He was unsure what to say. Part of him wanted to fling the watch back at his father. *Screw you! My mother made you do this,* but Ingeburg had never made the Old Man do anything. Freddie didn't know how to feel. He walked toward the subway, singing a Beatles' song, *He's a real nowhere man / sitting in his nowhere land . . .* He was ready to start his own life.

In 1989, Freddie's former wife, whom he'd never bothered to divorce, contacted him, screaming into the telephone, "Your father had no right to call my home! Who the fuck does that old man think he is? He says he's coming here. He can't do that. You don't even pay child support." She was out of breath. "What is going on?"

"I'll take care of it." Freddie would've said just about anything to hang up with Veronica. There was a groupie in his bed. She'd planted herself there a day earlier and, except for moving naked between the bed, the refrigerator, and the bathroom, showed no signs of leaving. This was a serious problem but not an uncommon one. Just the same, he didn't want the mother of his only child to know that there was a woman in his bed. Freddie reassured Veronica, "I will handle it."

"And I'm supposed to start trusting you now?"

"You called me. Isn't that why you called me?"

No one had said anything about trust.

Freddie phoned the Old Man in Bay Ridge, Brooklyn. They hadn't seen each other since Freddie had left home, age eighteen. Ingeburg picked up. Overcome by the sound of his voice, she whispered, "Wait a second." She crept upstairs, where she continued to whisper. "I miss you. I love you. Your father loves you. It's hard for him to say what he feels. I don't know about Prudence. He is insisting we go to Florida . . . No. No. I do not know when. I am not a mind reader. You have to be a mind reader to know what this man is thinking one minute to the next. But no, he is not crazy. I think he is too sane. He talks too much these days. I like him better quiet. I need a respite . . . How are you? I miss you. A mother is supposed to see her son." Ingeburg had to say everything in one fell swoop.

Downstairs, she told the Old Man, "There's someone on the phone for you."

"When did the phone ring?"

"You must not have heard it."

The Old Man looked confused. "Who is it?"

"Just take it," she said.

Putting the receiver to his ear, the Old Man said, "Who is this? What do you want?"

"Dad," Freddie began, "I don't want anything."

The Old Man looked accusingly at Ingeburg. "Freddie's on the phone." Ingeburg shrugged. To his son, the Old Man said, "You always want something. You would not telephone if you do not want something."

"I called to say hello."

"Hello. Can we say good-bye now?"

"Dad! Listen: Veronica called me."

"Is that your wife who is not Lithuanian and not German, and not worth a cent red? The one you don't live with? The one you never talk to? Is that the wife you married without anyone's consent?"

"Yes, that's her. But that's beside the point. She said you called her house. She said you called Prudence. Why did you do that?"

The Old Man looked to Inge and pointed at his cigars before beginning his dissertation. "Listen, my one and only son, Freddie, I am an old man, but I remember that when the Nazis came and they chased the Soviets away, the first thing they did was write everything down. First names and last names and your parents' names and their parents' names. I knew enough German. I could say 'Heil Hitler.' I could say anything they want after the Red Army. The point is, I know your name. You are my son. You know my music. You are my son, but I do not know the little girl who is growing up, and she is your daughter, and I do not think that even you know her since you do not live with her, so I am going to see her. She is blood. I am going to introduce her to our Lithuania, a country that exists in the hearts of a people. I am a speech maker these days, but really, I am just an old man, and this is something I must do. Can you be there in Florida to keep your strange wife away from me? Or maybe she will want to hear about my sisters and your grandparents. I do not know. I know you, son, and I was wrong not to know my own grandchild before now."

In Nashville, the toilet flushed. The groupie was back in Freddie's bed.

Freddie asked his father, "When are you planning to go to Florida?"

"I don't know. We are asking Andrei one block down to help for the plan. He has been to Florida before. And I am only joking about you being there. You are too busy for us. We do nothing for you but give you life."

"I'll come home." Freddie peeked into his bedroom. The groupie was examining her legs.

"You'll do what?" The Old Man looked to Ingeburg. "He says that he'll come home."

Using calf muscles she'd forgotten she had, Ingeburg jumped, her old feet rising a good inch off the ground.

"Calm yourself down. He won't come home."

Folding her hands together, Ingeburg pressed them to her lips.

Freddie told his father, "Tell Mom that I'm coming."

"That's what the boy says, Inge." He grumbled, "I'll believe it when I see it." Surprisingly, the Old Man did believe it, and he felt a kinship to the son he had nearly disowned. Maybe age had made the boy Freddie wiser. Maybe age had made the Old Man softer. Either way, their lives were going to change irrevocably. The Old Man felt it. It felt good, like if he opened his mouth to scream, to warn his sisters that something bad was coming, they would finally hear him.

9

Prudence

*T*he clouds rolled in and bore down on the Los Vientos pier. The brown baggers weren't catching fish, just an occasional skate, their tails and wings twitching, the whiteness of their underbellies writhing on the concrete. The black storm clouds came in from the north and settled over us like squat men in capes. We could feel the darkness pressing down.

In Brooklyn, the Old Man kept dreaming, and in Los Vientos Wheaton had his visions. He gave them permanence in his brown notebook, sketching my wings. Like the rendering of the ghostly girl, they were veiled, not fully realized. But I knew them. Meanwhile, I felt them: long feathered things tickling my ankles, making me feel that any four walls were too cramped. We were three individuals feeling global shifts, cosmic ripples, a wall cracking, an iron curtain torn like dusty drapes, the reunification of the Vilkas clan. These things filled us from the inside, a collective breath holding.

It's a bumpy landing, and we're in the back of the plane. Sam Kirk and I wait patiently for the other passengers to gather their carry-ons. I wonder how the pilot would react if I ran my fingers through his candy hair. Not very well, I think.

"I need a glass of water," he says.

He's sticky with booze. Apparently, neither of us is in a hurry to get up. I pass him my water bottle. "It's been opened, but you can have the rest."

"Luckily, I'm not a germaphobe." He guzzles it down, confessing, "I'm better at flying than being a passenger." He sits up straighter. We watch the other passengers hurrying to disembark, pulling down square suitcases, mothers grabbing hold of children's hands, middle-aged women complaining about the rough landing, the businessmen folding their papers, their *Wall Street Journal* and *New York Times*, securing their laptops, looking anywhere but at the other passengers. Sam Kirk, my new friend, says, "I'm going to see my mother." He reaches in the seat-back for a spiral notebook and a pencil.

"That's nice," I tell him.

He holds up the pencil. "Not really. I come once a month to write down her memories."

I'm perplexed, and it shows. Is the pilot also a writer?

He says, "Usually, I drink too much, but it's not like she notices. She has Alzheimer's, and it's getting worse. The only thing she wants is for me to write down her stories and then, when it's worse, and she doesn't know who she is, to read them back to her. She lives in Greenpoint, Brooklyn, and last month, she asked me, 'Do you know where I am? Am I still in Greenpoint?'" He grimaces. "She whispered, 'I don't know where I am, and I'm afraid to ask anyone.' Then she said, 'I'm scared. I'm really scared, Roy. I don't want to lose my mind.' Roy was my brother. He's been dead ten years."

Sam Kirk looks like he's going to cry, and I think about the Old Man. Is he really finally *old*? Will he know me? Does he know Oma? Nothing is more important to him than his family. *He can't lose us.* Then, I do the unexpected. I slip my fingers under Sam Kirk's blond curls. Instead of pulling away, he leans closer, and we stay like that, his sour breath under my nose, on my collar, and in my ear. We look like lovers.

The flight attendants have begun sweeping and collecting trash. Sam Kirk touches my hand, my fingers still twisted in his hair. His eyes are filled with tears. He says, "There's a woman who comes during the day, and my mother has neighbors and friends who stop by, but I don't know for how much longer." We separate slowly, gracefully. He opens the spiral notebook. The pages are filled with blue script, the pilot's hand. "I never dreamt that my mother would have so many things to say. I never imagined that it would get worse so damn fast, and that's what it is now. This month, I'm reading to her." I squeeze his hand, and he squeezes back. "I'm reminding her who she is." As I get up, he awkwardly pulls his wallet out. "My card," he says. "Here. Let me give you my card." Sam Kirk is lovely, but he has the wedding-band tan. Just the same, I take the card. He's going to see his mother, and I am going to see the Old Man.

Veronica is already at baggage claim. She still smokes, so she's eager to get outside for a cigarette. "Where were you? What took you so long?"

"I was in the back of the plane." We don't see her suitcase. "Maybe we should go to Oma's before the hospital?"

Veronica's features soften. "We can do that." She squeezes my wrist. "If that's what you really want to do." Sometimes I make my mother out to be this horrible person, but she's not. She's got heart. She doesn't always show it. She's terrified of being vulnerable. I guess we all are.

"I don't know," I waffle. We had to get to the airport three hours before our flight. "I mean, we could rest up a bit." Veronica knows what I'm doing—postponing the inevitable.

"Your Oma said that he doesn't have much time," she reminds me. "The Old Man is old. He's lived a long life." This is not what I want to hear. It's June 4, 2005, a Saturday. I think I understand the Old Man better than anyone, and this isn't a long life. Not long enough.

Freddie thought that his father lived in the past, but the truth was that the Old Man couldn't escape the past. If he'd been able to forget, maybe he would have. He's always felt guilty for surviving, but whenever he told his story, he kept them, each of them, his mother, his father, and his sisters, alive in some small way. Without a survivor, there's no one to tell the story.

On June 14, 1941, in Vilnius, Lithuania, the Old Man's mother,

Aleksandra, was carried away, a soldier's hand squeezing each elbow, her black shoes brushing the ground. She was a beautiful woman born exiled in Kazakhstan. She had walked with Petras, the Old Man's father, back to a home known only through song and story.

At the train station, the Old Man's little sister Daina, the songbird, squeaked, "I'm coming, Mother," and chased after, but a soldier pointed his gun at Daina and said, "*Begi!*," which Daina knew to mean "Run!" Her mother told her, "Go now!" Daina ran home to her sisters. Finding no one, she hid in an upstairs closet. As you've heard, *Daina* means "song." Run sounds like *run* in every language. Three years later in Germany, Ingeburg knew to run. The word *run* is conveyed in the eyes, in one look. Ingeburg had fallen and cracked her tooth, tasted blood. She could imagine the Old Man's little sister running, but there'd been no place to go.

Back at the train station, with the extra push of two Russian soldiers, Aleksandra boarded a cattle car bound for the northern Urals. In the center of the car, there was a hole for urination and defecation. In the center of the car, huddled around this hole, there were women and children and babies. In this place at this point, it was hardest to breathe. Bodies were pressed tight against one another. When the train slowed, there were mothers who dropped their babies through the cattle car's hole, counting on the kindness of a passing stranger to save their infant.

As the train rumbled north, growing colder, the dead were piled on one side of the locked car while the living cowered on the other. The survivors huddled close to keep from freezing, knowing that they were to be worked to death, possibly shot in the back of the head. Why were they singled out for such a cruel fate? Because they were educated? Because they'd been enemies of Russia at one time or another? Because they were landowners? There was no rhyme or reason.

My father heard pieced-together versions of this story from his father, but being a consummate optimist, Freddie imagined that the grandmother he never knew was in a train car that ran off the tracks. Freddie imagined this train car hurtling down an icy hill, the side of the metal car cracking open like an ostrich egg, launching Aleksandra and the other women high into the air. Up there, in the cold temperatures, the air would be frozen. Time would stop. It was easy enough to imagine the spirit of vast-winged birds, knowing the gift of freedom, inhabiting each woman and child, each soul reborn a big gooney bird able to traverse the Pacific.

Early in the morning on June 14, 1941, before the sun, before Aleksandra was taken to a waiting train, Russian soldiers came to the front door of the Vilkas home and shouted things too loudly and quickly. They said that the Old Man's father was a criminal, an enemy of the people. Daina and her sisters gathered behind their father. The Old Man's mother cinched a robe at her waist. Incensed and confused, she stood apart from her daughters. "What is going on?"

It was only then, half-asleep, that the Old Man, who was twenty, practically a boy, still Frederick, came down the stairs. "What time is it?" He yawned.

His mother was livid. She screamed at the soldiers, "Just what do you think you're doing?"

Frederick rubbed his eyes. "What's going on here?"

The soldiers struck Petras with the butt of a rifle. As he fell to his knees, Frederick, a bookish university student, threw his hands in the air. He had long supple fingers and strong narrow wrists. This is the unraveling of the Vilkas clan. Young Frederick's violinist hands are helpless, unable to disturb the universe. There is a war raging inside and out.

The soldiers pulled the Old Man's father to his feet and bound his hands behind his back. Frederick's three sisters crossed their hands like wings, covering their O-shaped mouths. If anyone had pried the girls' fingers apart, the pent-up squeals of horror would've made the soldiers' ears bleed. Frederick put his arms around his mother, demanding, "Let our father go this instant." The soldiers laughed at him. Frederick lunged, but his sisters, their hands still over their mouths, formed a blockade, their shoulders and legs entangling him. *No, Frederick. You are not going with Father.* The soldiers tore quickly through the foyer closet, laughing at ladies' hats and shoes. All the while, Frederick's father was bound, helpless. His lip bled. Aleksandra punched at one of the soldiers, who smacked her face. Frederick lunged yet again, but his sisters were fierce, even in their long nightgowns. Already, they seemed of some other world, like mythical sirens, whose voices if released would crack the center beam overhead—sending shards of pine and plaster onto the interlopers' heads, but the girls were silenced, their mouths puckered shut, their forces drained.

Petras Vilkas was taken at gunpoint across green fields to an area behind the slaughterhouse where a mass grave had already been dug by other captives. Frederick ran as fast as he could to keep up with his father, who was still bound, rolling in the back of a Russian truck. When his father was pulled from the truck, Frederick watched from a canopy of pine. He had to do something. He had to protect his father. He had to protect his mother and sisters. Frederick's father was propped beside the hole. The town banker was among the men whose hands were tied behind their backs. Frederick watched as the soldiers went from man to man, taking their jewelry and identification. "Get on your knees," they ordered. Most of the Lithuanian men knew Russian, but they didn't obey. The soldiers prodded them with rifles. From his hiding spot, Frederick felt like a coward, but he didn't know what to do. His father was on his knees facing a pit. It was a hole the size of which someone would dig to lay the foundation for a house or pour a concrete basement. It was not meant for the bodies of grown men. Frederick convulsed and wept silently. What could he do?

There were no cigarettes and no blindfolds, and it's doubtful that, as much as Freddie the hippie would like to think his grandfather had a song in his head, Petras Vilkas was thinking about anything but his family's fate. His beautiful wife. His daughters and son. From the pines, Frederick saw that his father still had his pocket watch. It glinted, sandwiched between his bound wrists, in the morning sun. Frederick watched as his father and eighty-three other Lithuanian men were shot in the backs of their necks and booted face-first into the mass grave. Some of the soldiers were laughing and smoking like this was all in a day's work. Frederick wanted to look away, but he didn't. Some of the men in the pit were still alive, but the dirt came just the same. It covered ministers and machinists. It dusted blacksmiths, accountants, and doctors. It fell in rich clumps over lawyers, shop clerks, poets, teachers, and musicians. It didn't discriminate. The rich Lithuanian soil tended by its people was being used to conceal their deaths.

More trucks arrived. More men died. In shock, Frederick watched. He did not blink. The image of mass murder, of his father's death, was stamped, a black stain, into memory. It was on this day that Frederick first became an old man.

When the soldiers were gone, he crept from his hiding place. Because it seemed like the most important thing to do, the Old Man clawed through the dirt to find his father. The Old Man was an innocent. Despite witnessing his father's demise, he never thought a bloody fate would befall his mother or sisters, who were surely safe at home. Like his future son, he believed, *Men don't butcher women.*

As the Old Man dug, he heard moaning and pleas for help. He was able to pull some men, half-alive, to the surface. One man, a local poet, helped him dig for and uncover his father.

Petras's body was face down, another corpse across the back of his knees. Just the same, for a second, the Old Man was able to raise his father's torso enough to see his face, his expression one of horror and disbelief. Even as his life had been snuffed, his gold watch, lodged between his wrists, kept time. The Old Man vomited in the pit. He hoped that the single bullet had killed his father. This was better than imagining him suffocating to death, the Lithuanian soil filling his lungs.

The Old Man rubbed the dirt off the gold watch and pressed it to his lips. The poet, who was named Arturas, thanked the Old Man for saving his life. Likewise, the Old Man thanked him for helping to find his father. They grasped hands, each man crying, wishing the other luck. There was nothing else to do. The Old Man secured the watch in his coat pocket, careful to push it down deep and button the flap. Then, he ran home as fast as he could to tell his mother and sisters that Petras was dead. They would have to flee, but he didn't know where they would go.

The Old Man had no concept of how long it had taken to help three men to the grave's surface, or how much time had elapsed since he'd followed the Russian truck. When he arrived home, his mother was on her way to Siberia. His sisters were gone. According to the neighbor, their bodies had been removed, heaved into the back of a truck. Nothing remained of his family, nothing but bloody bedcovers. That day, the Old Man lost any optimism that he might've inherited from his father. The Old Man looked around his empty boyhood home, picked up the family portrait they'd recently had taken, and sliding it from the silver glass frame, put it in his pocket where the watch was secured. Without his family, the house was a tomb.

On the back stoop, he surveyed the land and wondered, *What do I do? Where do I go?* He considered seeking refuge at the university. He didn't know that his professors had been the first men and women rounded up. He sat on the back stoop, staring at the forest. His mother had told stories about the trees marching to protect the Lithuanian freedom fighters. She told stories about black bears, reincarnated freedom fighters protecting the pines and the people. He stared unblinkingly at the forest. *Fairy tales.* His body was caked with death and dirt. When he saw his next-door neighbor Nelly Straż running toward him, he didn't move. She was sixteen, the same age as his sister Daina. "You have to hide," she said. Frederick didn't acknowledge her. He had no will. She told him, "They'll come back for you."

Nelly took his hand and tried pulling him off the stoop. He didn't budge. "Come with me," she begged. Frederick stared into space.

"They killed your sisters! You have to get out of here."

The Old Man was angry that he'd believed in the brave bears and marching pines. It was useless.

Nelly pleaded, "Come on. Get up now! We have to get out of here!"

The Old Man looked disappointedly at the forest. Of course, his mother told fairy tales. That's what mothers do. Nothing mattered anymore. He rose, letting Nelly lead him across the field toward her house. She said, "There's a bed in the basement. Mother's got a pot of soup on to boil." She patted his hand. "You'll be all right." She said it again, "You'll be all right." She said this as though she were the one who needed convincing. She was sixteen, the Old Man was twenty, and the world was mad, terribly, horribly so.

Within a few days, the Germans, who'd made a pact with the Soviets, broke this pact. Hitler decided that he wasn't going to let the Soviets keep Lithuania, or Estonia, or Latvia. Or Finland or part of Poland either. The German tanks rolled north and east. The Soviet tanks retreated.

The Straż family who hid the Old Man in their basement were Jewish—as the Old Man constantly reminded Ingeburg. In 1940, when Soviet tanks rolled into Lithuania, the Straż family had waved a Russian flag. They figured they had a better chance of surviving a Soviet regime than a Nazi one. But many of the Lithuanian families who hated the Soviets equally hated the Jews for waving their Russian flags. As the Germans marched into Lithuania, these families waved Nazi flags, hopeful that Hitler would be better than Stalin. There was no lesser of two evils.

Less than a month after the Old Man went into hiding from the Russians, the Nazis came to the front door of the Straż house. They informed the Straż family that they needn't pack anything. They wouldn't be gone long, just long enough to register as Jews. There were public documents testifying to their Judaism, and additionally, their neighbors had reported them as Soviet sympathizers.

They were certainly Jewish, but first and foremost, the Straż family was Lithuanian.

The Gestapo found Frederick in the basement and, grabbing him by his overcoat, pulled him up the stairs. He wasn't registering with the others. They already knew who he was, and he wasn't a Jew. They seemed to know everything. It was unnerving. One of the Nazis, a man twice Frederick's age, punched him playfully in the arm. "You hid among the vermin." The Nazi smiled before he spit on the Straż family room floor. The Old Man slid his finger into his trouser pocket to check for his watch and his photograph. They were safe. "Where's Nelly?" he asked.

"Where's Nelly?" the soldier mocked. "Never you mind."

The Germans advised the Old Man that he would be serving the Führer and the German people in the war effort. Words failed the Old Man. It was astonishingly clear that he was as significant as a nit on someone's scalp, irritating because he was there, but ultimately inconsequential.

On the eighth day of the Old Man's march toward Germany, the Straż family was exterminated, a bullet to each brain at the Ninth Fort, a former Soviet prison. They were Sasha, thirty-eight, Ibrahim, forty, Nelly, sixteen, Andrew, fifteen, and Yana, eight. Sasha and Ibrahim tried to barricade their children from the bullets, to no avail. Like the Old Man's family, they were guilty of nothing.

The Old Man marched, a young man caught between monsters. As he walked, he remembered his family's music: his mother's voice, his father's violin, his sister's flute, and he breathed in time with his memory. He was an old man hobbling over rocky terrain toward a foreign land. The Germans told him that Hitler had saved him, that he owed his life to the Führer. They were liars. All of them! The Nazis and the Reds. His feet were tired. As a boy, he'd been taught that good triumphs over evil, but it hadn't. It didn't.

The Germans searched him for weapons. Surprisingly, they let him keep his watch and his photograph. As a group, the soldiers were well fed and well ordered. Amid such insanity, it was uncomfortably *wrong* that there was the pretense of humanity.

The Old Man counted the days like beats. He tried to put the image of his father and the other men out of his mind, but it was impossible. No amount of steps or days would accomplish that feat. Nothing would ever be one note, one chord, or one pitch again. Not forgetting, not believing, and definitely not living. With the greatest clarity, he pictured his mother rubbing her throat, opening her mouth to sing, the songbirds perched around their summer home on the coast of Palanga. The Old Man kept this sweet blue memory lodged in his parched throat, like a robin's egg, making it difficult to swallow.

10

Prudence

Night after night, the rest of the world slept under a blanket of dark clouds, their window units buzzing and hiccupping, and I went alone to the pier. To Wheaton, I pretended that I'd given up on seeing the ghost of a girl, but I hadn't. She and I were connected. I needed to know if there were others like us. At first, Wheaton did not understand that this had nothing to do with him. This was about me. This was mine, and I plainly told him so.

In May 1989, my father kept his word to his parents and drove his Chevette, lovingly called a "shit-vette," north. I'm sure that he nervously rehearsed what he would say to the Old Man when they came face-to-face. Although he hadn't seen his father since leaving home, he had seen my Oma. She told me that they'd met secretly at a coffee shop in the Wall Street district while the Old Man sat in their Brooklyn brownstone, smoking his cigars, thinking Ingeburg was out shopping or getting her hair done or doing any number of things women do. Things he needn't be bothered with.

During their clandestine mother-son meetings, my Oma encouraged Freddie to file for custody of me. She didn't know that Freddie and Veronica were still married or that as much as he loved me, he couldn't ask Veronica to give me up. Even though she'd walked out on him, he felt guilty. Music had been his first love. Then it was me and music second. Freddie didn't suspect anything would change the order of things he loved. Veronica would always come third.

During their secret visits, my Oma held back judgment while Freddie talked about possible recording deals. She humored him by asking for specifics, but she didn't imagine a man who could love an instrument before a woman would have much luck in life, not at anything, even a musical career. It seemed to my Oma that a profound love was necessary to make beauty from any art, musical or otherwise. I can picture my Oma during these coffee-shop meetings with her chipped tooth and the pink scarf that always covers her set curls.

Then in 1989, the secret meetings ended. Freddie was coming to them. He was driving to Brooklyn. My father and grandfather were going to meet face-to-face. My Oma anticipated meeting her granddaughter shortly thereafter. She was as anticipatory as anyone. Myself included.

Freddie drove through the night, stopping only for gas. He remembered a song: *I don't care if it rains or freezes, long as I got my plastic Jesus.* He smiled. Music was his way of praying.

The brownstone had not changed. Downstairs, he smelled lemon-scented liquid Pledge. Upstairs, mothballs. His mother was hysterical, hugging him and retreating, hugging him and retreating. She covered her mouth, her chipped tooth. "I've missed you so much, Freddie. Sit down, or you can stand, but have a seat. Relax. It's so good to see you." She hugged him again. She couldn't stop. "When your father said that you are coming, I never believed it."

The Old Man was waiting in the downstairs study, playing Shostakovich's Violin Concerto no. 1. Seeing Freddie, he stopped. "I can't play how I used to because of the arthritis."

Ingeburg said, "Your father is fine. He exaggerates."

Freddie said, "It sounded good, Dad."

"You play, Freddie. Put down your guitar case, and you play for your father." He extended the violin to his son.

"Maybe later."

"Why not now? Play now."

Freddie didn't want it to be this way.

The Old Man said, "Don't you practice?"

"I'm beat, Dad."

His father pointed the bow at him. "You do nothing but what is best for Freddie. Always, and you never change."

Freddie looked at his mother. "It was a long drive."

"Go rest. Your room is nice for you."

At dinner, the Old Man sopped his plate with a hunk of bread. "Your mother is not going to fly in an airplane, so I arranged for a car to rent. It is settled."

"Nothing's settled," Freddie said.

The Old Man looked to Ingeburg. "Tell your son."

"We're going to meet her," she told Freddie, "with or without you."

The Old Man added, "It's time. We should've done this sooner. For this, I have regret."

Freddie had never gone against his mother, and he realized that he never would. He put his napkin beside his plate and cleared his throat. A change of heart. "I'll drive."

"We are taking a rental car. Do you have a valid license?"

"Of course."

"How do I know this?" the Old Man asked.

My Oma reached for Freddie's hand, feeling the striations on his fingertips. "Thank you." He was a good boy. Always, he'd been a good boy.

When Freddie called Veronica from his parents' house, he locked their bedroom door to use the phone. He was prepared to face his estranged wife's wrath. He could admit that he was a deadbeat dad, but he couldn't deny his mother her wish to meet her granddaughter—not anymore.

"You're not coming here," Veronica told him. "They're not coming here."

✳ ✳ ✳

It happened on this particular night, with so much at stake, that I felt my wings emerge once more, slicing like paring knives through my back. Outside, the crickets chirped, and inside, my invisible wings expanded, making a hushed sound that only I could discern. I felt this sensation like fingertips tinkling my flexed back. I stood near my mother, hoping she could sense them, the wings in the room. They were lush and majestic. I remember. Veronica told Freddie, "I am her mother. You can come, but this is on my terms."

I crossed my arms over my chest, feeling like that angel or fairy or butterfly Wheaton had mentioned when we were seven. God, I loved Wheaton. I don't know how I would've survived without him.

My mother complained to Freddie about child support, how she'd like to see some of that coming her way. I lit one of her cigarettes. My wings started to sag. I felt them pulling from my skin, at the itchy spot where my scars resided. It seemed like the wings wouldn't be around for very long, like they were too miraculous for me to possess. Veronica continued her treatise, her conditions. "I'm not leaving her alone with them."

The lushness of my wings was devolving into weightiness, two fists pulling me down.

My father never asked to speak to me.

Veronica put the phone down. My knees buckled from the heaviness of my wings. She said, "They want to meet you because they're old. Because they're going to die one day. Because everybody dies." It felt like there was a wet blanket draped over my shoulders, like the vinyl flooring and Styrofoam ceiling had conspired to come together and squash me like a bug. Veronica picked up her purse, and checking to see how many cigarettes I had smoked, said, "I'll see you later." I didn't know where she was going.

She hurried from the house, and I had no idea if she was ever coming back. I was sixteen. I wasn't so old, but I was painfully sad. Wheaton was out of town. He never went anywhere, but on this particular night, he was gone.

I heard the car start. I didn't know Veronica's friends or her boyfriends. I didn't know what she did when she wasn't working. Her life was work. Then she was backing out of our yard. I watched from the den window, where I saw the reflection of my wings in the glass. Somehow their presence only made me sadder. Ghostly wings are as useful as a ghostly girl.

Wheaton had traveled across state to a cheerleading competition with his mother and sister. Even though he'd had no choice, I remember being angry at that moment. Everyone had turned against me. My mother was right: these old people wanted to meet me, but I didn't know them. My father was only coming because *they* wanted him to. *Did any of this have anything to do with me?* I showered, letting the water beat down on my wings. I was still crying, trying to be hopeful, trying to think that someone gave a shit about *me*, but overwhelmed with an indescribable hopelessness, like a bottomless pit. I didn't really have wings. Some doctor had put me under anesthesia and taken them. My parents had let him. I didn't have much of anything. My best friend had visions. He could see this winged girl on the pier, but she wouldn't make herself known to me. I got to my knees, pressing my hands against the algae-stained tiles, the water streaming over the back of my head, my forehead to the drain. I was not and never had been any better or any more special than anyone else.

I didn't try to kill myself. Not that night. Not ever. There are some accounts, police reports, that claim differently, but they are just wrong. I would never take my own life, but there was something that compelled me on that stormy night to venture to the pier. Maybe it was the weight of my wings, the distance between me and my parents, the desire to be free of this place, or the proximity of possibility. Maybe I was afraid that my grandparents would come and then they wouldn't like me. I'd be a disappointment.

I wore a vintage lavender nightgown purchased at the Goodwill. I was barefoot, my hair pulled back in a ponytail. Later, when the police asked me why I went to the pier at midnight, I had no answer for them. I'm still not certain. Something pulled me there. When I stepped off my front stoop, the stars were like a map to the sea. I don't think I ever looked down at the sandspurs, tufts of brown grass, or briars but walked, a straight shot, to the pier. It felt good to have direction.

The rest is murky like Florida's stormy coast that night. I remember two lights blinking and swaying with a gale-force wind blowing out of the east. My nightgown clung to my breasts and legs, ballooning out behind me. The concrete felt good on the bottoms of my feet. I thought I saw the ghost of the girl, but I was squinting my eyes, wishing I had Wheaton's gift of sight, wishing that I understood my destiny. Did I even have one or was everything random? I had the distinct feeling that Freddie was probably telling his parents that he hardly knew me, that I wasn't worth their time or trouble. I remember thinking that my grandparents would hate my thick dark hair, my combat boots and black eyeliner. I wouldn't be the girl they hoped to see. My eyes were green with an orange starburst. My mother's were brown. My father's were a beautiful bright blue. Where did I come from? Who wanted to claim me? I think that if Wheaton had been home on the night of May 15, 1989, I would've gone to him. I would've told him my insecurities, and he would've said, "You have to have faith, Prudence. Wait and see what happens because something is going to happen."

But Wheaton wasn't there.

I did *not* jump. I know that I didn't. I wouldn't do that.

The salty spray and driving wind slicked my hair back. I licked the spray from my lips. *Dear Prudence, let me see you smile.* I started crying again, but the wind whisked away my tears. Did Freddie care about me? Did Veronica? Would I ever be whole again? I don't remember if I pulled my nightgown overhead or if it tore free. I remember the darkness, whitecaps on the water, an eggplant sky. I was perched on the ledge. I was careful, wiggling my toes. I remember thinking that I wouldn't fall because the wind was blowing against me, blowing me back toward the safety of the pier's walkway. It was nice up there. I was naked, licked clean by salt. My invisible wings expanding, growing, spreading, how they did that first time in the audiovisual room. Not heavy but pulsing. I wasn't going to jump. I'll admit that I did want to fly. I recall the wind spinning me up, tornado fashion, hurling me like a speck, and for a second, I thought I would drop safely, disappointingly to the pier, but my wings caught the wind. I ascended—for a second or more. For two seconds. Maybe three. I thought I would fly away. But these wings I carried were only ghost wings. I plummeted, dropped forty feet, my heels striking the water's surface. I submerged into the bottomless deep.

For a little bit, all was dark, murky, like that whole night. Below the surface, I awoke to luminescent jellyfish with tentacles like fingers, holding, caressing me. All around, there was luminescent plankton like stars. An octopus pulsed past. The jelly tentacles clung to me, the surf like boiling stew. Anemones and silver fish ripped past, then brighter fish, orange and green zip lines, the waves like puppet masters, maneuvering my arms and legs, lifting me up and dropping me down. I swallowed the sea and it likewise me. The puppet master left me pressed against a barnacle-covered piling. My body was limp, my strings cut. The barnacles scraped and sliced my skin, glowing now like the jellyfish. Then I saw the winged girl swimming toward me. She was real. I could see her. I had told Wheaton that she was mine. She belonged to me. Maybe I was dead. With black hair floating and wings enormous, she came. I reached for her hand and caught it. She grabbed back. Her fingers were rough, striated, how I remembered my father's hands. She was holding tight, pulling me away from the piling, but I didn't want to go. Her mouth was open. Her eyes were green with orange starbursts. Like mine. I knew her. That's the last I remember.

11

Prudence

On the night that I tumbled off the pier, I thought I had died. When I saw the ghostly girl beneath the waves, I thought I was in another world. But I did not die. My savior was a homeless man curled up under one of the benches halfway between the beach and my falling-off point.

He rolled over to pull his coat tighter where his zipper was broken, and seeing something in the distance, crawled out from beneath the bench to try and make out what it was. At one time, he'd worn glasses for astigmatism, but hadn't worn them in many years. Reportedly, he saw a giant bird perched on the ledge. Then he rubbed his eyes and saw a person standing there. He claims that I stepped off the edge. Hearing the splash, he went to the pay phone at the pier's entrance and called the operator. He told her, "At first, I thought I saw a bird, but then it had arms and legs." The operator notified the Coast Guard and the police, and they notified the local hospital.

Coast Guard helicopters were dispatched to search the choppy water. Because of the dangerous surf, I was presumed dead. I don't re-member being pulled from the water or flying in a helicopter to the hospital in Jacksonville. "She's not a bird," the Coast Guard men joked, but I was surprisingly easy to spot beneath their searchlight. Covered in bioluminescent plankton, I was a five-point star. Jellyfish tentacles were strung across my arms and legs.

When I woke in the hospital, I was examined by a smiling nurse and an icy doctor, who only made contact when he shined a light in my eye. At two a.m., I told the nurse my name and phone number. They telephoned Veronica. My next visitors were policemen. They told me that committing suicide was illegal, not just with the Catholics but also with the local government. At five a.m., I saw Veronica. She was pale, the crunchiness washed clean from her hair. Already she'd telephoned Freddie, who was still in Brooklyn. My room had its own phone, and while the nurse checked my temperature, Veronica was on with Freddie again. She told him that I would be okay, whispering, "I don't know what happened." She felt guilty, I think, for telling me that my grandparents only wanted to meet me because they were old.

Freddie wanted to talk to me. Veronica handed me the phone. I remember telling him, point-blank, "I didn't jump off the pier. I fell or something."

He said, "We're coming to see you. We're driving."

"I'm going home tomorrow." I started to tell him our address.

"Honey," he said, his voice cracking, "I know where you live." He said, "I love you very much." I refused to cry. Then he explained that my Oma had a propensity toward blood clots, so they'd have to stop every two or three hours for her to stretch her legs. He said, "I'm sorry that I didn't call on your birthday," and then he started crying. "I love you so much, little bird." He was crying so hard that it sounded like he was hyperventilating. I was callous, a little satisfied by his tears. He could cry, but I wouldn't.

The nurses were kind. They told me, "No more night swimming." They laughed a lot, squeezing my forearm, feeling sorry for me. Then a social worker came to interview me. I didn't mention my wings. I had learned from Wheaton not to say anything surprising or unusual, lest I get thrown into some institution like the Gardens. Instead, I told the social worker that I'd gone for a walk. I wanted to see what it felt like to stand over a dark ocean. I was pensive because I knew that my grandparents were coming. It was windy. I slipped. Basically, everything was true, except that I wanted to see what it felt like to fly. Maybe, for those three seconds, I did fly. Like Freddie and the Old Man's old man, I was an optimist. I was born with wings. How could I be otherwise?

On the afternoon of May seventeenth, a Wednesday, I was released into Veronica's care. I pretended to sleep on the car ride home. When we pulled into the driveway, Wheaton was waiting. I emerged from the car, stiff and bruised from the water forcing me into the piling, and Wheaton grabbed hold of me, pinning my arms to my sides, squeezing me harder than he ever had. I didn't think he was going to let go. Already, he was counting, murmuring, "You don't want to die," making sense of what had happened. *You don't want to die* is five syllables thumb to pinky. *You don't want to die* is much better than *You want to die*, which would leave you one shy, hanging on the ring finger. He said another five syllables, "Don't ever leave me," and stopped squeezing.

We spent the rest of that evening hand in hand sitting on a blanket watching sandpipers dart through the surf. Veronica packed us a picnic dinner. Wheaton never asked if I was trying to kill myself. I'm certain he knew the answer. He said that Tammy had come in second place in her cheerleading competition and he reminded me that I was his best friend. I already knew. I told him that he would always be my best friend, and we lay back, our faces to the waning light, digging our heels in the sand. Wheaton said, "I know that your grandparents are going to love you." It was only thirteen syllables, but it was the exact right thing to say.

On June 3, 1989, Veronica gathered dishes and opened windows to air out the smokiness. She wanted to impress Freddie and the in-laws she'd never met. One day earlier, she'd had her hair cut into a bob. No more hairspray. She looked good, better than the Barbie she'd become.

I didn't want to alter anything about myself before I saw my dad or met my grandparents. In a way, I wanted to be at my worst. I wore jean shorts and black boots with the tongues turned down. My Pixies T-shirt was torn *Flashdance*-style at the shoulder. I wanted them to like me for who I was. I couldn't pretend anymore, and I was too exhausted to be nervous.

Freddie drove the rented Oldsmobile across the bridge separating our island from Saint Mark's. This would've been his first time in Los Vientos, so I imagine he saw the shabby billboard proclaiming "Welcome to Los Vientos Beach," with "Welcome to" crossed out and the word *SUCKS* spray-painted in all caps. (We always met in Saint Mark's.) Freddie and my grandparents would've seen the neon pink and turquoise Bunny Motel, and possibly the Bunny's resident nudists, Earl and Liz—a Los Vientos treasure. They would've passed Big Sal's, serving "All-You-Can-Eat Hotcakes" and "Pig-Happy Barbeque," and the Dunes Smacker, a hole-in-the-wall frequented by the pier dwellers.

Driving even farther, they would've seen our concrete pier. It was *the* pier, the one I'd fallen from. I'm sure that Freddie slowed down, hoping I hadn't tried to kill myself, hoping that I wasn't going to do anything irrational. He'd told his parents nothing about my recent hospitalization. He hadn't wanted to upset them. I understood. I didn't particularly want them to know.

Past the pier, there were rows of squat homes, some coquina, some wood siding, others cinder-block, and then there was our house, and then there was me waiting on the front porch with Wheaton while Veronica was indoors dusting, wearing a real apron. The Oldsmobile turned up our driveway, which was no more than scrub grass and gravel. Veronica peeked through the blinds. I didn't know what to do, where to put my hands or how to pose, but I stood tall, my hands at my sides like I was ready for the firing squad. Freddie was out the driver's door fast, a cigarette dangling from his lips. He opened his mother's door while the Old Man, who was just sixty-eight in 1989, said, "Is this the place?"

My Oma told Freddie, "Enough with the smoking."

I looked at the Old Man and he looked back, each of us examining the other.

"Who are you?" he said, walking toward me. Freddie was still helping Ingeburg because her legs were stiff from the drive. Her varicose veins mapped the life of a woman who'd spent too many years on her feet. If you followed the blue veins north, they expanded into stretch marks, a gift from Freddie. If you followed them south, they led to hammertoes. There is something surprisingly beautiful about my Oma's imperfections, the black hairs growing above her lip, her chipped tooth and scarred lip. She is a testament to living. I watched her grab the cigarette from between Freddie's lips and drop it to the cracked walk.

"Who are you?" the Old Man said again, his voice gruff. He pointed at me. "Are you Prudence Vilkas?" Veronica was still watching from between the blinds.

"I am Prudence Vilkas," I told him. We faced one another. His hair was streaked gray. His eyes, the same blue as my father's, were familiar. The Old Man lit a cigar, puffing away, and squinted. "Come here, woman!" he said. He was not talking to me. I looked to my Oma, who was clutching her purse, getting her bearings, the sandy earth foreign beneath her orthopedic shoes. She didn't respond to the Old Man. He raised his voice. "She's got the baby's eyes." Then, comprehending that I was standing right there in front of him, he said, "You have my sister's eyes, the youngest sister's eyes. We called her Little Bird."

I hadn't felt my wings move since my late-night swim, but I felt them now. They swelled like two helium balloons, like I was going to lift off. Veronica was still indoors, while Freddie was walking my Oma step by step to the Old Man's side.

The Old Man said, "My sister's eyes have shooting stars like yours."

Freddie said, "You mean the orange starburst?"

"What is the difference?"

"Which sister, Dad?"

The Old Man and my father were practically twins except that my father's hair was still black. Around my father's eyes, there were wrinkles like pin scratches. The Old Man was seasoned—what I expected. His face was windburned, the lines around his mouth and eyes dug like ravines. When my Oma got closer, she began to cry, just a little, enough to use the handkerchief stuffed in the pocket of the jacket she wore despite the ninety-degree weather. She saw no resemblance to her own mother in me, which she'd hoped for, but that didn't matter. She saw her granddaughter for the first time. We embraced. For so long, she'd wanted to know me. Her face was round like a pie. Her eyes were brown moons. Around her chipped tooth, her skin was soft and loose. In the corners of her mouth, the pink lipstick, the same shade as her pink head scarf, bled. Even though it would take years to understand her, right away I loved her. She took my hand in hers, still holding on to me, and I remembered that Wheaton was there somewhere. I hadn't introduced him. I forgot.

Veronica finally came out wearing her apron. To Freddie, she said, "Well, just look at you! Long time, no see." It was ridiculously clichéd, but what else was she going to say to him and the in-laws who hadn't wanted to know her? Freddie nodded and she laughed, hugging him. I rarely know what my mother will do or say, but on this particular day, when her insecurity was palpable, she was quite easy to peg. She smiled awkwardly, her hands behind her back, waiting for someone else to say something else. I imagine that she didn't think anyone cared that she was there, and maybe the Old Man didn't, not right then, but my Oma certainly cared. She was a mother. Freddie was her son. She let go of me and told Veronica, "Thank you for allowing us to come." She knew that being someone's mother and someone's wife was very important.

The Old Man asked Veronica, "Where are you from?"

"Troutville."

"You are from a fishing village?"

Veronica wasn't sure how to answer. "Not exactly."

"Where is your family from?"

My Oma seemed to be worried about Wheaton, who stood there counting out the syllables of multiple conversations, none of them ending on the pinky. She reached out and patted his hand. Freddie interrupted the Old Man's interrogation of Veronica and said, "Dad, I used to call Prudence 'little bird.' That's what you called your sister?"

"Daina," the Old Man said.

I said to my Oma, "This is my friend Wheaton." When I think back, the six of us were standing in a circle, like a constellation. Connect the dots, me to Wheaton, the Old Man to Ingeburg, and Freddie to Veronica. Veronica slipped a pack of cigarettes from her apron pocket. She was better at selling real estate than selling a Betty Crocker image to her in-laws. "My sister Daina had wings," the Old Man said. I honestly think that I shook my head before blurting, "I was born with wings."

Wheaton said, "I can see them."

My Oma said, "What is it that you see, young man?"

Veronica said, "They weren't exactly wings, Prudence. That makes you sound crazy." She took a drag off her cigarette. "The doctor called them bifurcated protrusions."

Freddie said, "They looked like wings, Veronica. She was a little bird."

My dad is just like that. Sometimes I want to kill him, and then, with one or two sentences, he's Superman.

The Old Man dropped his cigar. "What are you saying?"

He opened his mouth to speak, to answer his own question, but no words came. He pressed his right palm to his forehead.

"Is he all right?" I asked my Oma. She stared hard at me like I wasn't real, more apparition than girl. "Daina?" she queried.

The Old Man looked at me the same way. With his mouth forming an O, he seemed incapable of speech. It hadn't fully registered with me that his sister Daina had been born with both orange starburst eyes and wings.

"Frederick?" my Oma said.

His cigar burned in the scrub. I bent down to pick it up. Wheaton said, "God, the ghost of the girl. It's his sister. That's who it is."

At first, I didn't understand. It was unimaginable. His sister? The ghostly girl? My wings? I grabbed hold of the Old Man's elbow. He dropped his hand from his forehead and, bending slightly forward, nuzzled his beard between my neck and shoulder. I felt hot tears on my back where my T-shirt was torn.

No one said anything. We stayed that way for a good while. Wheaton's fingers were quiet. While his world made no sense, mine was coming together. I was the first to speak. "I was born with wings," I repeated.

The Old Man straightened up, dropping his head back, the spot on his forehead as pink as the setting sun. Resting his hands on my shoulders, he said, "You have my sister's eyes. You too have her wings. You *are* a little bird."

This was one of the places and times in my life where I could exist forever. Play the record, let it skip. Play it again. Climb on and off the Ferris wheel. Pay the carny to leave me up top staring at the horizon. Let the sun set. The wheel is filled to capacity with me, Wheaton, the Old Man, Ingeburg, Freddie, Veronica, and the ghost of the girl who was a real girl named Daina. No one is getting off. We're going round and round, and on our way down, the stomach drops, and on our way up, the heart leaps. This is the best place to be.

PART THREE

The destiny of the world is determined less by the battles that are lost and won than by the stories it loves and believes in.

—Harold Clarke Goddard

12

On June 15, 1941, Daina used her hands, black dirt beneath her fingernails, to dig a hole beneath a tall pine. It was too shallow to be a real hole, but she pulled her dress overhead and sat in the dirt saucer, pretending to be invisible, her face hidden within a petticoat and skirt, her thighs exposed. As far as she knew, everyone was dead. She attempted to pray to Saint Casimir, Lithuania's patron saint, but no words came.

Dropping her skirt, she pulled her brown hair over one shoulder and braided it. Despite its oiliness and the knot at the nape of her neck, she twisted three ropes together—how Mother would do. Loose hairs fell to her shoulders, and she wished for death.

Then Daina heard a noise.

A rustling. Footsteps. Maybe a bear. Maybe a boy.

She pulled her skirt back overhead. Bear or boy, she did not want to see it or him coming. Daina did not know that her grandmother Aušrinė had hidden beneath skirts in this same forest. If she had known, she might've had voice to pray, she might've felt some kindred spirit, the protection of the pines, but Daina, like her sisters, had been sheltered from horror stories, and for now, she was terrified. Hopeless. She felt the dirt, not only beneath her fingernails, but streaked along her legs and chest. It seemed to have made its way down her throat, making it hard to breathe.

This morning, her mother had been forced into a cattle car bound for Siberia. Daina had run home to tell her sisters and brother. *What are we going to do?* But her brother wasn't there, and while Daina huddled in the wardrobe behind heavy furs with her two sisters, the heat unbearable, Russian soldiers entered the house. As their footsteps grew nearer to the girls' bedroom, Danutė, the oldest, put her hand over Daina's mouth, and Audra, the middle girl, grabbed hold of Daina's forearm. Together, they moved Daina into the corner, covering her with a wool shawl. The door to the wardrobe creaked. Daina squeezed her eyes shut. Audra and Danutė were pulled from the wardrobe while Daina cowered beneath the shawl. From behind this flimsy screen, Daina saw the ugliest man in the world force himself on Danutė. Afterward, he stuck his knife in her gut. From beneath her cover, Daina convulsed, but she did not peep.

Two days earlier, Danutė had taught music. She'd gone to university in Vilnius. She was gifted at anything and everything with strings. Now she was dead. Her blond hair stained pink. The plank floors swallowing her blood. On a perfectly fine day, a sunny June afternoon, while professors in other towns drank tea, Danutė died, but before she died, she bled.

Daina did not make a peep. Making two fists, she dug her fingernails into her palms and while Danutė continued to bleed, she watched the ugliest man in the world try to force himself on Audra—the middle sister—but something was wrong, and Audra, the middle sister, the quiet one, laughed and spit in his face. His boots and the cuffs of his pants were soaked with Danutė's blood. Daina bit her lip to stop from screaming. As stifling as it was in the wardrobe, she was cold now fearing for Audra's life. The wardrobe was jostled by one of the men, his forearms, lined with coarse dark hair, his shirtsleeves creased and drab. Daina did not breathe as two fur coats were pulled from their hangers. She imagined herself smaller, a mouse. Outside the wardrobe, two men held the coats while the ugliest man in the world stabbed Audra how one would gut a pig or a deer. Daina looked with horror at the sight and at the two accomplices holding the fur coats. How could they just stand there and do nothing? One of them was no more than a boy, her age maybe, with a gash above his left eye and a cut on his left hand. While he shut his eyes, Daina did not. She watched Audra vanishing. *Not a peep.*

Sometimes it's hard to imagine someone has a mother. How Frederick, Daina, Audra, and Danutė were born into a musical family, this ugly man with dirty hands was born stabbing holes into girls. Only there was very little blood, hardly any. It was the strangest thing. Even as he stabbed and twisted the knife, Audra would not bleed. It was as if Danutė had bled for both sisters, for their whole family, for the town of Vilnius, for the cause of independence, for all of Lithuania.

Daina thought that she had stopped breathing. When she did breathe, it was too noisy. The ugly man was going to find and kill her. She did not want to die. *Not a peep.* Not then.

If there'd been one man—just the one ugly one—Daina would've fought him. She would've burst forth from the wardrobe and wrestled the knife from him. She would've slit his throat. She could've done it, she knew, but there were three men, not one, and she was trembling. Then she yelped. She did not mean to. She covered her mouth, expecting the three men to turn toward the wardrobe, but no one had heard her. No one turned to see. The earth, vibrating on its axis, had hiccupped for Daina, tuning out her cry. She was going to be spared. Like her older brother Frederick, Daina understood that without a survivor, there's no one to tell the story.

After the men had gone, Daina fell out of the wardrobe and crawled through Danutė's blood, already cold, having turned the floorboards red. She tried to pull the two sisters together, to join their hands. Danutė was surprisingly light and Audra equally heavy. Daina tried to say a prayer to Saint Casimir. She tried to cover her older sisters with the shawl they'd used to hide her in the wardrobe, but it was too small. Daina attempted everything and accomplished nothing. She fled the house and ran into the pines.

There is a Lithuanian proverb that says, "If you flee from a wolf, you'll run into a bear." Sitting in her saucer, the sound of bear or boy approaching, Daina was ready. *Come.*

The rustle was not a bear. It was the boy from her bedroom, the boy with fresh wounds on his hand and above his left eye. The boy who'd shut his eyes. Daina would not fear him. She pulled down her skirt and stared at him. In her bedroom, she had wanted to survive for her sisters' sake, but now that they were gone, she wanted to die. Her mother was on her way to an icy fate. In truth, she knew that her mother was probably dead. Aleksandra was never acquiescent. She was never one to do as she was ordered. Daina assumed her brother had died alongside her father. They were gone, all of them, everyone she loved, and now there was nothing to do but join them. *Just kill me! Kill me, soldier boy.* On all fours, the boy who was not a bear scuttled toward her. Pulling a hunk of bread from his pocket, he set it by her boot and backed away.

Just get it over with. Daina had already dug her own grave, at least the beginning of a grave.

The wounded boy pulled off his Soviet coat and heaved it to his right. Beneath the coat, he wore a button-down dress shirt. He smoothed the collar and bib like he'd never seen it before. Then he fell to his side, whimpering like a trapped animal. He clawed the dirt the way Daina had done. Overhead, sunlight broke through the pines, spilling onto his shirt and soaking the earth. The brown bark turned rich like good chocolate. The dull earth took on the appearance of a starry sky. This boy wasn't going to kill her. Daina reached to feel the two stilled wings on her back. It would have been better if this boy were some bear instead of a sniveling murderous boy. He kept crying. She kicked her legs out, sprinkling dirt in his direction. It was a dare. *I dare you to kill me.* The boy who was not a bear sobbed. Daina kicked more dirt in his direction.

After a while, the boy got to his knees and wiped his face with the back of his sleeve.

Daina stared at him. Neither of them had spoken. Then the boy, reaching into his sack, pulled out an apple. He rolled it toward Daina. It was fresh and red in the light. Daina looked from the boy to the apple. She didn't want it. Then the boy, who was most assuredly not a bear, started talking. His name was Stasys Valetkys. He'd been kidnapped. He spoke Lithuanian and not Russian. He'd seen terrible things. What was her name? Did she have a name? "I am running," he said, "and hiding."

Daina could not speak, and he could not stop speaking. "I have seen the most horrendous things. I have lost my parents."

Daina knew firsthand what he'd seen. He'd seen her sisters butchered, but this boy had no idea that she had been there hiding. Daina stared at the apple. It was too shiny and the sun was too bright. She shielded her eyes from the dappled light. When she was born, Daina's mother called her wings a godsend. The midwife, wiping the wings clean, crossed herself. She thought that Daina was born from the devil. She didn't know that the mother, Aleksandra, was wild for birds, that Daina and her wings were a miracle. Petras, Daina's father, knew the folklore, the family history. His mother, Aušrinė, was born in Lithuania. She was born with wings. As a child, her wings had been bound, and as an old woman, they had dragged the dirt. The wings never meant that anyone could fly. Not Daina. Not Aušrinė. They were grounded birds, like ostriches and emus, long-legged, flying nowhere. Only in death did Daina imagine that she might soar high enough to see her family again.

Daina sat in her dirt saucer, staring at the boy Stasys. She was waiting to be a turnip or a bird, rooted or free. She was bothered by the sun and by Stasys. She wished he'd slit her throat or his own. The darkness came up from the ground, rising like fog. Daina bit into the bread that Stasys had offered. Why was this boy who watched her sisters die allowed to live? She knew that the boys and men in town had been rounded up and shot. Why was this one spared? Daina tried to shut Stasys out, to pray, but still no words came for Saint Casimir. Stasys said, "My father was a doctor. My mother was a teacher." Daina did not care what his parents were. She would've preferred a bear.

Again, Stasys asked her name.

She refused to speak. Stasys continued, "The Russians made me go with them."

Daina did not care. In the darkness, she grew ravenous, eating more of the bread and biting the apple without a thank-you. After some time had passed, she spoke. "Has the Red Army taken the coast?"

"I don't know."

"I want to go there."

"Where?" The cut above his left eye was caked with dried blood. Instinctually, Daina wanted to clean it, but she wouldn't.

"To the coast."

"Do you have family there?"

"Sort of." Her family had gone there, had been there every summer on holiday to Palanga. "Let's go there."

"Where?"

"To the sea."

"But your family," he said.

"Is gone," she finished.

Stasys said, "I don't know. We'll be picked up."

"If I'm going to die, I want to see the water one last time." Daina was thinking that time was short. She was thinking that on the walk there, she could recall her mother's voice, her mother singing arias. She could remember how her wings had responded to the light. And even if she and Stasys were stopped and killed en route, she would be going somewhere, not just sitting and waiting to die.

Stasys said, "Maybe we should hide deeper in the forest or find someone to hide us."

Daina said, "You can do that—if that's what you want to do."

He looked at Daina. "How old are you?"

"Eighteen." She lied.

"Me too." He also lied. "I can't let you walk off alone."

"Yes, you can." She had the spirits of her dead family to watch over her. Certainly it was a short matter of time until she joined them in the afterlife. Never in her darkest imagination, in her worst nightmare, had she conceived of anything like what had happened today. Now it seemed like there was no choice but to participate in the madness, to choose a course. Hers was Palanga. To remember birds and music. To pray for the dead. To try and pray to Saint Casimir—if words would come.

Stasys said, "I'll go."

"So be it."

Under cover of darkness, they started walking west. They used the North Star to guide their course. Stasys attempted conversation. He didn't talk about the dead. Instead, he asked for her name once more. What year of school was she in? Did she go to university? What did her parents do? In response, Daina asked him to please be quiet, and so the scarred boy who was not a bear mumbled to himself much of the time. He needed to hear a voice—even his own—to know that he was still alive.

After a few days, Daina resolved to tell Stasys her name. She would have to cooperate with him to some extent in order to get to Palanga. Some sort of story would have to be invented. The truth would not do. They agreed to tell people that they were married. If they were brother and sister, strangers might ask about their parents. It seemed easier to be married. Why were they walking? Because their grain store had been sovietized, leaving them homeless. They thought there might be work to the west. It seemed like a reasonable lie, a necessary one, but Daina and Stasys were clearly children, so their lies fooled no one. Just the same, it was 1941 and everyone told lies. No one minded that Daina and Stasys stuck to theirs.

On the road, Soviet tanks rolled east. Daina and Stasys traveled through the woods, individually pretending to be pine trees. As children, they'd both heard the Lithuanian folktales about the woods coming to life, and they wanted to believe. During the day, they hid in granaries and churches, wherever they could find a corner or crevice. On June twentieth, as they sat in a pew with their heads bowed, a hump-backed woman, her face partially hidden beneath a gray wrap, approached them. She kneeled beside Stasys, who, despite the woman's appearance, was worried that she was secret police. With his hands together, he stared ahead at the statue of the Virgin Mary holding the Christ child. The base of the Virgin was broken, her feet missing. The elderly woman whispered, "There is someone in town who will hide and feed you. He is a good man, and you can stay as long as you need." She crossed herself and passed a slip of paper across the back of the pew where their hands were folded in prayer. Stasys and Daina trusted no one, but out of desperation, everyone. They had no choice. At any moment, they could be discovered and charged with treason or charged with nothing. They could be shot or sent to Siberia or sent to Siberia and then shot. They didn't know who sent the old woman or why she was helping them, but they were hungry, and they hadn't turned down a good turn yet. After the woman left, they waited in the church, nervous that someone would find them. At least, Stasys was nervous. Daina was always expecting capture, and with this expectation had achieved a sense of calm.

When night came, they went to see the man called Tomasas. He lived in a small row house on a paved street. Green ivy covered the facade. Leaves encircled the front columns and laced the old bricks, and in the darkness, his house glowed lavender. When Tomasas opened the front door, he said, "Hurry up. I've been expecting you," and ushered them inside. He would've taken their coats, but neither Stasys nor Daina had one. Tomasas was tall. He clapped his hands together. "Follow me." He took them to the back of the house, to a small kitchen where turnips and garlic boiled. "There is good news," he announced. "The Soviets are retreating. They are leaving by tank, wagon, car, horseback, and on foot. By any means possible." At first, Daina and Stasys did not believe him. He urged them to sit and offered to pour tea. Tomasas was a man, but his mannerisms were more effeminate than Daina's. He spoke with his hands. Daina said, "Why would they leave? That doesn't make any sense." In one gulp, Stasys drank his tea.

"Why else? The Germans are coming. Marching from the south."

"No," Stasys said, disbelievingly.

Tomasas was tall and thin, a bright-green apron tied around his waist. He rolled out pastry dough. "Yes! Already, the Soviet flags are being pulled down and the Nazi flags unfurled."

"One devil for another," Stasys said.

"So it seems," Tomasas agreed. He sprinkled sugar on the dough and covered it with a cloth.

Daina laughed. At first a tickle, and then a full-on guffaw.

Tomasas said, "Have you gone mad?" and this made her laugh even harder. No one had laughed in very many days. Daina covered her mouth. Tomasas brushed flour from his cheek, his hands on his hips. "What's so funny?"

Daina restrained herself. "Your kitchen smells of garlic, baked apples, yeast, and cheese. Please don't take offense, but you remind me of my mother. She always fed us."

"Take offense?" He rolled his eyes. "That is the greatest compliment."

Daina, wanting to cry now, said, "It really is. She is wonderful. Her given name is Aleksandra." The laughter subsided. Daina had an image of her mother rolling out pastry dough. *Not anymore*, she thought. She would've given anything to feel her mother's embrace.

Tomasas fed them until their stomachs swelled. As they ate, Daina and Stasys wondered the same things: What would the Nazis *do* to Lithuania? Would things be better? Would they make it to Palanga? Would they ever have a home again?

It dawned on Stasys that he was an orphan. This was something Daina had realized right away, on June fourteenth, the day her family was murdered. This realization was why walking to Palanga was her only recourse. She was ready to die and join her family. She could be slain en route or after she saw the Baltic Sea one last time. But Stasys, because he'd been forced into the Red Army, was only now coming to terms with the loss of his family. He'd been too busy surviving to comprehend what had happened. His father had died a month before the Red Army invaded, and his mother, a professor of dramatics, had been picked up, along with her fellow teachers from the gymnasium, and taken to the forest. He'd seen the mass grave where she'd been booted. Because of the tree roots, it was a shallow grave. He glimpsed a red wool hat and a leather shoe, but he didn't dig. He was too afraid to bend down. Just standing beside the pit, he felt like the soil was falling over his head.

The Russian soldiers found him at the gravesite and took him into custody. They explained very matter-of-factly: "You will join us or die." Unlike Daina, Stasys did not want to die. At all cost, he wanted to live. He surmised that in time, he would escape from the army. He would live because his parents would want him to survive. To do otherwise would be a disappointment. He was brought up disciplined and educated. He knew history, and now he knew terror firsthand. He was taking this girl to the sea because it was a noble mission. It was survival.

Tomasas sheltered Daina and Stasys for two nights, until the ladies in town were lining up outside his boutique to get their hair styled and set. This desire for beautification was a good sign, a kind of normalization—this luxury, this treat.

Before departing, Stasys and Tomasas shared a cigarette in the hall-way that connected Tomasas's beauty parlor to his apartment. "Listen," Tomasas told Stasys, "my father was a Bolshevik. He openly justified the first killings, even the death of the royal family. He was a fan of Trotsky. Now, he is in Siberia."

"I'm sorry."

Tomasas shook his head. "Don't be, but I must tell you: I am worried about your wife."

"Who?"

"Your wife." Tomasas was still pretending to believe their lie. These fabrications were important for everyone's sanity. Tomasas continued. "I fear that Hitler will be no better than Stalin. He will not grant us our independence. No one will. They are all greedy grubbers. Mad monsters. We'll have to fight." He paused. "And your wife, I think she is set on dying. Not fighting. None of us are made from this cloth, but your wife will want to end it after she fulfills this quest to see the sea. She is aligned with the dead."

"How can that be?"

"The dead have a grip on her or she on them. With her, it can't be otherwise. Watch out for her. Life is precious." Tomasas leaned down and kissed Stasys on the lips. "I will pray for both of you."

Stasys felt the man's stubble against his cheek. He went to wipe the kiss away but stopped. Instead, he shook Tomasas's hand. "Thank you for everything."

The next morning, Tomasas packed bread, cheese, and salted meats for Daina and Stasys. He cried as they left. Daina wagged her finger at his sentimentality.

Continuing on their quest, the pair of orphans had something to talk about: Tomasas. "He was very nice."

"Very hospitable."

The farther Stasys and Daina walked, the closer they were to the ordered clacking of German boots. "My father always had good things to say about the Germans," Daina said.

Stasys shook his head at her strange optimism. She didn't seem like a girl bent on death. Just the opposite, but Stasys didn't know that Daina was anticipating the conversation she would have with her father after she joined him in death. She would tell him about the German invasion, and he would wonder how the Germans behaved as occupiers. Had they ransacked everything? Was Hitler as mad as the newspapers said?

Watching the sky alight with bombs, Stasys said, "I don't know if there is anyone we can trust." Daylight was beginning to break. They were close to the sea, hiding behind random hay bales in the middle of a field.

"Especially not each other," Daina answered. She was thinking of her sisters, remembering Stasys holding the fur coat.

He didn't know why she would be so cruel for no reason. He told her that he'd lost his parents, that he'd been forced to do the Soviets' bidding. He'd spent days witnessing the worst horrors, things he could never verbalize.

Daina thought that she could punch Stasys in the lip until it was fat and bled dark purple like blackberry jam. She thought that the Germans must be better than the Soviets who ravaged her sisters and killed her parents. Maybe they would grant Lithuania her freedom. "I am fine on my own," she told Stasys. "Just go home."

Stasys had no home.

Daina had ideas that she would take flight over the sea. Every summer except for this one, her family had gone to Palanga. Beneath the hot sun, they walked past shops and outdoor flower markets. Daina's sisters chatted about books while Daina looked toward the sky. At home in Vilnius, she tended to forget the wings sprouting from her back. Beneath heavy silk blouses and hand-me-down dresses, they were compact enough, flat enough to forget, like two hands against the small of her back, but in Palanga, walking cobblestoned streets in strapless sundresses, a backdrop of tall-steepled churches and towering pines, she felt them move, as if they yearned to be free of undergarments, wool and silk, as if the sea were where Daina belonged. She remembered running after pigeons, the birds scattering in her wake. Arms outstretched, she turned back to her brother and sisters. "With the right breeze, I'd be gone."

Danutė told her to be quiet. "You're always showing off."

Frederick said, "We should get ice cream. We're on holiday."

Daina remembered that overhead, all types of birds soared. As they tromped toward the sea, her mother ran up and pulled at Daina's scoopback bathing costume, draping a cover-up over her wings. "There, that's better. I don't want you to burn."

Would the birds still be there in Palanga? What about ice cream? Would Mother be drinking lemon tea with honey, preparing to sing? Would Father play his violin? Which books would Audra and Danutė discuss? Daina felt that walking to Palanga was walking home. She told Stasys Valetkys, "I am set on Palanga. You can go your own way."

Stasys countered, "I am going your way, whichever way that is."

13

*P*alanga was how Daina remembered, except for the Nazi soldiers parading up and down the street. She knew a little German. They were demanding to see her papers, and she was thinking about the sea, about undressing and exposing her wings. Stasys spoke German. He said, "The Soviets took our papers."

The German authority wanted to know where and when.

He recited their lie.

"Report to the Gestapo and apply for papers."

Daina wasn't the least bit afraid.

"Right now."

She pursed her lips at the police. She'd take her time. If they grabbed her out here in the open, it would be fate. After all, she was meant to be with her sisters and brother, her mother and father, not here with this boy who'd watched her sisters die a terrible death. But before her own end, there was the sea. The waterbirds and the salt air. That wasn't very much to ask, was it?

Daina and Stasys walked west. They saw Jews lined up in the street. Whole families: men, women, children, babies, all wearing yellow stars. "What are they going to do with them?" Daina asked.

"I'm sure they'll be okay," Stasys lied. The babies cried. Mothers, their hands resting on the heads of waist-high children, assured them,

"It's all right. Everything will be fine." The Germans shouted at them. Some passersby whispered about the abuse.

Daina was more intent than ever on joining her family. This world was not of her or for her. Stasys said, "They're probably going to move them to the countryside."

"As opposed to the seaside?" Daina knew that he was lying. She was sixteen, but she was not stupid.

"I don't know. Probably."

Daina and Stasys stood stock-still, watching the line of thirty or so people question and console each other. Daina's mouth was agape. Stasys reached for her hand, but she pulled it away. She didn't need kindness, not his. One of the Gestapo shouted at them to keep moving. Honestly, Daina and Stasys didn't want to see what was happening. No one did. They were glad to be ordered away.

That first night in Palanga, they did not speak, not even Stasys, who used the sound of his voice as reason to stay alive. Because he could hear the timbre and pitch change, he was real, just like his parents, who'd been real, who'd birthed and raised him. In his voice, he heard theirs. They'd loved him. He had his mother's eyes and his father's chin. Compassion and love were real when he remembered them. *Hold on to it,* he thought. *Otherwise, the madmen win.*

The first two nights in Palanga, they slept beneath a wooden pier that creaked with the tide. Daina tried to stay awake. She planned to venture far out into the sea while Stasys slept. She planned to submerge her wings in the black water, but Stasys did not sleep. Remembering Tomasas's warning, he kept vigil, plum-colored caverns appearing beneath his eyes while Daina's eyes closed and she lost consciousness.

During the day, Stasys nodded off for ten minutes here and ten minutes there.

"You look terrible," Daina told him.

He shrugged, not caring how he looked, only that she didn't run away.

On the third day, they were chased away from the pier by Lithuanian soldiers under German authority. That night, they found an empty warehouse two streets from the coast. Stasys's eyelids were too heavy. He used his fingers to hold them open. His fingers failed. He hadn't slept in days, and he hadn't slept well in months. He slept, awaking to smoke, coughing. Daina was beside him. He nudged her. "It's burning. We have to go." She didn't open her eyes. "Fire!" he shouted.

"We're supposed to die."

"The warehouse is burning."

She wasn't moving.

"Let's go."

She wouldn't budge. She had gone on long and far enough.

Not much taller than Daina, Stasys grabbed on to her boot heels. He pulled her from the smoky confines, her skirt up her back—how he'd first found her with skirt overhead, pretending to be a turnip or a bird. *You're not going to die.* As flames raged, Daina lay in the dust, her dark hair gnarled, her starburst eyes explosive, reflecting the firelight. Her legs and buttocks had dragged the floorboards. She was splintered and filthy.

"Get up," Stasys said.

She rolled onto her side.

"Get up!"

"There's no point."

He tried to pull her farther from the flames, but he was too exhausted. He lay down on top of her to protect her from the fire and to hear her breathing. She didn't care. Perhaps she would sink into the earth and be swallowed up. It is a mortal sin to take one's life, but it is no sin to raise your arms in submission and let the world destroy you.

Less than fifty feet away, the fire raged, but it never came any closer.

On the fourth day, they went back to the Baltic Sea. They bathed and rinsed their smoky clothes, hanging them on the bordering pines to dry. Stasys glimpsed the wings folded against Daina's back and thought that he was hallucinating from exhaustion and hunger. They sat apart, huddled and hidden between dunes, Daina's hands covering her small bosom. She called to Stasys, "Where are we going to stay now? Do you have any ideas, soldier boy?"

He hated that she called him soldier boy.

"I'm not in any army," he said.

"But you'd like that, wouldn't you? Carrying a gun around and shouting commands? You'd like to be the one telling people what to do!" Daina hugged her knees to her chest.

"Why are you being spiteful?" Stasys wanted to cry.

She would never tell him, *I saw you there, in my bedroom! You watched my sisters die! You're a monster!* She could never tell him. Right now, Stasys, half boy and half monster, was all she had. *Men are mad, but not the sea.* She peeked over the dune, and Stasys caught sight once more of her wings. *How can that be?* he wondered, rubbing his eyes. He wanted to ask about the wings, but what if he'd gone mad? She'd have even more reason to leave him. He kept quiet.

Two days later, they went to the Gestapo for their papers. It was a large office in a former warehouse. There were cubicles. Electric typewriters and adding machines whirred. Papers were penned in black script. Cards were stamped. Food ration coupons dispensed. Stasys was told that there was an apartment for rent. "Do you have any money?"

He did not. They'd lost everything in their make-believe and real worlds.

"You have thirty days to make payment." A lease and bill were produced in triplicate. Stasys signed. As did Daina. Stasys pocketed their copy. Daina kept her eyes to the floor until one of the German soldiers raised her chin and studied her face. In German, he said, "You're like a baby. So fresh." Daina did not know what to say. Stasys said, "Thank you." They moved through the lines, Stasys thanking everyone for their help. Many of the Germans were dismissive, but some of them smiled at the young couple. Daina would not smile.

The apartment was in a residential square by a florist and next to a bakery. Furnished, it held the possessions and breath of a Jewish family.

It was as though at two in the afternoon, a mother, father, and daughter had disappeared. There were clothes, cigars, ashtrays, canned meats, coats, and family portraits. On the kitchen counter, there were recipe cards, a clue to the former residents' last supper. There were books with places saved and words underlined. There were knitting needles laced through unfinished hats and scarves. In the little girl's room, there was a porcelain doll upright on the bed, her porcelain hands resting on her lap, as though she were waiting patiently for the girl to return.

Rather than packing up this doll and these many possessions, Stasys and Daina left them where they were, choosing to live with the ghosts, never dismissing the possibility that the family might return. Everything was make-believe, but not in a good way. In a horrific way.

In the beginning, Daina and Stasys pretended to be eighteen to each other and then they pretended to be twenty-two for the Gestapo. With their papers in order, Daina took Stasys's surname. After all, they were married. Reality was an invention. Daina sat on the floor with her eyes closed. She was thinking about the porcelain doll. Not so long ago, she'd played with dolls. She realized she'd been in shock during the walk to the sea. She'd had no idea that men were capable of such cruelty.

Stasys said, "Are you all right?"

She'd forgotten he was there. With her hands pressed to the floorboards, she was back home.

He said, "At least we'll be warm tonight."

"No," she said. "I'm not all right."

"I'm sorry." He wished there was something else to say. He wished that his mother were here because she'd know how to console two children forced to play grown-up. Daina opened her eyes, staring right through Stasys. He was unnerved. "I'll make something to eat."

She didn't respond. Tonight, she'd go back to the sea. She'd go alone. It was no good being in someone else's home, longing to be a little girl again. Whenever she considered the possibility that this family whose home she inhabited had been killed, she felt a stabbing pain in her stomach. She wanted to believe that the family was on holiday. Perhaps they went to visit the Louvre in Paris. Perhaps they were on a steamship bound for some tropical destination.

Stasys made potato soup. As Daina stabbed the undercooked potatoes with a fork, he said, "You'd better eat."

"Where are you sleeping?" she asked.

"Where do you want me to sleep?"

"I'm not hungry." She got up to look for a hairbrush. "I'll have a bath. There are two bedrooms. Which one do you want?"

Stasys planned to sleep outside whichever bedroom she chose to make sure she didn't leave him. "Either one," he said.

Daina went to take a bath, an unbelievable luxury. In the bathroom folded on a shelf, there were plush towels that smelled of lavender. On the bathtub's edge, there was a bar of oatmeal soap. From the tub, Daina saw a squished bug by the door. Someone had stepped on that bug. For some reason, it made her smile. Here was another trace of what had been, of real people knocking around living real lives. Stasys tapped at the door. "Are you all right?" Daina slipped beneath the water. He opened the door and peeked in to see her emerge. She was breathing heavily. There they were again: her wings. Somehow, they didn't surprise him as much now. She covered her breasts with her hands. Stasys quietly pulled the door closed.

From that first afternoon he saw her sitting in a saucer of dirt, he knew that she was different: his salvation. Why should wings surprise him? It made sense for an angel to have wings.

After her bath and once Stasys was asleep, Daina planned to slip away from this ghostly apartment, but the lavender overtook her. She slept in the double bed, the door closed, Stasys sleeping against it. He couldn't let her leave. He couldn't be alone. Not now. Not yet. He worried that she was the only force keeping him sane, giving him voice and reason to survive. *God in Heaven, she has wings.*

In the morning, Stasys washed up, and Daina took advantage. This was her chance to escape. She hurried down the steps. The day was warm and sunny. Pulling the door shut behind her, she ran toward the dunes. She thought she might've heard Stasys calling her name. She ran faster. She didn't stop until her boots were covered in sand. Despite a raging war, there were tourists and sunbathers. A man in a black bathing suit with a Winnfield moustache said, "The water is lovely." He and a little boy chased the surf. Daina was surprised that anyone could be happy. She pretended to be a sunbather, to be happy, to be one of them. She agreed with the man. "Yes, it's beautiful." In truth, it was. There was not a cloud in the sky. She listened for her mother's voice but heard the squawk of gulls and gleeful tourists. She sat in the sand and untied her boots. Walking north, she looked for Mother and Father. She sought out Frederick, Danutė, and Audra. All around, she saw people who resembled each of them. Everywhere she looked, there were boys about Frederick's age, kicking the foamy surf and chasing the tide. There were blue-eyed girls with blond hair, girls like Audra and Danutė. Beneath a straw hat, there was a woman with a braid down her back. It could've been Aleksandra. But it wasn't.

The hard-packed sand felt cool on the bottoms of Daina's feet. She swung her boots, nearly approaching the woman who looked like her mother. *Is it you? Why can't it be you?* Daina walked until the sun kissed the sea, an uproarious gay pink spread out before her, a gift from God. She stopped in awe to watch. Everything was the same as it had been except that everything was different, so awfully different. She changed direction. She would join her family. They were with God. She would be there too. She belonged with them. God would make sure that she returned to them. Maybe not tonight, but soon. If only Stasys had left her in the burning warehouse, she'd be with them now. Maybe they'd be on this same beach, but there would be no death and no war. There would be no bullets and no yellow stars. Her sisters would be laughing. Her mother would be doting. Her father would squeeze her tight, and her brother would call her little bird. With the state of the world, she wouldn't have to wait long to die. She crossed herself and sat on the cold sand to lace up her boots.

When she opened the door to the apartment, she saw Stasys, gaping and red-faced, standing on the cramped entryway steps that led to their apartment. "What?" she asked him. "What do you want? What do you have to say?"

"Where did you go?"

"It's none of your business."

"I was worried."

"I took a walk."

Daina smelled like the ocean. Sitting on the soft velveteen settee, she unlaced her boots. She hadn't worn stockings. Her feet were covered with sand. Her face was sunburned.

Stasys's face was moist from crying. While she'd been gone, he'd broken down. He didn't think she'd return. He said, "I was chopping onion."

"I don't belong to you," she told him.

"I didn't say—"

"I know what you think."

"All right." Stasys went to bed with the porcelain doll. He didn't like how the doll looked at him, so he set her on her back to make her eyes close. *What do I think?* he wondered. *Do I think about my parents? Do I think about our apartment in Kaunas? Do I think about my friends? Do I think about the death and torture I've seen? What do I think? What do I do?* He took a deep breath.

I think about a girl I found in the dirt, a girl with wings, a future. That is what I think now.

By August, Daina got a job sewing buttons, and Stasys got a job working for a butcher. He was quick with a knife. At first, the Nazis seemed more civilized than the Soviets, but as days and weeks passed, it became evident that they thought the Lithuanians were an inferior people. They didn't buy Lithuanian products. Goods were imported from Germany or the Germans nationalized the stores, taking all profits before shopping in them.

One particularly sunny September day, when everything seemed to glimmer, Daina walked home from the button factory. In front of her, a police car was parked and the Gestapo was out on the street shouting at an old man. "Get a move on! The street doesn't belong to you!"

The old man stopped. In Lithuanian, he said, "I'll walk how I please," and pointed his cane at the policeman.

Without hesitation, the Gestapo shot the man in the head. The man dropped to his knees before toppling to the pavement. The Gestapo looked at the passersby, including Daina, her eyes now fixed to the bloody pavement, and he shouted in German, "See that this trash is picked up!" As the Gestapo drove away and the dead man's wife knelt by his side, Daina ran to a synagogue that had recently been vandalized and boarded up. There, she vomited between the synagogue's steps and a row of young pines. *I've seen too much blood spilled.* She prayed. *Please God, take me. Please.*

At dinner, Daina told Stasys what she'd seen. "What are we supposed to do?" she lamented. "How are we supposed to keep living?" This talk was unusual. She never expressed her feelings to Stasys.

Without thinking, he got up. As did she. He took her in his arms, the two of them pressed and nestled against the kitchen window. Stasys buried his chin between her cheek and collarbone. She smelled like the oatmeal soap in the bathroom.

Without thinking, Daina let him hold tight.

He whispered, "I don't know what we are supposed to do."

She opened her hand and touched the back of his neck.

"But it's going to be all right," he concluded. With his left hand, he felt one of her wings. He thought, *If she can fly, she can take us away from this place.* He smiled. *Who thinks such crazy thoughts?* Then he kissed the spot between chin and collarbone where his lips rested against her skin. He couldn't help himself.

She pushed him away and said, "I'm sorry." She didn't know what she was sorry for. Certainly not for pushing him away. That didn't make sense. "I'm tired. I'm going to bed."

This was the first night when he felt compelled to say, "I love you."

He wouldn't apologize for grabbing on to her. Never. But instead, he said, "Good night."

It was cold. The wind blew whitecaps off the sea. Daina had one nightmare after another. From the doorway, Stasys watched her toss beneath the bedcovers. He wanted to go to her and make it better. He wished that he could make the world the kind of place it should be, the kind of place it used to be, the kind of place they both deserved, but that was not possible, so he kept watch.

That first year, 1941, word spread fast that all the Jews in Vilnius and Kaunas had been killed. Mass graves, the kind Stalin liked, had been dug and filled by Nazis and Lithuanian conspirators.

Daina and Stasys had once upon a time hoped that the Germans would let Lithuania rule itself, but that wasn't to be. The Nazis were no better than the Soviets except that they were *slightly* pickier about whom they killed. Every day, the local newspaper depicted the Jews as having allegiances with the Soviets. Many Lithuanians believed what they read and saw, blaming the Jews for every past Soviet deportation, torture, and murder. Daina and Stasys were no longer naïve. They were surprised by their fellow Lithuanians who inhaled the anti-Jewish propaganda like ether.

In 1943, Stasys and Daina turned eighteen. In their pretend world, they were twenty-four. Daina slept in the big bed. Stasys slept in the Jewish girl's bed, the porcelain doll on the nightstand, sometimes eyes open, sometimes eyes closed.

Stasys thought about very little other than Daina. She was the only good thing he had. Everything about her impressed him as disciplined and strong. She worked hard, her fingertips striated from needle and thread. Every day after work, she walked on the beach. Most nights, if he got home in time, he accompanied her. If she wanted to go alone, he followed, fearful that without him, she'd ascend over the black water and fly west like some strange bird camouflaged by night, gliding through dark mist, invisible but for the hushed flap of wing. He could not let her go.

14

*I*n 1944, there were bonfires in the street. The Germans were leaving. The Red Army was returning. Anyone who'd been identified as conspiring with the Nazis was picked up and killed or deported to Siberia. Daina and Stasys had no allegiance to Hitler. So far, they had not been reported.

Daina continued to work sewing buttons and Stasys got a job writing educational pamphlets. The pamphlets detailed, as ordered, that children belonged to the state more so than to their parents. "Children who report on their parents for fascist or antiproletariat statements or deeds are the people's heroes. Stalin is their Father, and they are the new and greater future." Stasys also illustrated these pamphlets, which had to be freighted to Moscow for approval before being returned to Lithuania for distribution.

Years passed. Daina worked. Stasys worked. The world was monotonous. Everyone was a "comrade" and Stalin was a hero. Lithuanian culture and customs were suppressed, and the rest of the world seemed to forget that Lithuania and their neighbor Baltic states, Latvia and Estonia, had once been sovereign nations.

At night, when they felt brave or could no longer tolerate being comrades, Daina and Stasys laughed at the ridiculousness of the propaganda. "Can you imagine *believing* that Stalin is our great father?" They'd look around, afraid the house was bugged, but so bored with the grayness of their lives, they were willing to take the chance. "But we're nobody," Daina would say. Always, they whispered.

Stasys would shrug. "Everybody's nobody."

Stasys was so adept at his job that he was eventually hired to write a scientific report stating that communism made people physically and mentally stronger. (He was not a scientist.) He wrote, "There is strong evidence that communist men and women will outlive their corrupt capitalist counterparts."

Daina said, "I hope you never start believing those lies."

"Have a little faith in your husband."

At this, she laughed. Their marriage was as real to her as the propaganda Stasys penned.

In 1949, Stasys was assigned a full-time illustrator to work on his pamphlets. Her name was Olga. She was Russian. Here in Palanga, she'd take direction from Stasys, who took direction from a man in Moscow. Olga's artwork was meant to complement Stasys's pamphlets. Pictures spoke louder than words. Olga was not educated at university. She was educated on the street. Orphaned, she'd been apprenticed by a prostitute who worked along the Moskva River, though Olga suspected that her artistic gifts were inherited from the mother she never knew. Olga was born in a Siberian gulag in 1928. Her father was called Andrei Petrovich. He was a guard who delighted in leaving scars like Braille along the torso and thighs of Olga's mother. For the slightest infraction or for no reason, he relished torturing all female enemies of the people. Olga's mother was not special. When she became pregnant, he beat her harder, running his fingers along the bloody striations crisscrossing her back—accusing her of being with someone else, which was ludicrous. *The lines*, he thought, *are mine. They belong to me.*

When there was a baby, Olga's mother begged Andrei to spare the child's life. Babies did not survive where "Labor is a matter of honor, glory, courage, and heroism." Andrei obliged the poor woman, putting the infant on a transport train bound for Moscow.

Olga's surrogate prostitute mother found Olga bundled alongside the Moskva River. Prostitute or not, she figured she had as much right as anyone to have a child. Besides, orphaned children were an embarrassment, a black smudge on the glorious beauty and wealth of Moscow. To avoid this besmirchment, dirty, hungry children were rounded up and shot. Not knowing Olga's exact age or birthday, her surrogate prostitute mother celebrated it on the anniversary of the Bolshevik revolution— November seventh. In this way, when there were fireworks and bonfires, they could pretend that the revelry was in honor of Olga's birth.

Olga's surrogate mother died when Olga was sixteen. Olga had already joined the family trade. She was beautiful, blond, her face and limbs supple, with skin the color of alabaster despite the harshness of the ice and snow that turned so many young faces ruddy. After Olga's surrogate mother passed, Olga upgraded her clientele, entertaining Central Committee members and sometimes their wives. There was no one to garnish her wages, and she didn't have to discriminate between men and women. Anyone with money was fair game. Olga rejected sentimentality as though the wounds that had crisscrossed her mother's back and thighs were her own. But truthfully, her wounds were deeper. Unlike Stasys and Daina, Olga hadn't had a real family to lose. No real mother. No father. The Siberian winter of her birth had been tattooed on her bones. She was always cold, never satiated. Never enough wool. Never enough bread. Never enough anything.

Her dream was to leave Moscow, to live by the sea, to find a good man and have children. When she petitioned a Moscow government official, she knew that she would either have the opportunity to start over, to make believe she was someone other than a prostitute, or she would be sent to Siberia, to a lifetime of hard labor. She showed the government official, an oafish man who liked to watch her undress but was capable of little else, her drawings. Olga held her breath. "You see," she told him, "I am good at more than one thing. Do you see?" She was nervous, kneading her hands in her lap. He looked at her drawings, tossing them to the floor. "You stupid girl," he said, "I have been wanting to help you. I am not heartless."

On June 15, 1949, Olga Grishin received her illustrator post in Palanga, the Western Province of the Soviet Union, the former Lithuania.

She was glad to meet Stasys. His Russian was good. Her Lithuanian was poor, but that was no matter. Everyone was required to speak Russian in the workplace. After two weeks of working civilly side by side, Olga spoke up. "You are a very handsome man."

"Thank you, comrade."

"You are welcome." Her blond hair was braided over one shoulder. She was what Stasys would describe as a "pretty girl," but he had no interest in any girl except for Daina.

"Do you think I'm nice-looking?" she asked Stasys.

He looked up. "Nice enough, but I am trying to work."

"Do you think that you would like to know me better?"

"I'm married."

He went back to work.

The next day, she asked, "Why won't you flirt with me? It's no crime to flirt with a girl. It's so boring being here all day, and it's just the two of us. What's the harm in a little flirting?"

Stasys was bothered by Olga. At home, he told Daina that she was "fine." He'd get by. He didn't want to burden Daina with his problems. She worked a long, tedious day operating a sewing machine and attaching buttons to coats.

Every day, Olga had some new shocking thing to say. "Why doesn't your wife produce progeny for Stalin? Is she barren? I'm sure that I'm not barren."

"I don't want to know whether or not you are barren. Leave me alone, please." Stasys nervously felt for his shirt buttons to make sure they were in place.

"You don't like to have fun," Olga complained. She stuck her paintbrush in her mouth and leaned with her back against her drafting table.

Stasys ignored her. She made it difficult to concentrate. He was a man, twenty-four, not a boy, and he was a virgin. He took a deep breath and went back to work. There was nothing he could do. He couldn't report her. She was Russian. He wasn't permitted to complain. He would continue to ignore her. Eventually, she'd stop. Maybe he could find a man who would like her, and she would leave him alone. Olga glanced at him, taking the paintbrush from her mouth. "The more you push me away, the more I am determined."

"I'm married."

She shrugged. "Marriage is a piece of paper."

Stasys lacked even that. His love for Daina was unrequited.

"I am Russian," Olga told him. "You should think that I am beautiful."

"You are beautiful. Please stop!" He smacked his hands hard on his desk. "I can't concentrate. I am working here."

"Look at my lips. This is not lipstick. These are my real lips." She pursed them together.

Stasys began to perspire. He brushed his fair hair back from his eyes. "You can look at your lips!"

"Don't be rude to me!" She huffed. "I am new to the Western Province of the Soviet Union. You should be kind." She wagged her finger.

This woman is dangerous. "I apologize," he said, "but I do not want to judge your beauty." At this, she put down her illustrator's brush and approached Stasys's drafting table. "Look at me!"

He kept his eyes focused on his typewriter.

"I said, 'Look at me,' comrade!"

What kind of woman are you? Stasys got up, knocking over his chair, and rushed from the room.

That night, he told Daina, "Comrade Grishin is strange. I don't understand why they sent her here. I can illustrate the pamphlets. I can glorify Stalin the same as anyone. Put a big halo around his fat head."

"Don't be so hard on her," Daina said. "I'm sure she has a story like the rest of us."

Stasys didn't tell Daina the specifics of what Olga had said, what games she kept playing, only that she was a peculiar and difficult young woman.

Olga continued daily to hound Stasys. Not comprehending such sentimental notions as "love," she repeatedly cornered him in their cramped office. Stasys talked a blue streak about the Soviet Union's good news for the people. Olga swallowed audibly. "Why hasn't your wife given you any children? Why is she denying Mother Russia her offspring?" Olga exhaled into Stasys's ear. He was a man. When his right hand dropped to his side, it touched her thigh. "No," he said. "My wife is not barren." He stepped back. "I am tired of this."

"I'm warm," Olga said, unbuttoning her sweater.

"It's cold." Stasys looked up. Without wanting it, he got an erection. Olga pointed and laughed. "You want me."

"Please stop," he told her.

She was thinking, *I can call someone in Moscow. I can find some reason to get rid of his wife. Why does he resist me? Here is my chance to start fresh, and he won't let me.*

I want you, Stasys Valetkys. I get what I want. Olga regularly strolled past his walk-up, admiring the red geraniums planted around the bottom step. She sometimes knelt to smell the flowers and imagined herself within, a part of this world. She'd bake traditional Russian sweets to welcome Stasys home from work. (Olga loved sweets.) She'd wash dishes and fluff pillows and whatever other domestic chores were required of a wife. She did not belong in some cramped boardinghouse. She deserved a real home. She deserved to be a real wife and maybe one day a real mother. She hadn't come all the way to this western province to be a spinster. And she liked Stasys—as good as anyone. He seemed nice, and he was playing hard to get. In that respect, he was an unusual man. She liked it, his peculiarities.

Olga never *intended* to be cruel. She simply never comprehended that Stasys and his wife were real people with real emotions. Emotions that did not include basic needs like hunger and warmth were incomprehensible to Olga Grishin, who was only just venturing into notions of love, like a young girl discovering romance novels.

In November 1949, there were rolling blackouts. Stasys stood in the street watching Daina undress. He couldn't help himself. She was all shadow through the window except for the roundness of her wings catching the moonlight. The heart-shaped wings were intoxicating, and Stasys knew that he'd never be with another woman. Unrequited or not, his heart belonged to Daina.

Olga walked home from work, thinking about how she would successfully seduce Stasys, when a golden-haired mutt, fur nearly the color of Stasys's hair, crossed her path. "Hi, little one," Olga said, extending her hand to the dog's snout. The dog retreated, and she continued on her way. "Bye, little one." Hearing the dog whimper, Olga turned back and saw the mutt staring at her. The dog's eyes were crusty.

"Come on, if you want. I don't care." Olga kept walking. A few seconds later, she turned back to see the dog following.

"That's all right by me," she said, smiling. "I don't mind the company."

If she had the salted ham from the day's lunch, she could offer the dog something to eat, but she'd finished everything. She had been ravenous, filled with adrenaline after calling a government comrade in Moscow to report Daina Valetkiene as a traitor. It was as easy as that. Certainly Stasys's wife, like most of these sniveling Lithuanians, was in some way conspiring against the Soviet way of life, undermining Soviet thinking, and perpetrating crimes against the great father by sullying his grand name.

Olga laughed as the dog trailed her to the brick row house where she rented a room from a blind man named Bohdan. All day, Olga had been happy, anticipating Daina's arrest and her own union with Stasys. She turned the doorknob and checked to see if the dog was still behind her. Pets were not permitted, but she did not care. She would do what she liked. The blind man was as anti-Soviet as they came. One day a week, he collected the rent, and then he got drunk and listened to American jazz records like Benny Goodman, Billie Holiday, and Louis Armstrong. He'd be arrested sooner than later. Olga thought daily about turning him in. He was flaunting his wealth with booze and music when the money belonged to the state. She often thought that her landlord was the perfect subject for a propagandist poster: *Capitalists are stricken blind because they do not serve the common good.*

The mutt followed Olga through the front door past the blind man rubbing furniture polish on a banister and past a little neighbor girl sitting cross-legged, reading a book.

Shutting her bedroom door, Olga retrieved a handkerchief from her bureau and wiped the dog's eyes. As she cleaned, the dog licked her face. "Look at you," she said, wiping the muzzle next. "You're a pretty girl." The dog sniffed Olga's bed and walked in three circles before jumping onto the mattress as if it had lived there always. Bohdan knocked at the door.

"What is it?" Olga said.

"I need to speak to you." It was the blind man.

Leave me in peace.

"I'm not decent," Olga said. She was never exactly decent.

"What do I care? I don't see."

To the dog, Olga said, "I'll call you Emma."

Since she was a little girl, Olga had imagined living the life of the bourgeoisie. She'd imagined having a horse and a little dog or a kitten to love.

Bohdan knocked again.

"Go away!"

Olga was on her knees scratching the dog's neck. "It's all right. You'll see. You're safe." The dog whimpered. "But you will need a bath."

Bohdan knocked harder. This time, he said, "Is there an animal in there with you?"

Olga said, "Leave me alone. I paid my rent."

Turning on her hot plate, Olga cracked an egg for the dog. "A little something on your stomach. That'll be nice." The mutt closed its eyes, rubbing its paw against its nose.

Olga put the egg down on the floor, and the dog eyed it and then Olga.

"It's all right. I'm not going to poison you."

Later, Olga took Emma outside to the spigot and, using a sliver of lye soap, lathered her fur. She pressed her head against the wet dog's neck. This sentimentality toward an animal was new. In Moscow, she had not been afforded such luxury. She knew some girls who'd had pets, but they were thinner, less prosperous than Olga, because they weren't just worried about feeding themselves.

That first night, the dog slept at Olga's feet.

In the morning, the blind man knocked.

"Leave me alone," she said. To the dog, Olga said, "Shh." She put her finger to her lips. Bohdan was blind, but he wasn't deaf. He said, "I brought some breakfast scraps. A bit of sausage and egg. Can I come in?"

When Olga opened the door, Bohdan said, "We used to have dogs when I was growing up." He felt for Olga's hand and gave her the plate of scraps. "What does the dog look like?"

"Like honey. But with dark eyes like Egyptians in the films. I'm calling her Emma."

"Can I pet her?" He got down on his knees. Surprisingly, Emma came to him, and Bohdan settled on his haunches hugging the dog's neck as Olga had done. "Nice dog," he said, pressing his cheek against her wet nose. To Olga, he said, "I can help you take care of her."

"I don't need any help." But she did. She worked all day. The blind man was home, doing whatever it was that a blind man does all day in a creaky house. Dusting? Drinking? She didn't know.

"Okay," Olga said. "All right."

"I'll walk her when you are at work."

"Okay."

Bohdan smiled. Olga stared at his vacant gaze. *I'm never going to report this man to anyone, capitalist or not. Maybe I want to be a dirty capitalist.* At the thought of this, she laughed unabashedly.

Ignoring her laughter, Bohdan stood up. "We'll take good care of her. Bring the plate to the kitchen tonight. And if you want, I can let her outside later. Or I can take her for a short walk."

"That would be helpful, comrade," Olga said. This was Olga's way of reminding him of her allegiances. His position as a landlord could be a cover. He might be Soviet police. She couldn't trust anyone. No one could. It was always wise to say "comrade."

Bohdan smiled and bent down to feel Emma again, but the dog had returned to Olga's bed.

He patted Olga's hand. "Thank you." He didn't call her comrade.

She stopped him. "Your surname is Straivinski. That's Polish."

"Lithuanian."

"You're Russian."

"No," he corrected her, "I'm Lithuanian. My mother was Lithuanian."

Olga rolled her eyes. "But your father was Russian? You are a Soviet now."

"Like all men, my father was whatever they called him."

"All right," Olga said. "Never mind."

"All right," he said. "Never mind to you too."

15

On Sunday, January 8, 1950, the secret police came to arrest Daina. She was twenty-five. In her pretend world, thirty-one. She was painting a tiny bird on a teacup. When the men in black trench coats grabbed her by the arms, the teacup dropped from the table, smashing into pieces. Red and blue paint splattered the floor, the paint bleeding lavender.

"What are you doing with my wife?" Stasys demanded.

"She's being taken for questioning."

Daina felt her wings move. Just a smidgen, but it was enough. A sign. She was going to die now, nine long years after her family's murders. In the Heaven she imagined, there was the beach, like in Palanga, but without secret police. Without bullets. At the Heaven beach, children laughed. There was no shortage of food. There was no shortage of fine wool or silk. There was ice cream. Her fingertips were uncalloused, brand-new, perfect for dancing hand to hand. Her face was smooth—no windburn—perfect for dancing cheek to cheek. Her mother was there, happy, singing. The little Jewish girl was there, holding on to her porcelain doll once more. Daina smiled as the Lithuanian police, acting on orders from Vilnius, orders that had originated in Moscow two months ago, carried her, similar to how they'd carried her mother, her slippers dragging the floor, from the house. Daina was a slight thing. One of the policemen put his hand on her head, guiding her into the backseat of the hearse-like car. Everything was white with new frost. Stasys saw that Daina was not upset by her arrest. He stood on the front stoop, knowing that the neighbors, every one of them, were wiping at their windows to see. It was like the windows themselves, the two rubbed-out circles, were eyes. Soon the frost would fill them in again. Everyone would know, and no one would say anything.

On Monday, January ninth, Stasys paced his office and waited for Olga.

She brushed snow from her sleeves and started unbuckling her galoshes. "It's freezing out there." For two months, she'd left Stasys alone, and he had been glad for it.

Stasys said, "You reported her, didn't you? You fucking reported her!" He wasn't prone to using expletives.

Olga had forgotten what she'd done. She'd forgotten the plotting that had finally taken root and grown from one phone call to three men tromping up Stasys's steps to steal his wife. "Calm down," Olga said. "I didn't do anything. I didn't report anyone." She hung up her coat. There was a lump in her throat.

"You're like a snake."

"Oh, Stasys, don't say that. I didn't do anything." But she had done something. She remembered the phone call all too clearly now.

And Stasys could imagine Olga doing something terrible. She was from Moscow. She must've done it. Who else would've done it? "You need to get her back," he said.

"I'm not the secret police. I can't 'get her back.'"

"Just get her back."

She showed him her hands. "There's nothing I can do."

"What do you want? I'll give you anything. I need her back."

"I don't want anything." She searched the desk for her cigarettes. "I only wanted you to be sweet to me, Stasys. I only wanted you to love me how you love your precious wife, but I don't want anything anymore."

"You did it!" Tears formed in his eyes. "I need her back."

"I'm sorry about your wife, but I had nothing to do with it." She fumbled with her cigarettes, dropping them on the floor.

"You're a liar." Stasys crushed them with the heel of his boot, then bent down and picked up the crumpled pack. "I'm sorry," he said, "but please help me."

"I can't do anything. I'm sorry."

"Is there a chance?"

"I didn't do anything." Her palms were sweating. She rubbed them down her slacks, and Stasys grabbed on to her hands.

"Help me, please."

Groveling, in all its forms, disgusted Olga. Such overt displays of weakness were sickening. She said, "Your wife is probably working for one of the resistance movements."

"No, she's not."

"You can't know everything about your wife."

"But I do know that." Stasys pulled Olga's coat from the rack. "Fix it. We're running out of time."

"I can't *fix* this."

"You have to help me."

Begrudgingly, she took her coat.

When he heard Olga's heels on the stairs, Stasys got down on his knees. He wasn't a praying man, but he prayed now. Pressing his ink-stained knuckles to his lips, he prayed, *Dear God, bring her back to me. I can't live without her.*

In a holding cell in Palanga, Daina's wings were discovered, literally un-covered as she was ordered to strip. Pale in contrast to the rest of her sand-and-wind-worn limbs, having been bound by undergarments and coveralls, the wings were slightly askew, the right wing fuller and higher than the left. Daina favored her right hand, and the wing was in propor-tion to the difference between her right and left breasts and her right and left forearms. She was tired of guarding them. For the nine years she'd been tangled up with Stasys, she had not acknowledged them to him, to anyone, whereas at home in Vilnius, they had been common-place, envied by Audra and Danutė, who, in their own right, were gifted, in possession of beauty and brains: Danutė, the scholar and musician, and Audra, the caretaker and beauty. Their father used to tease that Audra would never have any girlfriends because they'd all be jealous of her looks, so she'd better be good to her sisters. Audra was beautiful with pink bow lips, blue eyes, and hair like wheat. She never had a cross word for anyone, and then, Daina remembered, she'd laughed at her murderer's impotence. Daina missed Audra. She missed all of them, but soon they'd be together. Finally, Daina would meet her maker.

Too many young people had been taken too soon. It was devastating to think of the wishes and kisses left unfulfilled, the musical scores and stories left unwritten, the songs left unsung. With bone too new and bone too brittle buried and burned, there was no one left to mourn, no one left to say prayers for the dead. Daina was ready to join them now. She'd been ready for nine years. Being alive was paying penance.

The Lithuanian guards, in awe of this birdlike woman under their command, were speechless and afraid.

"Why is she here?" one of them asked.

"Who sent her?" Both men suspected that God had sent her to the jail.

"She's an enemy of the people."

"Do *the people* know about her wings?"

Another guard said, "What if she puts a curse on us?"

"She won't curse us," the police captain said. He'd gone with two others to pick her up. "She's some kind of angel or something." He crossed himself.

Daina heard what they said. Huddled in the cell's corner, her wings cold against the bricks, she thought, *Here I am to join my family; here I am to meet my fate. I've been found out.*

The captain said, "Where are her clothes? What are you fools doing?" One of the guards retrieved her nightgown. The captain averted his eyes and passed it back to her. "I'm sorry." It didn't seem right or wise to put her in dingy prison garb. When she was deported, they'd do what was required, but for now, they wouldn't demean the winged woman. Not until they had no other choice. The captain said, "We should have someone take her picture while we wait to hear from Moscow."

A new guard, a kid on loan from the army, said, "I know someone with a Zorki. He's a real photographer. He moved here from Leningrad."

"Pick him up."

The captain asked Daina if she was warm enough.

I'm waiting to die.

He got her a blanket. "I'm sorry it's not softer," he said. "They don't issue anything of quality anymore. Are you Lithuanian?"

"From Vilnius," she said.

The captain asked, "Are you an angel?"

"No. I'm not an angel."

"But your wings." His voice echoed. *Wings.*

She nodded. The cell was big and gray. Its distinguishing characteristics were six metal beds attached by iron to brick walls, a single lightbulb, four barred windows packed with sand for insulation, and the institutional ticktock of a clock manufactured in Klaipėda, Lithuania—a seaport city ravaged by war, then razed and resurrected as an industrial proletariat wasteland.

"I'll get you some tea. Would you like that?"

Daina nodded.

While the captain steeped her tea, he sent one of the guards to his own home to bring softer blankets, to transform a stainless steel bunk into a cozy nest. The captain divided the dinner his wife had delivered. Whatever happened to this miraculous woman was out of his hands, but he could be good to her while she was in his care. He did not want to sin against one of God's angels. He did not want to burn in hell.

Daina said little more than, "Thank you." She hoped her death would be quick.

In the morning, a tall, thin man with wispy black hair and piercing blue eyes entered her cell. He held a camera. "Can I see them?" he asked. "I'm not KGB. I'm a photographer." He handed her a stained, crumpled business card. *Lukas Blasczkiewicz, Professional Photographer.* He said, "We're going to take your picture."

"What do you want to see?"

He stammered. "Wings . . . your wings? Can I see your wings?"

"No," she said.

Lukas Blasczkiewicz, professional photographer, said, "I don't think you have a choice. I didn't have any choice coming here. They made me bring my lights." He gestured with his hands. "They woke me in the night and forced me to come."

Daina said, "I'll talk to Captain Vincentas. I'm sure there's some mistake." But there was no mistake. Everyone was in agreement that they wanted pictures, proof that an angel had been in their Palanga holding cell. "A flash of light won't hurt her," the guards agreed. They even took a vote, which was not the most Soviet-minded thing to do. Whatever Daina was—angel, girl bird, or demon—they wanted evidence, before Moscow or anyone else got to see.

"It's indecent," she insisted. "It's obscene."

Captain Vincentas explained, "You're the one with the wings."

She countered, "I don't mean my wings. I mean," and she whispered, "taking off my clothes for a camera."

"You've got nothing to lose. You're being transported to Moscow within the week. From there, you'll probably be on your way to a gulag. If I could stop this from happening, I would. But I'm no one of importance."

"Can you just kill me?"

"I would never do that. Of course not." He held his camera up as proof that he was a photographer and not a murderer.

Daina refused to cry. She could undress by herself or the guards would do it—not Captain Vincentas—as there was some grace in being in charge. Daina chose the first option. To an extent, the policemen permitted her and the photographer some privacy. In the corner of the room, Captain Vincentas kept vigil to make sure that the photographer, whose hair and dress were unkempt, and whose eyes were eerily vivid, didn't violate the winged girl.

The photographer positioned Daina in front of a flexible screen. Turning on one light after another, he said, "Just try to relax." Then, he took a deep breath, glancing at the captain in the corner. *Here we go.* Lukas was nervous. He'd never taken pictures under these circumstances. He'd never seen a woman with wings. He'd never shot a naked woman. He took another deep breath and began snapping photographs, concentrating on the subject and light.

Daina heard the depression of the shutter and the film spindle turn. At first, she faced the photographer, one arm across her breasts, the other between her legs. To empty her mind, she recited in Latin Saint Casimir's hymn to the Virgin Mary. She turned when the photographer told her to turn, but she wouldn't move her hands. She bit her lip and blinked in the spotlight. All the while, she wished she might hide her wings, but there weren't enough arms or hands for that. She imagined the nudie photographs being passed from one man to another. Disgusting. She knelt and she bent over. She stood on tippy toes and held very still. The wings were folded in on her back like a baby bird's. Then Lukas Blasczkiewicz, the photographer, said, "Look at me. Look at the camera." Daina's face was hard. She stared squinting at the awful light. "Just like that," he said. He thought he could see the wings expanding on either side of her long arms. Daina thought she saw Saint Casimir inside the spotlight. Despite the light's intensity, she opened her eyes wider to see better. Lukas saw the orange starbursts in her eyes pop like fireworks. At the same time, Daina saw the saint's robes and then his cherubic face. The saint stretched out his arms, unbelievably long, for her to come, to come and be brave, to have no fear. She was bathed in this heavenly light, and she heard him say, *Don't be afraid.* Saint Casimir revealed himself to her. The prayer and words had come from her lips, and in turn, the saint had come to save her. The room glowed. The light from his embrace warmed her. Finally, he'd heeded her words. God had given her wings. No one could do anything to soil them. They were her birthright. She basked in Saint Casimir's light, dropping her hands to her side, eyes wide. *I don't want to die. For the first time in nine years, I don't want to die!* These two men could take all the photographs they wanted. It didn't matter. They would never know her or possess her. They would never take her faith. Her wings undulated and spread. There was no reason for shame. Not now. Not ever. Men will pass nudie pictures back and forth. That is what they do. So be it. Lukas Blasczkiewicz wanted to shout, "Turn around!" to get the wings in all their glory. *This is the mother lode!*

But his plea was unnecessary. Daina turned on her own. She spread her arms, her calloused fingers wide, like veins within the wings. This was between her and Saint Casimir and God. She was no longer afraid. Daina gave Lukas Blasczkiewicz the shot he wanted. His mother lode. His life's gold. She turned her wings to his spotlight, feeling them open further, growing, spreading, extending, until they filled the room, until she and Saint Casimir touched in the cold, damp cell. Daina felt enormous, brilliant.

Meanwhile, Captain Vincentas and Lukas Blasczkiewicz were thinking the exact same thing: *She is sent from God to right our wrongs.* Captain Vincentas said, "I can't breathe. I have the asthma." He rushed from the room. The photographer mumbled, "You're amazing. This is incredible. You're an angel." He repeated, "You're an angel," "Dear Lord," and "miracle." At one point, he ran to the bathroom, but when he came back, he mumbled some more about miracles and gifts from God. He mumbled, the letters losing their order, like speaking in tongues, until the film ran out. "Genius!"

Captain Vincentas returned, his hands on his heart.

Daina glowed. She did not want to die. God did not want her to die. She smiled at Lukas and Captain Vincentas. She was grateful that the police had come for her. She was grateful for another turn.

16

Lukas Blasczkiewicz

Lukas Blasczkiewicz, the photographer, could be a side note or an asterisk, but after he witnessed the illumination of Daina Vilkas Valetkiene, a desire and impetus to make all things beautiful took root in Lukas. From that day forward, he spent hours studying and basking in wonders that others overlooked, from starflowers to weeds, from inchworms to cockroaches and everything in between. He transformed his world into a shrine, a place of worship for breath and motion, and then the oddest thing happened: Lukas Blasczkiewicz stopped aging. Not one gray hair. Not one wrinkle. People noticed his wispy black spikes, like his hair had been whipped, and they regarded his long purposeful strides, the silhouette of a man on stilts. Lukas halted with the same purposefulness when something caught his eye, his upper body swaying forward like a reed.

I was born to a giddy Bolshevik in 1914. Few people know that there were giddy Bolsheviks, but there were, men and women with a fever for revolutionary change. When Czar Nicholas II sent Russian soldiers to fight in the Great War, it was a giddy time for those proletariat-hungry Bolsheviks like my father: a Marxist-Leninist man. A learned man. An earnest man, a real believer in the people. He'd traveled abroad. He'd met Lenin. He knew exiled theorists. He wanted to stake his claim in the reformation of a new Russia. He wanted to do something grand—to get rid of the monarchy. *Who do they think they are? The world is aflame!*

I was born taking pictures. I'm a photographer, and even as a boy, I saw things in pictures, moving and still. So picture a man, so happy that he is kicking his boots in the air, heel to heel, *tap tap* in your head, and he's nearly horizontal. This was my father.

A prankster. He was not as serious as the other famous revolutionaries, like Lenin, Stalin, Dzerzhinsky, and Trotsky. He laughed too much. Like Dzerzhinsky, he was born in Poland, but unlike Dzerzhinsky, he'd never been tortured or jailed. His jaw was intact. And he was never famous. Just giddy. A jokester, a fool.

When Czar Nicholas II abdicated the throne, my father celebrated with spirits. He made merry. My sisters and I were babies. My mother told us these things. In 1918, when my father read in the newspaper that Czar Nicholas II, his wife, and their five children had been killed by the Bolsheviks, he hid his face behind his drafting hand. According to my mother, he said, "Well, it was necessary. We will discuss it no further. I don't think." He paused. "It's terrible, but it's for the people."

She said, "That's no good, killing children. We have three girls and a boy. The czarina had four girls and a boy. Her boy was not much older than Lukas. They used cold steel."

According to my mother, my father told her that some evils are necessary, and that we should not think too closely on it. All his life, he'd wanted to think too closely, nose-deep in everything, but not this. "After all," he said, "one of those children might've claimed the throne."

"And rightfully so. It's their throne." Mother smacked our father. She did this whenever his notions infuriated her. She was not a revolutionary. She was a mother with a hot temper and swift hand.

The revolution came—just as my father had hoped. But what had he anticipated? There was no great parade. No celebrations. The churches were closed. The shops were rationed and nationalized. Food disappeared. Then there was the Red Terror, the Cheka—hundreds of henchmen donning long black coats, rounding up landowners, the top military officers, their wives and children, the clergy, the bourgeoisie. Everyday people on the street.

Thousands were shot on suspicion of being enemies of the Bolsheviks and then "enemies of the people." The numbers were printed in the newspaper as a warning. According to Mother, Father justified these murders by saying, "Lenin can't have another revolution. Russia can't have another revolution. He's doing what's necessary." Mother smacked him. In 1920, Father worked as an illustrator for *Pravda,* one of Russia's newspapers.

Six years later, the men in dark coats came to our door. Perhaps Father expected it, but I don't think so. Like I said, he was giddy with revolution, always wanting to be part of something big. We knew this. So when the henchmen came, we all wondered, *Why are they here? Father is a Bolshevik. He is true to Lenin. Why is Father being arrested?* I was twelve. My sisters were five, seven, and nine. I remember thinking that we might be going with him. I knew of other children who'd disappeared, but they did not want us, only Father. I had suspicions as to why we were spared. These notions had to do with my mother. With long black hair, and eyes like sapphires, she was exotic-looking. More importantly, she was admired by a man who knew a man who knew Joseph Stalin, Lenin's successor. Thankfully, this man was not a friend of Joseph Stalin's. To be Stalin's friend meant that you would inevitably be suspected of trying to undermine him, which meant that you would be shot in the nape of the neck or sentenced to hard labor. These were the options. Stalin was a great liquidator and exterminator. He quickly learned that the cleanest and quickest way to kill someone was to have them bend over, to point the gun upward at the nape of the neck and pull the trigger. Less blood. Less mess. Less writhing and moaning. I think this was partly learned when the last czar and czarina and their five children were killed. Rumor has it that they fought. Rumor has it that bayonets ended their young lives. Too much mess. It was that cold steel Mother mentioned. I see these things in color. I always have. Too much red.

My father was sentenced to twenty years hard labor. It had something to do with one of his cartoons, some suspicion that he was spreading anti-Soviet propaganda. Father denied this claim until he was faced with death or prison. Admission meant prison. Denial meant death. With this in mind, he confessed to a crime he hadn't committed.

The portly man who was a friend of a friend of Stalin's was named Anton. He visited the house when my father was working in Petrograd—before Father's arrest. My mother had told us that we were not to tell my father about Anton's visits. We never disobeyed Mother. Besides, for some time, Father's giddiness had been waning.

After the Cheka—the secret police—took my father away, Anton visited more frequently. I think he gave my mother ration coupons. I know that he gave her furs. My sisters and I pretended that nothing was wrong. We weren't permitted to do otherwise. There were to be no tears. I understood that to cry, especially in front of Anton, meant that I might join my father in some tundra prison. Anton often said, "Tell the boy not to look at me. His eyes are like ice." I had my mother's eyes. I still do.

My mother drank tea and acted like the bourgeoisie we were supposed to despise. She met with other ladies who wore plumed hats, and she talked about Anton, waving her hands, the cuffs of her blouses adorned with gold thread. She wiggled her pinky finger to describe Anton's manhood. The ladies laughed. In his absence, my father's giddiness had apparently taken hold of Mother. She took to drinking hard spirits and laughing too robustly for someone whose husband had been sentenced to hard labor.

I was thirteen when Anton bought me my first camera. I thanked him, averting my eyes, shaking his hand like the young man I was supposed to be. He bought my sisters all manner of dolls with eyes that opened and closed. Somehow, he had money. I knew too that he had his own wife and children in Kiev. My sisters and I called him Uncle Anton and sat on the front steps when he and mother went into our father's bedroom. If you can picture us there, me and my sisters lined up smallest to tallest, all of us with our mother's raven hair and blue eyes, licking our fingers, eating the sweets Uncle Anton brought—you'd see that we were smiling. I wish I had snapped our photo on one of those afternoons, but there was something deeply sad in us. I never thought of it then. Back then, I only thought of the sugar on my tongue, how lucky I was that there was a man bringing candy, but now I remember the sadness.

We grew up. Mother grew disoriented. Anton died. Father came home in 1944, eighteen years after he'd been taken away. I was thirty years old. My sisters were married. The oldest was a doctor. The middle sister was in a sanitarium. The youngest sister was in Siberia. She and her husband had been declared "enemies of the people." No one knew why. When Father came home, he was no longer giddy. His jaw was intact, but he walked with a limp. His right hand had been broken three or four times, so he started drawing dark disfigured faces with his left hand.

I worked for a local newspaper, taking pictures of farmers and factory workers.

I lived at home with Mother and Father. In my spare time, I worked as a portrait artist, taking photographs of those who could pay for developer and lighting, plus a few extra rubles for necessities or extravagances for pretty girls. And then, in 1950, I was reassigned to the former Lithuania. The Soviet Union was deporting Lithuanians to Siberia and simultaneously sending Russians to Lithuania, repopulating the state.

I won't lie to you. I was ambivalent about going. My mother's beauty and joy had turned to the purest ugliness. Her cheeks sagged. Her chin, which had been slightly dimpled, was like a crevice. I think my father was unconsciously drawing her disfigurement as he mumbled about hard work, how it was the path to righteousness. I think he believed this. They were sickening. I was suffocating, turning into a mumbler myself. I told you: I saw the world in pictures. I still do. There is nothing linear in my mind. There never has been, and Father's deportation to the gulag, and Anton's gift giving, and my sisters' later marriages, the one prison sentence, and my mother's dementia, none of it follows a straight line. It was all foretold in 1908 when my father embraced Bolshevism. I will always paint in blues, yellows, and blacks, the colors of bruises. I will always curve a line and drop graphite fast like gravity, like the world should be. I will never take an oath or swear any allegiance without changing the words in my brain. This is how I survive. If you are in a situation near to mine, do the same. Keep your brain tidy. Set perimeters.

Recently, I've begun painting my eyelids blue, setting the timer on my camera to capture just how blue an eye can be. My hair is long, twisted beneath a trapper's hat. I live in a third-floor walk-up in the Western Province of the Soviet Union. Above a shop. Out back, I raise rabbits, soft fuzzy things with pink and gray eyes. I work hard, taking pictures of the giddy people of this Western Province of the Soviet Union. Sometimes Mother writes to tell me that Father is doing poorly. Sometimes she writes to say that my sister, the one in a Soviet prison, might come home soon, and sometimes she writes to say that she's thinking of murdering Father or taking her own life. She's a complex woman, but when I think of her, I remember her before the revolution, before Father went away, when her beauty was her own and thereby ours.

I will not succumb to history. *Never.* My name is Lukas Blasczkiewicz, and if I learned one thing from my father, it is "Never embrace another man's idea of the world." I have my own ideas. This is a constant. In an inconsistent world, constants are a comfort. When I was thirty-six, I was awakened in the middle of the night and driven to a police station in Palanga to take photographs of a winged woman. Depending on your beliefs, she was like a bird, like a magic fairy, and most certainly like an angel sent from God. Because of her, I developed a thirst for miracles. I am on a quest like a knight. And no, I am not mad. I don't suffer dementia like my mother. I am sane. I am the sanest man in all the world. At least, I believe I am.

17

On January 9, 1950, Olga walked home. She felt sick, and this sickness was a biting, caustic, jabbing pain in her gut. Waves of nausea sent her to the toilet. Never had she felt anything like this, like the sickness was born on the inside and coming out, not like she'd caught something somewhere and she had merely to take an aspirin and dispense with it. This illness started in her trunk. It spread. Her scalp hurt. Her hands felt crackly. Her elbows were scaly. She was no longer a beautiful woman. She was like a monster, only she was just now recognizing her scales and claws.

She called the man in Moscow and said, "The woman I told you about, the woman named Daina Valetkiene . . . She is not a traitor." Her voice broke. "Can you send her home? Can you send her back? Is she . . . dead?" Olga's chest tightened. There was a fist in her throat. She was telephoning from the kitchen. Anyone could be listening.

The man said, "The woman is still in Palanga. I don't know why. They like her there, I guess."

"Can you do anything? Can you make them release her before she's transported?"

"She ought to be on a train by now, but she's not. The Western States are incompetent. I don't care how many Russians we send west. Incompetence and laziness run rampant."

"Will you see about helping her? She is not an upstart like I thought."

"Why do you care about this, Olga? It sounds like the sea is making you soft."

Olga bit her lip. "That's not it." She tried to sound upbeat. "You know me: I'll never change."

The man laughed. "No, I don't guess you will. Come see me when you are back in Moscow. Will you do that? I miss you."

"Of course."

"I'll see what I can do for you. No guarantee. For all I know, the Lithuanians killed her in their bumbling. What is she like?"

Olga didn't know. She'd never met her.

In the jail cell, Daina ate a zeppelin: a traditional Lithuanian potato-and-pork dish that long predates the *Hindenburg*. Captain Vincentas's wife had cooked up a batch for Sunday dinner. He'd told his wife about what he'd seen, about the wings, and at first she didn't believe him.

"You're drunk all the time," she said.

He said, "I swear on my father's life."

His wife wrapped up three zeppelins for the girl. "Maybe she's an angel."

"That's what I think."

It was Sunday, a week since Daina had been imprisoned.

Daina ate hungrily. She said, "Please tell your wife thank you. This is delicious."

Captain Vincentas said, "We got a call this morning." He looked disappointed.

"What kind of call?" Daina took another bite. "Is it time for me to go?" She looked up at the dark ceiling, thinking of the waterbirds that might be feeding on the jail's winter lawn or flying overhead. Maybe she'd see the birds when they moved her outside for the transport to Russia.

Unconsciously, the captain touched her face. He couldn't help himself. Her cheeks were rosy despite the grayness that permeated the jail. "You're not being deported."

She didn't understand.

"You're not being deported."

"What's going to happen? What is it?"

"I think you're going home."

"You think?" She felt her wings, flat beneath her nightgown, pulse. "Home?"

"I think." He looked at her plate. "My wife is a good cook."

Daina nodded.

"No one wants you to leave."

"When can I go home? Can I really go home?" This was the first time that she thought of her apartment with Stasys as home. She belonged somewhere.

"They've already sent someone to get your husband. I wanted to share a meal with you, to show you kindness."

She put her hands together in prayer, pressing them to her lips. *I'm going home.*

Daina Vilkas Valetkiene was desperate to live.

Stasys rode to the jail in the same black car that had picked Daina up. He sat in the backseat, praying. *Please, God, let her be all right. Please . . .* Inside the jail, she was waiting, wearing the nightgown he'd last seen her in. A blanket was draped over her shoulders. It belonged to Captain Vincentas. She tried to give it back to him, but he said, "No, keep it. It's cold outside." He wanted to hug her, but his subordinates were watching. It was unprofessional, and considering her wings, it might also be a sin. There were no formalities, no papers to sign. Everyone in Moscow would pretend that this had never happened, and everyone in the Palanga jailhouse, except for Lukas Blasczkiewicz and Captain Vincentas, would do the same.

Walking to the car, Stasys held Daina close. "Are you all right? Did they hurt you? Oh, Daina." He kissed the side of her face and the top of her head. "I love you so much." He'd never spoken the words aloud, but he couldn't stop from saying them now.

"I know you do, Stasys." She saw it in the way he looked at her. For her part, she'd grown accustomed to him, to their daily rituals. She'd even become fond of him, his kindness. The man she knew as Stasys

Valetkys couldn't be the same boy from her sisters' bedroom, not here in Palanga, not after pledging allegiance to Hitler and then to Stalin, not after nine long years together.

The same frosty windows that had watched Daina leave watched her return. She was covered by the captain's blanket and her husband's coat, climbing the front stoop. "Things are going to be different," Daina told Stasys, as he turned the key to the front door. "Things are going to be better."

"It's already better." There was no point in inquiring about an explanation for Daina's detention, because if there was something in writing, it was usually "Fascist, Enemy of the People, Traitor to Mother Russia"— which meant traitor to Stalin, Russia's father. Really, it meant nothing. That was the problem. People disappeared and died for nothing.

On the same night that Stasys retrieved his wife from prison, Olga went to Bohdan the landlord. She knocked at his bedroom door. She was going to tell some cute story about the dog Emma. She was maybe going to ask for a glass of something stronger than water—because she needed it. Instead, she hiccupped. Then her left eye twitched. Then her face itched and a prickly rash spread across her chest and up her neck, shame made manifest.

When the woman who'd raised Olga contracted influenza, coughing herself to death on a straw-filled mat, Olga did not cry. When other women, supposed friends, met their ends, Olga would nurse them to the last, but she would not cry. Always, she felt a gnawing chill. She felt the cold most in her femur bones, and the sensation made her wonder if there was something more than this exhausting fleeting life, a compilation of pleasure, pain, and death. Tears were a sign of weakness, and weakness was sickening, but then, standing in front of a blind man, a man who couldn't see her tears, Olga succumbed.

When she tried to speak, Bohdan said, "You don't have to say anything." He put his hands to her face and pressed the tears hard against her cheekbones—like he was trying to bury them back under her skin.

Olga fell asleep on his couch, and when she awoke, he said, "Let's get out of here." In the darkness (the world was always dark for Bohdan), they walked Emma six blocks to a squat cement building behind a taller brick building where Bohdan left a satchel behind a stack of wood. He said, "Come on," and they walked out of sight. When they returned twenty minutes later, there was whiskey and raspberry-filled chocolates where the satchel had been. Even though it wasn't rent day, Bohdan splurged. When they got home, he played Ella Fitzgerald and Billie Holiday. Taking his hand, Olga said, "I'll teach you to dance."

He said, "I'm blind. I'm not deaf. I can dance!" And he could. Old man that he was, he could dance. He took Olga in his arms and spun her gracefully in the cramped space, telling her, "Before the Russians, we had dance halls. We went out every night." He laughed. "Communists aren't much for dancing. They more fancy marching."

Olga laughed. *It's true! We much more fancy marching.* She was a card-carrying member of the Communist Party and proud of it. There were few things in life for which she was proud, but her allegiance to Stalin and the Party was something she took seriously. Stalin was like God. He giveth and he taketh away.

Bohdan ran his fingers along Olga's cheek and chin. "You are young and beautiful." She searched his eyes. Even though he couldn't see her, he sensed something in her—she knew. She took his calloused hand and put it at her waist.

He said, "You're young, too young for me."

She whispered, "My body is tired and I am sad."

He said, "That's no good. You're too pretty to be sad."

Two days later, eight blocks away, Daina climbed out of bed and went to the little Jewish girl's room where Stasys slept. She knelt on the floor, whispering Stasys's name. For nearly ten years, he'd been a light sleeper. He said, "What are you doing?" It was one o'clock in the morning. "Is everything okay?"

"I don't know."

He sat up. "What's wrong?"

Daina said, "I don't know how to tell you."

"What is it? You can tell me."

Daina kneaded the thin cotton nightgown bunched in her lap. "Will you be my husband? Will you show me how to make love?"

His heart felt like it would beat out of his chest. His hands quaked. He never imagined that she would want to love him. Slowly, Stasys made his way to the floor. "Are you sure?"

She nodded.

He pressed his lips to hers. He could inhale her, her wind-chapped lips ripe like fat berries against his. He didn't remark on her wings. He'd known about them for so long, they seemed as natural as her arms and legs, which were lean and sculpted. He saw her limbs and sometimes her wings when she climbed the dunes and bird-watched at sunset. When she was in their apartment, she was clothed head to toe. At home, her hands, calloused from work, were always busy with some chore, but not on the beach and not now. Not here. Beneath Stasys's blanket, Daina was the woman he watched on the beach. She was sublime. He'd never even held her hands, so he did that now, feeling the striations on her fingertips and breathing deep the rich smell of pastry still clinging to her hair. He'd waited so long, and he'd been willing to wait forever. In the early morning hours, he felt breathless. Her legs were wrapped around his. Neither of them spoke.

Hours later, a sparrow flapped ice from its wings, darting outside the window, and Stasys told Daina that he loved her, anticipating that she might respond in kind. Instead, she smiled contentedly and shut her eyes to the morning light.

Stasys was perplexed and disappointed. He naïvely thought that if a woman gave herself to a man, she must love him, but now he was annoyed with himself. Olga had been willing to *be* with him. Certainly, she did not love him, nor he her. It was stupid of him to think that words were more important than actions. Additionally, he couldn't know what Daina was thinking. She'd never been transparent. No one had. No one could afford to show the outside world who she was, on the inside—not in this world. Stasys had to believe that Daina loved him. He'd been with her nine years, a boyhood, and he'd loved her from the moment he'd found her sitting in the dirt. His love was enough. Nothing else mattered.

After their night together, Daina talked and laughed more. She told Stasys about her coworkers and about the birds she encountered on the beach. She smiled. For Stasys, this openness was better than any confession of love. Days and weeks passed. Daina and Stasys slept in the same bed. Stasys thought that she sometimes looked at him strangely, almost accusingly, reminding him of when she'd called him "soldier boy," and he had to look away because it was like she saw something threatening in him, something he didn't know about himself. It unnerved him, so he tried not to think on it. Sometimes he felt her wings shift and move, but they were always tightly folded against her back as she lolled beneath the sheets. She was not the girl he'd met in the dirt saucer. The jail cell had changed her.

In 1951, Daina lost a taste for her favorite cheeses. She ate broth and complained about indigestion. Stasys worried that she was sick. "You should stay home," he said, but she wouldn't hear of it.

"I have to work."

"And make everyone else sick?"

She threw up and felt better. Every day, she threw up at five p.m., just before leaving work. It was a purging. Maybe now that she was finally loving life, she would join her family. Maybe that was all that Saint Casimir had wanted from her in order to release her: a lust for life, an understanding of its worth—but now that she understood, now that the world's beauty wasn't wasted on her, she *wanted* to live. Eventually, she wanted to join her family, but not now, not yet. Her hair grew thicker and shinier, her stomach rounder. She worried that she had a tumor. One of her comrades at work told her, "You're going to have a baby."

Daina didn't understand.

"I've never seen anyone more pregnant."

"Pregnant?" Why hadn't she or Stasys considered this? They knew where babies came from. Daina crossed herself and concentrated on the sewing machine in front of her. Her back ached. Her ankles were swollen. She'd thought it was from the job. She could sleep anywhere. *Oh, Saint Casimir.* They were expecting a baby.

When she got home from work, she sat at the kitchen table waiting for Stasys. Her own breath seemed loud. When Stasys came in, he dropped his wallet on the table and went to the breadbox. "I am too hungry." She hadn't been cooking dinner or packing his lunch.

She sat there, watching him, a blissful expression on her face.

"Are you all right?" He bit into a hunk of bread.

"I am having a baby."

"No, you're not." He was chewing. He couldn't chew fast enough.

"Yes, I am."

"You're having a baby?"

"We're having a baby."

He swallowed the hunk of bread and pulled a chair up to sit across from Daina. "How?"

"How do you think?"

"So, you're not sick?"

"I don't think so."

Stasys began to cry, wiping the tears with the back of his sleeve. "I'm sorry." He couldn't have stopped the tears from coming and so he wasn't sorry, but "sorry" had felt like the right thing to say. He wasn't sure what a man was supposed to say in this situation. He sometimes forgot that he had grown into a man. He squeezed Daina's hand. "I'm going to be a father." Stasys Valetkys remembered his own father, a smart, generous man. A good husband with a gentle soul. Stasys's mother had been the disciplinarian and his father had been the consoler. "You'll be all right, son. You're a smart boy." He'd shown Stasys affection. Stasys would be a good father. He would show affection. Right away, he imagined a son.

"And I'm going to be a mother," Daina said.

"I love you," he said. And then Stasys imagined a daughter, a beautiful smart girl like Daina. It would be a baby, a new life, boy or girl. Whichever. It did not matter.

Daina was grinning. She was not going to say "I love you." That was fine by him. He had enough love for all of them.

Expectant, quiet in anticipation, their apartment took on its own voice as well as a hopeful breathing. In and out. Soon. Very soon. Life was coming. A beginning. There were new sounds and new sensations. They both heard the sea, even though it was nearly a mile away. In July, they felt the baby kick. In August, three days of heavy rains beat down and sounded like drummers squatted on the roof. The voices of children on the street floated through the open windows. The teakettle whistled and the bathwater ran. Tourists came and slept in the master bedroom. Daina and Stasys slept in the Jewish girl's bed, the porcelain doll at their side. They were in a waking dream, nesting and clasping hands. At night, Daina prayed to see a vision of her mother. Sometimes she thought she heard her mother singing. Daina had been to a doctor, who said that she should have a healthy baby. There was no reason why she shouldn't. Daina believed that the spirits of her family would be at the birth. Stasys was worried. What if their child was born with wings?

What would the doctors do? Would they let Daina bring the baby home? Would they hurt the baby? Would they let his wife come home? Every night, he prayed for a healthy child. He didn't care if there were wings, only that they could bring the baby home. He'd lost too much. He couldn't suffer the loss of a baby he hadn't even met yet.

In September, the tourists went home, and Stasys and Daina went back to the big bed. He stayed awake listening, resting his head on Daina's belly. Soon. Very soon. The house continued to whisper and breathe.

Across town, Olga and Bohdan danced three or four nights a week. In the darkness, Olga lay still while Bohdan used his fingertips to draw maps and diagrams of places he'd seen—before he'd lost his sight—across her stomach and thighs, up and down her legs. She closed her eyes. Bohdan was not too old for her. He was just right. They did not engage in sex, only intimacy. In the daylight, they played with the dog, Emma. Olga helped Bohdan in the kitchen. The other tenants whispered behind their backs. Bohdan could hear what they were saying, but he paid them no mind. "I bet the Russian girl doesn't pay him rent," they said. "I bet the old man pays for sex with her." Life was too short to be concerned with gossip. He did not care if Olga was Russian. She could be German or French. Even American. When he touched her face, which he did a lot, she always smiled for him. He knew that she was *not* always smiling. He sensed pain in her voice, but for him, she smiled. Sometimes they drank black-market whiskey. Always, they had a good time. When Olga told him about her sordid past, he said, "You were a child. It's not your fault."

She touched his face the same way he touched hers, sensing his youth, the man he'd been, not the old man that he was.

At work, Olga kept insisting that she'd had nothing to do with Daina's arrest. She'd come to Palanga with a mission. Olga, the card-carrying Communist, had a capitalist sensibility. If you worked hard enough, you got what you deserved. You got the handsome man. *Nothing is out of reach. I can have whatever I desire. I must be ruthless and single-minded.* Something in the slow pace of Palanga, the sweetness of Bohdan, the unconditional love of Emma had changed Olga. Something in the orderliness and cleanliness of this new life had transformed her. She couldn't fully own what she'd done. Not for the rest of her life. She only told Stasys, "I'm glad your wife is back."

He nodded.

Olga worked hard at her job. Her illustrations had a fierceness that Olga, the woman, now lacked. The red lines, the hammer and sickle, were sharp. "What do you think, comrade?" she asked Stasys, seeking his approval.

"Fine," he said. He couldn't make her go away. Sometimes he'd forget, for a split second, what she'd done to his wife. He'd start to talk to

Olga about Daina and the baby on its way. Then he'd remember and stop himself. *Never mind.* From the corner of his eye, he watched her work zealously, a contentment on her face that hadn't been there the year before, and he understood too that if Daina hadn't been imprisoned, she might never have wanted to live, she might never have let him be the husband he yearned to be.

Stasys glared at the ridiculous words he was writing. He elbowed his typewriter, five and six keys clacking the paper at once. He chewed on his pencil. It was hard for him to think about anything but the baby on its way. The information office he and Olga shared fermented with hope.

On October 6, 1951, after twenty-four hours in labor, Daina delivered a daughter with a cone-shaped head and black eyes. The doctor told Daina that her eyes would change color, "and her head will round." Daina looked in awe at her baby. She didn't see the black, sharklike eyes or the conical head. She saw the most beautiful baby in the world.

In the hallway, upon hearing that he had a healthy baby girl, Stasys asked the doctor, "Is there anything unusual?"

"What do you mean?"

"Anything different or peculiar?"

"I told you about her head, but that's standard with a forceps delivery."

"Is Daina all right?"

"She lost a lot of blood. She's a bleeder. Weak, but she will be fine."

Stasys took a deep breath and pushed the door open. His wife was most certainly not weak.

Walking past three other women in recovery, he went to Daina. "Are you disappointed?"

"About what?" Her eyelids were droopy.

He whispered, "That she doesn't have your wings?" He bit his knuckle. They had avoided this topic, but he couldn't any longer. He had to know how Daina felt.

"Of course not, Stasys." She shook her head at his silliness. "Did you see her? She's amazing."

Stasys peeked at the swaddled baby, at her five fingers on one hand, five on the other, at the smallness of her back. "She is." He opened the blanket to touch each toe. Her eyes were squinty, her complexion ruddy, her chin dimpled. He kissed her forehead and tiny ears. Resting his palm on her fuzzy blond head, he looked at Daina. "I love you."

Daina kissed him. "I'm tired."

All total, there were six women in the recovery room. Each of them had had a healthy baby. Each of them had had her first baby. Today was an epiphany, a birthday for six mothers and six children, a wish that each of these children would one day raise the Lithuanian flag.

Stasys sat on the edge of Daina's bed, telling her, "You did it! You're wonderful. I love you so much." Daina tugged at Stasys's shirtsleeve. Neither of them knew what the future held. Since the day they'd met, they'd merely been surviving. "I would like to name her Audra after my sister. Is that all right?"

"Whatever you want."

Daina kissed the knuckle Stasys had been biting when he'd first asked if she was disappointed about the wings.

She whispered, "Come closer."

Stasys leaned in, pressing his face to Daina's. "What is it?"

"I love you," she said. "I'm glad that you were a boy and not a bear." She scratched her cheek. "But I am very tired now."

Daina handed the baby girl to Stasys, who was unsure what to do. He cooed and made *tic-toc* sounds with his tongue. Daina rolled over and closed her eyes. Stasys told the baby, "Your mother loves me. Did you hear that? She loves me." He sat at Daina's side. He'd given up needing to hear those words, but just the same, they were music to his ears. When Audra started to cry and Daina didn't wake, he tried rousing her. The other mothers were feeding their babies while nurses in green uniforms skittered past. What had the doctor said? She's a bleeder? What did he mean? Stasys stopped one of the nurses. She was Russian. "I'm worried," he said. The baby was wailing. "Can you check on my wife?" The nurse was petite with short, dark hair. She had deep lines above her lip that disappeared when she smiled. "The baby is hungry," she said.

Stasys agreed.

The nurse checked Daina's wrist for a pulse, and then, shaking her head, lifted the blankets covering Daina's legs. "She's lost a lot of blood. I'll get the doctor." Daina wore a peaceful expression. Audra's cries of hunger fell on deaf ears. Unconsciously, Stasys slipped his finger into the baby's mouth and whispered to Daina, "Don't go to sleep on me. You have to wake up." He thought, *You've gone and done it to me, haven't you, Daina? You finally told me that you loved me, and now you're going to break my heart in two.* The nurse took the baby. Helpless, Stasys was herded toward a small waiting room while Daina was wheeled in the opposite direction.

The waiting room walls were the color of pea soup, and Stasys pressed his forehead to one of two small windows frosted with ice. He was reminded of the windows with eyes. There was always someone watching, always someone who knew things he didn't know, like that his parents were to be exterminated. Someone knew that some girls refuse to bleed while others are born with wings. But Stayis hadn't known any of these things. Someone or something knew everything that had been unexpected for Stasys, the slices of life that had knocked him off his feet and to the ground to grovel in the dirt. He was a survivor, but he didn't know if he could do it anymore. The Lord gives and the Lord takes away, and too much had been taken.

The doctor found Stasys with his nose and cheek pressed flat against the glass. Stasys saw the doctor's reflection and felt the man's hand heavy on his shoulder. The doctor smelled of antiseptic. Stasys presumed the worst. Despite the cold, Stasys was sweating. The doctor said, "She's going to be fine," and patted Stasys's back. "She's a tough bird." Someone or something knew that Stasys could endure no more. He turned to shake the doctor's hand, holding it in his grip, both men understanding the weight of this simple gesture.

Two days later, Stasys and Daina took their healthy baby girl home.

Audra's head did lose its conical shape, and her eyes did change from black to blue. The first year, she slept in the same room as Stasys and Daina, but when she was nearly two, they gave her the little girl's bedroom and the porcelain doll. It was 1953. On March fourth, they secretly celebrated the Feast of Saint Casimir. Daina had told Stasys about Saint Casimir's visitation in the prison cell. They would always celebrate his feast. The next day, March fifth, Joseph Stalin, general secretary of the Communist Party Central Committee, died.

Comrades wept in the streets. Presumably out of grief, but truthfully out of jubilation. Daina and Stasys wept. The greatest butcher the world had ever known was dead. It didn't matter why anyone wept. It was a mass catharsis of the people, and that bastard Stalin would've liked it.

A month later in the quiet of two a.m., Olga pressed herself against Bohdan.

Bohdan was old, but he was not too old, and he would not pretend that he hadn't fantasized about feeling himself inside Olga. A man can't listen to jazz and swing and smell a woman and trace her figure with his hands without wondering, *What if she wants to be with me?* On this fortuitous night, Olga told Bohdan that she was crazy about him.

Bohdan laughed because he was an old man and he could scarcely remember the last time a woman was swooning on his account.

Olga guided his hand along the curve in her waist, stopping at the bend in her knee and then at the bend in her arm. She pressed his hand beneath and between her breasts.

Olga had always thought there was something bright within herself. If anyone could see this potential, it would be a blind man. Bohdan climbed on top of Olga, pouring himself like molten iron into her. Olga's skin was the stuff of Chinese lanterns, paper thin, and Bohdan was the flame causing her to rise high above the hovels of her past. Bohdan illuminated the night and, if only for a few seconds, saw the luminescence of Olga's face.

Across town, Daina was awake. She saw light spurting like firecrackers, spilling from a window, buoyed by the cloud-filled night. It settled like a shiny halo over the seaside village.

As Time will do whether we want it to or not, it passed. It passed quickly. Daina and Stasys grew older, and Audra grew up. Nothing was as scary as it had been when Stalin was alive. He was a mythic figure, the great father, who'd ensured the nation's success. This is what Stasys now wrote in pamphlets that were distributed to schools throughout Lithuania. There were fewer deportations to Siberia. No one felt as nervous about smiling or even laughing. Stasys joined the Lithuanian resistance. With ample access to paper, he participated in the underground newspaper, smuggling news about Lithuania's terrible economic condition to the Western world, especially to Lithuanians living abroad.

Olga still worked alongside Stasys, but nowadays, she talked a blue streak about her blind man. "I love him," she told Stasys. After so many years, it was hard for Stasys to hold a grudge against Olga. They saw each other every day, and even though he felt in his bones that she was responsible for Daina's arrest, he couldn't hate her. As Daina once said, "Everybody has a story."

PART FOUR

It may be argued that the past is a country from which we have all emigrated, that its loss is part of our common humanity.

—Salman Rushdie

18

Prudence

My Oma and the Old Man returned home to Brooklyn. They had a trip to Lithuania to plan. During those months of planning before our actual journey, my Oma's worry lines doubled. Her fear had nothing to do with flying and everything to do with her past. In order to fly to Lithuania, officially known as the Western Province of the Soviet Union, we would first have to fly through Moscow. The East Germans, under orders from Moscow, had built that dreaded Berlin Wall that my Oma feared. At first just barbed wire, but later, concrete and watchtowers; the border guards had shot anyone who tried to cross, and she knew that too many boys had bled to death in the no-man's-zone between East and West. And now she was supposed to willingly enter the Soviet Union? It seemed like begging for death. She'd never been back to Germany. Her cousins were trapped in East Berlin. In order for her to even telephone one of them, her call was routed through Moscow. And now she was traveling to the Soviet Union? She couldn't imagine. Or she could imagine . . . which is why she wouldn't go. She couldn't go. Not to Lithuania, and certainly not to Moscow.

She explained this to the Old Man, and he dismissed her fears. "You worry too much."

"And you are too optimistic."

Certainly, the Old Man couldn't remember the last time anyone had called him optimistic.

I was not afraid. Rather, I felt that I had lived my whole life to take this trip. It was late summer, but already I was counting the days. In Los Vientos, blue crabs were fat, the size of dogs, a sign that the worst of the heat was nearly behind us. I remember that I no longer had time for Wheaton. I'd replaced him with father-daughter dates, phone calls with the Old Man, and dusty history books. I'd also started taking lone walks to the pier because I coveted the ghost of my great-aunt Daina. She did not belong to Wheaton. I remember that when I did see Wheaton, I was usually relaying the Old Man's stories. Wheaton's eyes reflected the Atlantic. He stopped telling me about his visions. I guess he knew that I had other things on my mind. He never complained. He couldn't find fault or place blame. He understood my desire to see my homeland and discover my birthright. I suspect he was counting beats: *the closing curtain.* Five.

From the pier, I admired the horizon, imagining what was on the other side. I didn't tumble again. There was no reason. Soon enough, I'd be crossing over. I felt the pulse and beat of bird wings like a musical interlude, a drumroll of sorts.

On November 4, 1989, we boarded a flight from New York to London. My Oma warned each of us that we were flying into the belly of the beast. "We should turn around in London and fly home." On our flight from London to Moscow, her knees buckled in the aisle, and Freddie had to basically carry her to her seat. "We shouldn't be doing this." When she started hyperventilating, the Old Man pulled a bottle of tranquilizers from his pocket, and Freddie ordered her a whiskey on the rocks to wash it down.

After a while, the sedative took effect. My Oma tinkled her ice and fingered the small bag of pretzels on her lap tray. "She is fine," the Old Man assured us. Veronica and Freddie held hands. The Old Man regarded them with curiosity. Veronica was the woman who was neither Lithuanian nor German, but she was my mother, so she couldn't be the most terrible woman in the world. I had my father's dark hair, but other than that, I resembled neither of my parents. They'd started dating in September, after Freddie took up residence across the causeway in Saint Mark's. Never mind that they were still married. At sixteen, I could not be bothered with their ridiculousness.

My Oma took another pill and ate a package of sugar cookies. After her third sedative, she lost consciousness, her head slumping onto Freddie's shoulder. Many of the passengers on our plane spoke Russian, and somewhere in the sky above the Republic of Volgograd, the Old Man was out of his seat, starting conversations with them. "I'm Lithuanian. I am taking my family to see our homeland." The Old Man was very proud of his return. According to him, everyone on the flight told him that he would love Moscow. "It is a golden city."

At some point, we all nodded off, awakened by the pilot's announcement that we would be landing shortly. Ingeburg was white-knuckled, gripping the armrests. As the landing gear came down and the wing flaps came up, she had a noisy, foul burst of gas. When the tires touched down on the freezing tarmac, she vomited on Freddie's lap. The interior of the plane rattled as Freddie grabbed for the sick bag. My Oma apologized. Then she refused to move. "We should not be here," she insisted. We were stuck in our seats while the other passengers made putrid faces as they were trapped in the aisle by her row. We were the last ones to disembark.

Surprisingly, there was a car, courtesy of a branch of the Soviet Union's Diplomacy Office, waiting for our family. The Old Man had never been in the Soviet Union, but he liked the changes that Mikhail Gorbachev had instigated—what he'd seen on the news, the new concepts like perestroika and glasnost. Change was happening fast. Of course, the Old Man believed in the fall of communism. He'd always believed in it, but what had once seemed impossible now seemed to be coming to fruition. It was emotionally overwhelming.

We managed to clean my Oma up and get her off the plane, but she did not want to get in the waiting car, certain it meant transport to our deaths. The other passengers had descended into the underground rail system. "It's okay," Freddie told her. The Old Man was surveying the landscape, telling everyone to hurry it up. "Inge," he said, "get in the car and stop being not smart."

The colorless November sky reminded me of how Wheaton's eyes sometimes looked.

As our official car headed through the city, we saw high-rise utilitarian housing complexes, row after row of gray and tan buildings. Nearing Moscow's center, we crossed a grand bridge over the Moskva River and encountered gold-domed Gothic cathedrals and palaces. Our hotel was on a busy street, not far from the Kremlin. Lined with flags, it looked more like an embassy than a hotel.

At the front desk, a woman with a blond coif and bright blue eyes informed us that they'd had two luxury suites reserved for us, but then they'd had a celebrity—whose identity must remain a top secret—come and insist on those suites. She smiled, apologizing for the inconvenience, explaining that this was to be expected as we were now in Moscow, the richest, grandest city in the world.

On the elevator ride up to our floor, the Old Man told me that the hotel reminded him of the fun house at Coney Island, all trickery, smoke and mirrors. I thought it was quite lovely, with high ceilings and red velvet drapes, but as we entered our adjoining rooms, he pointed out just what he meant. Our drapes were dusty and cinched with jute rope. The writing table was wobbly. The ceiling was stained with watermarks and black mold, and the windowpanes were loose, the glazing nearly gone, the draft vicious. Our two rooms shared a bathroom, and although it smelled of bleach, many of the floor tiles were cracked or missing. Outside, a heavy snow fell, and if you stood close to the window, you felt the cold. Being from Florida, I liked the cold. It was new to me.

While Freddie and Veronica unpacked, my Oma curled up on the bed. The Old Man checked our room for bugs, not the crawling kind. He told me that he never imagined himself in Moscow, but he would do whatever it took to show me our homeland. "Just wait until you see our Lithuania." He put his hand to his chest. I put my hand on top of his and thought I felt his heart beating. I could not wait!

19

Prudence

*T*he radiators clunked and sighed as water gurgled through the pipes. My poor Oma was freezing. She'd brushed her teeth twenty times, but her mouth still tasted bad. Her stomach hurt. She sat in the middle of a twin bed, the covers gathered at her neck. The Old Man said, "Our guide is meeting us in the dining room for dinner."

My Oma said, "I can't do it."

I remember that the Old Man kissed her forehead and pulled the dusty duvet tighter around her neck, telling her that she had to get well before we left for Vilnius, the former capital of Lithuania.

I pressed my hand to the window. The cold felt delicious. Breathing out, I could see my breath, Moscow in November. My Oma's feet were sticking out beneath her blanket. They were old feet with hammertoes and bunions, and I remember draping a blanket over them. Selfishly, I wanted her to hurry up and recover, afraid she'd ruin our trip. We'd come so far. I had to see Lithuania.

The Old Man was smoking his cigar, having a fine time telling one of his long history lessons about the Grand Duchy of Lithuania, at one time the largest nation in Europe. We'd already, without requesting it, had a bottle of Russian vodka brought to the room, and he was helping himself. "Vodka," he said, "is the one thing the Russians will always have." The Old Man was explaining in his didactic way that Lithuanians are nationalists, but not in the same way as the nationalism that spawns wars. "We live and let live." I remember thinking that nationalism has five syllables. Wheaton would like it.

At dinner, we met our guide, a petite woman with spiky blond hair and cat-eye glasses. Her name was Natasha Sluska. (She has since moved to the United States and works as a translator for a national charity, but back then, she was as red as they come.) We soon discovered that it was her job to subtly and not so subtly prove to us, despite the declining economy, that the Soviet Union was superior to the United States. I remember her thin-lipped smile and how she pushed her glasses up the bridge of her nose with one finger. From birth, she'd been indoctrinated to believe that the United States of America was bent on her destruction. Natasha was neat in appearance, wearing a pencil skirt and fitted jacket, one of the last vestiges of an orderly Soviet Union. Mass changes were afoot. Despite her position, Natasha was unaware. She gently informed us that she would be our guide for the duration of our visit, including our trip to the Western Province.

The Old Man didn't hide his disdain for phrases like "Western Province." He tugged at his beard, pursed his lips, and shook his head. "I'm not going to any Western Province. I'm going to Lithuania."

Natasha smiled politely. "And where is your wife, Mr. Vilkas?"

I explained that my Oma was sick to her stomach.

"We will send something to the room."

The Old Man opened his menu. It was imposing, the size of a poster. Natasha Sluska explained, "We have everything here, anything you could possibly want. This is the land of plenty."

I wanted soup. This was doable. There was cabbage soup and turnip soup and Beluga caviar, but nothing else: not the steak Freddie and the Old Man wanted. Not the green salad Veronica requested. There was vodka and a mashed beet blintz. Even I tried the vodka. The Old Man wanted to know why it was that the restaurant had nothing listed on the menu, and Natasha explained that we had just ordered the specific things that were late in being delivered to the restaurant.

Later, the Old Man slipped away to the kitchen. He knew enough of the language to ask a cook how he might get a steak. It came down to American dollars. How many American dollars was the Old Man willing to spend? According to the Old Man, after some tough negotiations, a deal was struck. He also finagled chocolate ice cream.

Thus, on our second night in Moscow, we feasted on steak and ice cream, and Natasha Sluska proclaimed, "I told you that we have everything you could possibly want in Russia." She truly believed what she said. The Old Man guffawed but said nothing of his bargain with the cook.

My Oma was still sick, refusing to leave our hotel room. I remember that she scratched the backs of her knees and elbows until the skin flaked white on the red duvet. She threw up the toast and hard-boiled egg she'd eaten for breakfast. The hotel concierge sent up a pitcher of hot steeped dandelion tea to help settle her stomach, but nothing helped. Each day, the rest of us had an itinerary to follow, a guided tour designed to impress and enchant, while Oma stayed in bed.

On our first day, we visited the Tretyakov Gallery, a museum housing some of Russia's greatest art. It was stunning. Even the Moscow Metro was worth seeing. The underground train had reflective marble walls, high ceilings, and shimmering chandeliers, another testament to the proletariat's brilliance.

Back in our room, the red velvet duvets were soft, but underneath, the sheets were scratchy and threadbare in spots. My Oma remained in this drafty room, her fear festering like a rotten plum in her gut.

She had lost her mother and father and brother, and then she'd lost her cousins to an iron curtain, and here we were behind the borders of this imposing red-star state, awakened each morning by its image on the television announcing the start of a new day.

It was November 9, 1989, and none of us knew that in Berlin, Germany, a wall was being torn down. In the rest of the world, it was on the front page of every newspaper, the story running continuously on cable television, but not in Moscow. Only recently had the 1969 moon landing by the United States been shown on Soviet television. Every morning, there were exercise programs and news reports about the evils of capitalism. At night, there were symphonies, the music of Tchaikovsky, and special programs on the glory of Lenin. In between, there were montages of happy, marching children, red stars, and the Soviet flag. I thought it was strange but alluring, and I thought it would be easy to believe the Soviet mirage.

For two days while we toured the Kremlin, my Oma remained in the hotel room. That black plum was rotting and wouldn't let anything else, neither soup nor bread, not even water, remain. The Old Man thought we might have to cut the trip short. She was pale. Soon we'd need to get her to a hospital. She was dehydrated. On the third day, Natasha Sluska called for a physician. He started an IV and injected fluid under her skin. Then she looked puffy. I told her about the grand cathedrals and palaces, the great works of art. She stared blankly out the frosty window.

Fear breeds sickness. Few things breed it as deeply or as quickly. I know that if my sweet Oma had seen the first sledgehammers knocking against the Berlin Wall, she would've tossed the bedcovers aside.

If she'd seen the pickaxes gouging out concrete and rock, she'd have thrown her hands in the air.

If she'd seen the strangers from East and West holding on to one another, hugging, and patting each other on the back, she'd have eaten cake.

If she'd heard the newscasters shouting above the flag-waving crowd, she would've raced outside in the freezing cold, bunions and hammertoes be damned, and my sweet Oma would've danced in Red Square. I know it. I wish that we'd all known what was happening in the world, but we were in a protected proletariat bubble. Of course, we'd know soon enough. That's the thing about bubbles. At some point, they burst.

In the middle of the night, my Oma shook me awake. She said, "I don't care that I missed the art. I do not like Russians, nothing about them. Not even Russian babies because they'll be indoctrinated." She looked like a specter in a long white polyester nightgown. Before I could respond to what she'd said, she shuffled back to her own bed and went to sleep. I was awake.

This was our last night in Moscow. In only three days, we'd seen

Lenin's tomb, Red Square, Victory Park, and Saint Basil's Cathedral. We could've spent three days alone touring Red Square. There'd been so much to do. At three in the morning, I went to the Old Man. He sat alone in an upright chair in the corner making gruff, bearlike sounds.

"I'm worried about Oma," I told him.

"She is a tough bird, Prudence." He scratched his salt-and-pepper beard. "Do you want a cigar?"

"Do you have any cigarettes?" He shook his head that he did not, and continued, "This is shit, you know . . . Their charades. Nothing here is what it seems to you. Your Oma is lucky she did not see it. Not lucky to be sick, but she will be better when we are away from this."

The skin beneath the Old Man's eyes was puffy. I don't think he'd been sleeping. We were all antsy to get out of Russia, and he couldn't hold his vodka the same way he could hold his beer. The vodka made him sad. He told me that they dug their own graves, and I asked him, "Who?"

"The Russians gave them shovels and they digged in the dirt until it was deep enough to bury them, and then they got on their knees, and if anyone tried to run, he was shot."

Like my father before me, I did not want to hear such things, and as if he could read my mind, the Old Man said, "Do you think I want to remember?"

The Old Man puffed on his cigar and looked at the rotting ceiling. "Who cares about shit?" I remember that he spoke to me in the present tense like everything was just happening, like forty-eight years hadn't passed. "If they have it their way, they will murder everyone or send us to work, to fish or dig iron ore until our hands bleed and we die." The Old Man's voice was sloshy and guttural.

I felt a lump in my throat, pressing against my trachea and pharynx, filling my voice box and spreading like thick jam over my vocal folds. I started to cry because I could imagine the men in that pit. I could imagine the Old Man digging for his father.

Right away, he changed the subject. He hadn't meant to upset me. He used his thumb, which smelled sweet like his cigar, to wipe the tears from my face. He said, "I will teach you some songs. There is every kind of song in Lithuanian. There are hunting songs, milling songs, harvest songs, herding and plowing and haymaking, but the most important song is the song for the heroes who fight for their freedom. When I was a boy, there were always festivals and singing, and my mother, she was the greatest at singing." With this, he sat up straighter and touched his throat. "Even I used to sing! You would never believe it. And my sister Daina is named after the word for song. She had the wings. She had a beautiful voice." His anger and sadness had evolved into excitement. "I remember singing."

His face glistened in the dim light. I asked if he was crying.

He gruffed, "There is something in my eye."

I loved my grandfather how I imagined a girl should love her father, unconditionally, wholly, and without reservation. Despite everything he'd endured, the Old Man was soft on the inside, a young man in an old man's dress.

I feel dirty from the plane. The rental car has that new car smell, and my mother is smoking, rolling down her window. There were house sparrows in the parking lot when we signed for the car. House sparrows were first brought to the New World and released in Brooklyn, New York, in 1850 because they were thought to feed on the insects that were then feeding on crop populations. Rather, as ground feeders, the sparrows ate those very crops that they were thought to protect. Because they've endured and thrived, simultaneously crowding out native bird species, sparrows are regarded as pests. I have old cookbooks filled with sparrow and blackbird recipes. Sparrows belong to the Old World, not ours.

The Old Man is from that world. We are driving to the hospital. My mother offers me a cigarette, but I don't feel like smoking. I'm not thirsty and I have no appetite. It doesn't matter where the sparrow originated. It's the most abundant songbird in the world. I want to be close to the Old Man, feeling his beard tickling my shoulder, hearing his gruff voice tell me that everything is going to be all right because I am a Vilkas. Like the house sparrow, I know how to adapt. If it weren't for the Old Man, I don't know that I would've survived losing Wheaton.

20

Prudence

Wheaton and I parted ways two years after my trip overseas, when the scrub of Los Vientos was no longer underfoot. I was accepted to the University of Florida and Wheaton was accepted to Saint Mark's College, a private liberal arts school only fifteen miles from home. Wheaton still carried his brown notebook, bulging with folded drawings and held together by thick rubber bands.

For acceptance to Saint Mark's, Wheaton spent six months compiling a portfolio, none of the work as brilliant as what I'd seen crumpled in his old brown recipe book.

Wheaton's father, Rick, had always wanted to attend the small yet prestigious Saint Mark's College, but instead he impregnated Lily with Wheaton's sister and procured a job as a proofreader for a local tourist rag. Growing up, we never saw Rick. He quarantined himself in a small room off the den working on his novel. While Wheaton and I ate dinner with Lily and Tammy, Rick was in the next room click-clacking away. About once a month, I saw him emerge from his cave and talk gibberish about people we didn't know. These people, Wheaton explained, were Rick's characters, and they were more real to him than Lily, Tammy, or Wheaton. Rick certainly spent more time with them.

Wheaton's mother was having an affair with a building contractor who lived four houses away. She liked the contractor because he made things with his hands and not his mind. She could see and touch the things he made. Wheaton, Tammy, and I knew about the affair. We didn't discuss or mention it. I think Lily knew that we knew, while Rick was oblivious, caught up with the fictitious lives of his characters. His real family was not welcome within the borders of his imaginary world.

I was busy at the University of Florida, with plans to be a marine biologist. I had no foresight.

It was during my first semester, October 1991, that Wheaton quietly left me.

In 1989, he'd feared my departure from his life because I had found my birthright, but in all our years together, I had never considered his sudden exit from mine.

The last time I remember speaking to him, he was telling me about his new friend Skye Bouvier. He'd known her for little over a month, and already I was sick to death of hearing about her. She was studying social work, and he'd told her about his visions. I was jealous, fearful of being replaced. The last thing he said to me was that he'd never be a leading man with me. I thought he was drunk or in the midst of some vision. I made light of what he said. I planned to see him over fall break and then again at Thanksgiving. But he was not there. He didn't come home for fall break. His college was fifteen minutes away, but he'd made "other plans." He didn't go into specifics. At Thanksgiving, Lily said, "He's not coming home." I didn't know that she meant *ever again*. I asked her if Wheaton was involved with Skye Bouvier. She had no idea to whom I was referring. I sent him cards and silly notes. When he didn't respond, I gave him the space he clearly needed. I suspected that he was engaged in his first serious relationship. I would see him at Christmas.

Then Christmas break arrived. I took over a plate of cookies and a carton of eggnog. "Where is Wheaton?"

It was ninety degrees.

"He's gone."

"Where?"

"He's moved on."

Had I done something? I couldn't think of any good reason for Wheaton to run out on me. I tormented his mother. She had to know his whereabouts. Finally, a few days after New Year's Day, 1992, she said, "I can tell you that he's fine, Prudence." She took a deep breath. "He's written you a letter." She took another deep breath. The door was open only enough for me to see her face. She looked tired. Wheaton's father, Rick, came up close beside her and extended a note for me. Lily looked like she might cry.

"Where is he?"

In unison, they shook their heads.

Had they somehow put him into a Magnolia Gardens for grown-ups? For a split second, I wondered if Lily was still sleeping with the contractor. Was Rick still struggling with his novel? But Wheaton's parents, for my purposes, were more like appendages than people. They were a link to Wheaton, little more. They closed the door and I crossed the street with my note. Sitting on the front stoop where I'd first sat, knee to knee, seven years old with Wheaton Jones at my side, I opened his letter. It was printed in pencil on notebook paper. The *W*s looked swirly and capped like waves. Those were Wheaton's *W*s.

Dear Prudence,

    I have to go away now. It's bittersweet to end on a grand number like ten, thumb to pinky two times. You were the most important person in my life. I wish that I had told you once that I love you. Why didn't I say it? I do. I love you.

    This isn't about you. You'll be all right.

    Remember: I can see things no one else can see, so I know that you're going to be just fine. Good luck with the birds.

Love,

Wheaton

What upset me most in his letter was the use of the past tense. I *was* the most important person in his life. I had been replaced. Ours was a platonic relationship, and although I'd had a few dates in high school, as far as I knew Wheaton had not. He was a virgin. At first, I assumed that Skye Bouvier had stolen him away from me. I knew nothing about her, but when I visited Saint Mark's shortly after receiving Wheaton's letter, I tracked her down. She seemed harmless. They'd been friends. She thought he was interesting. My accusations of a tryst bothered her. She had a boyfriend. She and Wheaton were never more than friends. She'd tried to help him.

Apparently, at fall break, Wheaton had left school and never returned. Shortly thereafter, he'd written a letter to the chair of the arts department, explaining that he did not belong at Saint Mark's. By the time I started investigating, Wheaton was no longer enrolled at Saint Mark's.

Skye said that she could show me his old place—if I wanted. She was sorry that I'd lost my friend, but she didn't know where he was. Maybe his parents knew? I didn't tell her that he'd left me, that there'd been a note.

I didn't know what to do.

Skye took me to his warehouse studio. It hadn't been rented yet, and she still had a key.

I nearly got sick on the concrete floor. In addition to finding the usual things, like clothes and toiletries, pen-and-ink, charcoal still-life drawings—what looked like early class assignments—there was a separate pile of drawings done on kraft paper. These were drawings of wings, but they were rendered architecturally, with an eye for utility, including formulas and measurements, things I didn't understand. In the warehouse's center was an eyesore, the culmination of Wheaton's designs: a winged monstrosity. In the winter of 1992, I still felt my wings, and I felt them at the sight of this thing Wheaton had wrought. I felt them sharp and bulging against my back. Wheaton had made hulking wings, heavy and robotic, like someone's penance for a crime. They were composed of metal, riveted, each one the length and width of an average-size dining room table, the edges ragged and rusted, serrated like steak knives. Upon closer examination, it appeared that the edges had been intentionally sharpened with some kind of tool. My wings were ghostly, naked to the average eye, felt from the inside out. Wheaton's wings—if you can imagine something so ugly being called a pair of wings—were connected by three butt hinges, leaving the faintest smell of WD-40 on my hands. Beneath the hinges, there were two industrial-size red-and-white-striped canvas straps that Wheaton presumably wore over his shoulders. Skye and I could not lift the contraption, but she assured me that he had in fact spent a good deal of time donning the metal wings. She showed me where a pulley had at one time been attached to the wings—causing them to open and shut. There was no way to tell Skye that I'd been born with wings. It wasn't her business.

I asked to be alone.

Skye obliged, calling Wheaton "a sweet kid." After Skye had gone, I rifled through his things, searching for clues, coming up empty-handed. His vanishing was like a scene from a bad science-fiction movie, where someone disappears from their bed and winds up on an alien spaceship. I started to think that maybe his letter was forged.

His mattress was on the floor. I sat down to catch my breath, to gaze at the mechanical wings. What was Wheaton doing? Men don't fly, not without meeting their doom. Bird girls hardly fly, only for a few seconds, only a few feet off the ground. I fell back onto the mattress, wrapping myself in his blue pinstriped sheets. He was gone. I was alone.

Freddie and Veronica sat in our old den. It was theirs now. They were in love or something. Freddie tried to reason with me. "Wheaton must've had his reasons."

"Like what?"

That was the question no one could answer.

Veronica suggested I call the Old Man. "If there's anything the Old Man can understand, it's the business of getting on with life." At this, Freddie laughed. "I'm serious," Veronica said.

I have always taken my studies seriously, and so I returned to the

University of Florida and completed my spring semester. After my last exam, I flew to New York to see the Old Man. I rehearsed a hundred ways of explaining my feelings of helplessness. When he opened the door, I fell into his arms. I felt guilty because I was upset by the loss of one friend when the Old Man had lost nearly everyone he loved. Loss, I soon learned from him, is not measured in numbers. It's not comparative. It's in here. I'm touching my chest now.

I showered and my Oma fed me. In the den, the Old Man acted the part of maestro playing his favorite records. He smoked his pipe and drank his Black Label beer. "You are chasing a ghost," he told me. "When it is the right time, you will find Wheaton again. You are not in charge of the universe."

"I never said I was."

"You are arrogant because of you being young. You can't help it. You think you are the bandleader. You are not."

"No, I don't. I'm not like that."

"Quiet," he told me. "I want to hear the music."

My Oma smiled at us. "I'll get a snack for you."

The Old Man puffed on his cigar. "How many years did you know Wheaton?"

"Twelve."

"Were they good years?"

Of course they were good years.

The Old Man said what I was thinking: "Of course they were good years. You love him, and he loves you. So what is wrong with you? Are you greedy? Is twelve good years not enough for you? What number of years will make you happy?"

There was no magic number. There was nothing to do. Like humans, birds mourn the loss of fledglings and mates. There are a thousand variant weeping songs to sing. I had to sing mine and get on with it. That is what I did. Now I am supposed to do it again, this time for the Old Man.

21

November 1989

*F*our hundred ninety-two miles west of Moscow, in Vilnius, Lithuania, Lukas Blasczkiewicz unrolled a sheet of canvas. Squinting at the speckled material, he looked for the outline of an angel. In everything, he looked for the winged girl who'd probably met an icy grave in Siberia. Because of *her*, he was not only a photographer, he was a painter and collector of wings—real wings, paper wings, wings formed from clay and glass, discarded cardboard, wrapping paper, particleboard, and packing material. Lukas Blasczkiewicz believed in miracles. After taking *her* photograph, he'd kept his own roll of film, developed it in secret, and printed the black-and-white photographs. With the negatives, he used milk and paint to add color. He experimented with techniques, curious about the bright light surrounding the girl. Each time he manipulated the negatives, he discovered something new.

Drawing inspiration from the photographs, he painted the girl singularly white, singularly red, singularly wrapped in her angel wings, cocooned as she might've been in that holding cell. He loved *her*, always and forever, for giving him the gift of sight. Every time a bird flew past, Lukas caught his breath. *God lives here now.* Twenty years ago, his mother died. At the funeral, Lukas had dropped a small locket with a picture of *her*, the winged girl, into the grave. His sisters were at the burial. His father was not; he was bedridden, dying the next year. His family was a shambled lot:

one of his sisters was taking medication for something called manic-depressive illness; another had lost three children to influenza. The third was so emaciated, self-starved, she looked like a corpse. Lukas might've been sad if he didn't see a little light in each of them, a glimmer of possibility. Because of *her*, he saw this light in everyone and everything.

Lukas's shop dated back to the seventeenth century and was located near the former Church of Saint Casimir. Under Soviet rule, the church was now the Museum of Atheism. Lukas couldn't pass the former church without snickering at the irony. He remembered that the winged girl had paid reverence to Saint Casimir. The fact that the Soviets would convert a church into a museum of atheism amplified the absurdity of the communist state. A former Polish and Lithuanian prince, Saint Casimir was a pious man who reportedly waited predawn for the chapel gates to be unlocked so that he could pray to the Virgin Mary. At age twenty-five, Saint Casimir died from tuberculosis. In 1522, after miracles were reported and attributed to him, he was canonized. It was rumored that his coffin, removed by the Russians, could cure illness. Lukas believed in such things. In fact, he was the kind of man to buy magic beans. He never considered himself foolish. Just faithful.

In the early morning, while the town slept, Lukas collected scrap metal in the form of tin cans and wire. He melted the metal down, cutting out and soldering wings. With a circa 1955 camera, he took moving pictures of the wings fluttering in the light of Vilnius square, outside the Museum of Atheism. He hung them, each pair, from the ceiling of his shop. Some of them he left metallic, while others he painted every color of the morning and night sky. Inside, he'd built a bubble machine that vented onto the street and filled the narrow passageway running perpendicular to his storefront with iridescent bubbles of all shapes and sizes. Children and adults passing by pointed at his three-story home. "An inventor lives there."

"No, he's a magician."

"He makes movies."

"He paints."

"He takes photographs."

"I think he is mad."

Lukas Blasczkiewicz spent his life making and creating. Ceaseless and devoted, he thought always of the girl with the wings who'd saved him from selfishness, depression, and self-loathing. Because of *her*, he saw the miracle of life everywhere. In butterflies and beetles, in the sky and underfoot. The antithesis of his Bolshevist enthusiast father, Lukas believed in more than men and their egoistic ventures. Solitary, he never felt alone.

In November 1989, on the same night that the Vilkas family prepared to fly west, first to Saint Petersburg, and then to Vilnius, Lukas Blasczkiewicz pulled open the heavy drapes that hid the interior of his shop from the curious passersby. He walked out onto the sidewalk, snowflakes the size of fists falling fast. The world was white like a photograph before it develops. Full of possibility. He stood back, looking through the plate-glass window to admire what he had wrought from the outside in. Cupping his face to the glass, he smiled to see his handmade paper lampshades, lit by candles, conical and square, suspended at different heights, hanging from his tin-plated ceiling. The shop emanated warmth. It was a refuge, a montage of who he'd become. The walls were covered with bright paintings and black-and-white photographs, each work, each wing rendered in as many forms and hues as he could imagine. The wind whipped his hair, and the black cat, her whiskers streaked white, meowed to return indoors. Lukas scratched his chin, thinking, *It is good and right to look from the outside in. Too many people don't stop to see themselves inside the snow globe, the big hand shaking the sphere.* Lukas grinned at the staircase he'd built from wrought iron. It spiraled to a second floor where he kept his books, everything from Beethoven to Byzantinism, but his favorite books were about flight, about the Wright Brothers—Orville and Wilbur—about Charles Lindbergh and Amelia Earhart. He prized picture books with fairies, *Angels in Art, Birds of Eastern Europe.* He'd made this. The cat wound round his ankles and the wind gusted from the east. Lukas held up his finger. Something other than snow was blowing, heading their way. His thighs shivered. He bent down for Cat. She nuzzled and burrowed in his sleeve.

22

Old Man, 1989

No one warns you that when you grow old, your heart that's been cooperating and keeping quiet, like it should do, is suddenly going to speak up and make you a driveling wreck.

I was a curmudgeon. I often wish that I had remained that way, to keep these blasted tears at bay. I feel my heart broken how it was nearly five decades ago, when the death of my family was raw, before I survived Germany and met Ingeburg.

When we were in Moscow, I knew that we had to get the hell out before Ingeburg succumbed to her fears. I knew that once we were in Lithuania, she would feel the land that I had been telling her about for so many decades. Because she was my bride, I thought of Lithuania as her home too. After all our years together, it seemed like she had to have known my sisters and my mother and father—even though she dismissed these notions, calling me crazy, insisting she was German and not Lithuanian. She could not be with this old man and not have some of my Lithuania rub off on her.

First we flew from Moscow to Saint Petersburg, and from there we boarded a plane for Vilnius, Lithuania. We sat on that damn plane for seven hours. It was like being held hostage because we were ready to leave the official Soviet Union for the so-called Western Province. We were ready to be in Vilnius, a grand city for six hundred years. I could not believe that finally I would see my homeland again. Finally, my son Freddie would see where I was born, where his family came from. And dear Prudence would see the steeples and the stained-glass windows filled with angels' wings.

It was worth the wait. I can tell you that it was worth Moscow. Part of me had feared that the Soviet Union had razed the churches and the university, my university, the largest university in Europe, but they had not. They had spared my city. The Gothic and Baroque churches, dating from the fifteenth century, were the same as I remembered, only the crucifixes were gone. Many of the stained-glass windows were covered with plastic tarps. It was an odd thing to see. One of the churches was a garage and another was a warehouse. There was even one turned into a radio factory. But my university where I had attended for one semester had been spared. It is the oldest university in Eastern Europe. I told Freddie and I told Prudence and even Veronica, who is not Lithuanian or German but from some fishing village or something. There were gardens and thirteen courtyards. Even in November, flowers bloomed. When I was seventeen, I had climbed to the top of the bell tower with a girl I fancied, and I remember it was May or June and the sun was setting and we could smell jasmine from the garden below, and that girl kissed me. I wish that I remembered her name.

On the streets in Vilnius, I took hold of Ingeburg's hand. I was never afraid that she would *die* in Moscow, because she is the strongest woman I have ever met, but I was worried about her. In Lithuania, she was regaining her strength as I knew she would. Prudence was skipping in the sunlight and I mistook her for my sister Daina. She wore black tights and short boots, a wool skirt like a Scottish kilt and a matching hat. It was an outfit like my sister would've worn. It is not easy to feel things, not pain or joy, because pain sits with you, and joy is fleeting, easily swatted like a bee. I know all too well these things, and even in the city I cherished, I contained my joy because seeing, touching, and smelling my birthplace, walking streets I remembered vividly as a child was untenable and unimaginable. Sometimes I feared it was a dream. The life I knew would be gone and once again I would be screaming, waking cold between the sheets. It is hard to feel deeply. It is easier to erect walls. When I listen to the great composers, I can settle in their world and hide. I am safe. Music is a refuge. I think the boy understands this. I used to think that he understood very little, but there is more of me in him than I thought. If there had been no war and no purging, would I be more like Freddie? It was stupid to imagine such things. If there had been no madness, there would be no Ingeburg. There would be no Freddie. There would be no Prudence. I might've married the girl whose name I can't remember, the one I kissed on the bell tower. These were the mad thoughts of an emotional man seeing his homeland after forty-eight years.

On our first day in Vilnius, I took my family toward the Upper Castle. I wanted them to see the splendor that surpassed anything in Moscow. On the way there, I grabbed hold of Natasha Sluska's gloved hand, startling the woman. "Do you like your job?" I wanted to know. She pushed her spectacles up her nose and declared that she liked it very much. At this nonsense, I told her that she was not a smart woman. Ingeburg gasped and told Natasha Sluska, "He does not mean it. Do not listen to him. He says that to me all the time." Natasha Sluska smiled her polite Russian smile. Her thin lips were chapped white, blending in with her face. I told the Russian woman that I was tired of her company. She sneezed and Ingeburg said, "Gesundheit."

Natasha Sluska told us to go on our way. She would go back to the hotel.

"If I knew we could be rid of you, I would've spoken up sooner," I said.

"It's easier here than in Moscow." Natasha smiled at us and patted Ingeburg's hand to reassure her. "It's not as strict."

We continued without Mrs. Sluska, passing another church, one used to house grain, but its stained-glass windows were intact, an image of the Virgin Mother holding the Christ child, an angel on each shoulder, a rendering of Our Lady of Perpetual Help.

As I remember, the others were in awe of my city. They regarded everything as sacred ground, but me, I could not shut up. It was growing harder and harder for me to contain my happiness. My God, but it was strange that everywhere we looked there were turrets and steeples, but nowhere could you get on your knees before a cross and praise God. My mother was a woman of faith. She believed in God and angels and girls born with wings.

Approaching Pilies Street, I breathed a sigh of relief because it still was a market street with vendors selling linen and amber, jewelry and art. Shielding my eyes, I gazed at the Upper Castle. I will never, not for my whole life, forget what I saw or how I felt. Even as an Old Man of sixty-eight, I was strong, but right then, I was weak in my legs. Wobbly even, blinking in the sunlight that accompanied my joy. Up there, where I had last seen the Nazi flag fly and before the Nazi flag, the Soviet flag, I saw my own flag. I had no words for anyone just then. Instead, I pointed, and for all my attempt to contain emotion, a rush of tears harbored for decades spilled down my cheeks. My beard was like a wet sponge. I was not embarrassed. I felt no shame.

Ingeburg demanded to know what was wrong. She was talking about going for Natasha Sluska, worried about one thing or another. I vehemently shook my head to indicate that she should call no one. She should not be a fool, but she should look up to where I was pointing. There was a young man, a university student with a satchel passing by, and I grabbed hold of his arm. I couldn't help it. I said, "Look there! Look up there! They've raised our flag. How is it that they've raised our flag?"

In Lithuanian, he explained that last year, a group of students had taken down the Soviet flag. A crowd had gathered. The young man had been there. He shook my hand excitedly and told me how he and the others had sung the national song of Lithuania. They'd feared someone would be shot. Certainly, they supposed there would be some terrible reprisal, but then nothing bad happened. Within hours, our flag had been raised in its place and remained.

The student and I were pointing at the flag. Pulling my handkerchief from my back pocket, I thanked him. I was still crying and then I was singing, not quietly, not fearfully, but unabashedly and with gusto, and this young man joined me. Freddie, who knew our national song because at one time he was a good and obedient son, joined us. We sang: *"Lietuva, Tėvyne mūsų, Tu didvyrių žeme, Iš praeities Tavo sūnūs Te stiprybę semia."*

I heard Prudence asking Ingeburg, "What does it mean?"

Ingeburg explained, "They love their country." As I've said, she is sometimes not as smart as she thinks. Sometimes she is much more German and American than Lithuanian. She cannot help it. Our national hymn means much more than loving one's country. The hymn's power soon became evident to everyone. On the street, men and women stopped and turned toward our flag. They also sang. I imagined that these men and women were like those men and women who'd been murdered over four decades ago. I imagined they were teachers and lawyers, doctors and butchers, poets and locksmiths, students and mechanics. I was proud. This was the Lithuania that I had described to Prudence.

Ingeburg said, "Someone is going to see and report this. We'll be picked up. They won't let us leave."

I ignored my wife and her fears.

When the song was done, everyone erupted in applause. Then, as if nothing extraordinary had occurred, the people continued on their way. I think my granddaughter understood then that this was also her homeland. Of course she came from this place—a country where everyone was always singing—and I think my son felt it too. He patted me on the back. There were tears in my boy's eyes. I turned to Prudence to explain. "Our hymn means don't forget history. Mankind is our duty. Unity. Lithuania forever . . . We are Lithuanian. We are not the Soviet Union." I wiped my face with my coat sleeve and smiled. "We never give up trying to be free."

Ingeburg said, "What if we get reported?"

"Stop it with your worry! Stop it this instant!" I was irate with my wife, tired of her fears, and I told her, "No more!" In Moscow, I could understand, but not here.

We continued down Pilies Street. We were walking and I suspect that my wife was worrying that Natasha Sluska was reporting us to someone in the KGB, but then we heard a man speaking in Polish.

23

Ingeburg

*T*he stranger was leaning against a railing on the front stoop of a brick house and smoking a Russian cigarette. There were three other men smoking with him. He told his friends, "They're tearing down the Berlin Wall. I heard it on BBC."

I stopped and looked at the man. He wore a thick leather coat and checkered wool cap. "What did you say?"

The man wasn't paying attention to me. Then, in German, I asked him again, *"Wie bitte?" What did you say?*

"Pardon me, ma'am." He tipped his hat, explaining himself all over again. "It's the beginning of the end. The wall is coming down. You can see cement being chipped away on the television. The East and the West are crossing over. The border guards are standing around useless; some of them have left their posts." At this, he laughed and clapped his hands, his cigarette ashing on the stoop.

"In the no-man's-zone?" I asked.

"Yes."

"And no one is being shot?"

"No!" he said. Then the total stranger, his cigarette dangling from his lip, grabbed me around the waist and pulled me to him. I could not believe what he was telling me. I reached my arms around his neck, and the other men on the stoop applauded. This was as incredible to me as men and women raising the Lithuanian flag and breaking into spontaneous song.

The stranger and I parted but clasped hands. The Old Man asked if what the stranger had said could be true. I knew that it had to be true. I believed. No one would say something so impossible to believe. Then the fear that had taken hold, that purple rotted plum, was replaced by the goose's golden egg. I had it. The gold was mine. I owned it. The fear that had poisoned my bloodstream was replaced with the memory of good schnapps and garden waltzes. *The wall is coming down. Hunks of concrete are falling to the ground.* I recalled the sweetness of marzipan on my tongue and for the first time in so long, I felt safe.

The world is changed, and no, Old Man, I am not a Lithuanian. I am a German girl. I am that pie-faced German girl you kissed when my face was unmarred, when my tooth was intact. Germany is my homeland.

I grabbed the Old Man and kissed him.

He said, "Are you all right, Ingeburg?"

I was better than all right. Wrapping my arms tight around his neck, I kissed him again. I do not think I had ever loved him as much as I did at that moment.

24

Prudence

The Old Man took us to one of the garages in town (formerly a church), and there he hired a car to drive outside Vilnius to the farm where he was born—where he'd grown up and lived twenty years. Understandably, my Oma was grinning. I don't imagine anything could've wiped that smile from her face. She was suddenly fit as a fiddle, talking about the crumbling wall, her cheeks rosy. She was planning her trip home to Germany. She intended to see her long-lost cousins and visit the house where she'd grown up. Thomas Wolfe said you can't go home again, but back in 1989, we were all giving it our best shot, and to me, at sixteen, it seemed that we were succeeding.

But the Old Man's road home had changed. When he'd lived there, it was paved, but in 1989 it was gravel and dirt. Along the road, the tall pines the Old Man remembered still towered majestically beside us. This was ancient forest. The Old Man told us that bears were rare in the pines, but once when he was a boy, out playing and looking for bugs and toads, he spotted a brown bear. He said that he kept very still, but his heel came down on a twig, and the bear looked at him. He told us that the bear had blue eyes. They were sad and lonely eyes, and the Old Man didn't look away, nor did he move. He and the bear stared at one another. When he went home and told his mother about the bear, she told him and his sisters that many of the freedom fighters who'd died in the forest had turned into animals, and that bears were good fortune. The Old Man and his sisters halfway believed her stories. She was always dancing and singing and telling stories, and that was the reason Petras had fallen in love with her. Petras also believed her stories. The Old Man said that a child should always love his mother, but that he and his sisters didn't just love their mother. They preferred her company to that of their friends, making up excuses to be with her. She liked to wear long pants and fitted shirts rolled at the sleeves. She kept her blond hair pinned in a bun except at night, when she took it down and she and the Old Man's sisters took turns brushing one another's hair. "She was never old," he told me. "Not like me." He seemed to think on this for a long time.

As the Old Man pulled into the spot where he knew his house to have been, we saw a sterile radio tower in its stead. "It was right here." The Old Man sighed loudly and resignedly. He was sad. His house, he told us, had been brick, and his neighbor's house had been brick. He'd hidden in the neighbor's cellar. There had been three families on the land.

The Old Man showed us where each of the houses had stood, pointing out where they'd had their garden and where they'd kept their sheep and chickens. Surrounding the radio tower was a weedy field, a few pieces of broken brick the only evidence that anything like a family's home had ever been in this place. The sun was shining. A glimmering piece of a hair barrette caught my eye. I picked it up and gave it to the Old Man. He kissed the top of my head and slipped the piece of metal in his pocket. I pointed out a rabbit not too far from us.

The Old Man straddled the radio tower's lowest beam and said, "This is where our living room used to be." When he was twelve, he'd helped his father add a large kitchen to the back of their house to replace one that had originally been separate from the house. His mother loved to cook. She was a wonderful baker, and he and his sisters were often shooed from the kitchen for picking at cakes and bread.

He said that his parents' house was the biggest of the three. It was also the first house built after his mother and father had walked to Lithuania from Kazakhstan. Before his father's brother left for America, they'd built two of the three houses. The Old Man looked up at the tower.

I remember that his sadness was palpable. He'd carried his family photograph with him. He'd wanted to show us where the photograph had been taken. He wanted to show Freddie the room in which he'd slept. He'd imagined that some other family would be living in his home, and he'd tell them his story, and they'd embrace him as their kinsman, and they'd be glad to meet a Lithuanian living in America. They'd want to know what was happening beyond the iron curtain. The Old Man imagined that Freddie would be proud of him. He didn't realize that already my father was overwhelmed, incredibly moved by the singing and the architecture, feeling a connection to this foreign land. While the Old Man sat uncomfortably on the metal beam, we stood around him like mourners at a funeral.

There was nothing for us to see, but then I saw it. Up high, at the top of the tower, a massive nest, big enough for the Old Man's blue-eyed bear to take up residence.

"What kind of nest is that?" Veronica asked.

We were all squinting to see. Even at sixteen, before my ornithology degree, I knew my birds. It was a black stork's nest. The black stork was practically extinct. It was November, but the bird would've nested in Lithuania in the spring. In November, it would be somewhere warm like India. The black stork is a big bird, the kind of bird the Old Man's mother would've loved.

I told them. I explained that in all likelihood the bird would return in the spring. It was no easy feat to build such a nest. Her mate would've built it and she would lay her eggs here.

We remained at the Old Man's boyhood home, where so much had begun and so many stories had ended. We stared at the empty nest, believing the black stork would return, knowing the bird had chosen this spot because of the Old Man's mother. It wasn't impossible to suppose that the loony-gooney Aleksandra, lover of birds, would be reincarnated as a black stork and nest where she had nested before. We each felt this dreamy sensibility. Maybe the blue-eyed bear was watching from somewhere beyond the field, noting that the little boy he'd once been face-to-face with had returned. Perhaps the bear was faintly aware that things were changing for the better.

Back in Vilnius, clouds squatted low over the city, and it snowed. There was a music to the hushed sound of flakes falling and boots treading, the white sky nearly indistinguishable from the ground. Natasha Sluska was in the hotel nursing a cold. My Oma's itchiness and nausea had long vanished. I'm sure that she imagined the watchtowers toppling, the concrete and barbed wire coming down.

Down, down, down, trampled underfoot, nothing more than twisted shards of metal.

I was imagining it.

We were tromping through the snow, marching down a side street. It's hard to describe the sense of camaraderie our family felt, even Veronica, who was as caught up in this swirling hope as anyone else. Snowflakes fell and clung to our dark clothes. Our footprints disappeared behind each step.

I remember that a man carrying an unwrapped side of beef hurried past us. It was four in the afternoon, and would've been dark but for the iridescent ice that turned the street electric. Most of the shops were closed except for a butcher's and a frosty storefront, its red window box piled two feet deep with snow. A warm glow emanated from the glass facade, and within, a fire burned.

It was intriguing. There was a red door to the side of the plate-glass window with a copper engraving glossed with ice. I brushed it off with my glove. *L. Blasczkiewicz, Photographer, Artist.* Returning to the storefront, I pressed my face to the glass, rubbing clockwise to get a better look. Inside was beautiful. Flitting lights darted across the ceiling.

The Old Man said that we should keep walking. We didn't need to bother with a photographer and artist.

A cat jumped to the window's ledge, startling the Old Man. It rubbed itself against the glass, just where my gloved hand was resting. My Oma announced that she liked cats. They'd had a cat in Berlin. My Oma wanted to go inside. I was in agreement. Freddie and Veronica were ambivalent.

Pulling the door open, the wind gusted out of the east, knocking it back against the plaster and brick of the exterior wall. The Old Man grabbed it for me, and we hurried inside, where it was toasty and quiet. The wind whistled inward as Freddie helped his father pull the door shut.

The five of us huddled within, watching the black cat wrap its way around spindle-legged easels. There were a dozen or more easels displaying paintings of angels and fairies. There were statues too: birds and beasts, and the squeak of metallic wings opening and closing above our heads. We started to spread out, each of us drawn to different corners of the room. There were black-and-white images of butterflies, birds, and dragonflies, enormous pictures, draped from the high ceiling.

There were charcoal drawings, nearly all black except for single spots of light accenting a cheekbone or the curve of a wing. The drawings hung from picture molding. There were brighter drawings too—stunning monochromatic wings in pink and gold, the bend of a knee, the crease of an elbow rich with vibrant reds and glossy obsidian. Silver-foiled butterflies, strung along transparent filament, flitted across the room while metal dragonflies, propelled by pulleys and fans, zipped past.

The Old Man put his hand to his chest. Freddie and Veronica held hands. If I remember correctly, our mouths were agape. At least, I'm sure that mine was. We belonged here, and collectively we felt this place also belonged to us. The wind had carried us here.

Just then, a willowy man with black hair came out from behind a red curtain. I remember clapping my gloved hands together because this somehow seemed appropriate to me. He'd created this place. First and foremost, all of this belonged to him. He took long strides, bending down to scoop up the cat, and asked, "How may I help you?" Even though we already sensed that we'd been called here, he didn't recognize us, nor we him. He spoke English. He told us that he had photographs of Russian ballerinas. Did we like the foil butterflies? Were we interested in our own bubble machine? How about fairies? Did we like fairies? Walking toward me, he said, "You have long legs like a dancer." He was so tall and slight, it seemed like he could disappear if he turned left or right.

The Old Man asked him, "What is this place?"

"A little of this and a little of that. I take pictures and paint pictures and make pictures, the moving kind. And sometimes, if I can get sugar, I make candy. My name is Lukas Blasczkiewicz."

Freddie said, "We are visiting from the United States."

"I do not know many Americans," Lukas told us.

The Old Man said, "I was born in Lithuania."

I remember thinking about dancing and ballerinas. When we lived in Nashville, I had a velvet-lined jewelry box that played music. When the box was opened, a plastic ballerina spun around, and I remember envying her pink toe shoes and wondering what she did when the box was shut. I couldn't imagine that she just lay down. There had to be more to her than that.

Lukas Blasczkiewicz approached Veronica, who was studying a photograph of lemons spilling from a wheelbarrow. Above the lemons, there appeared to be a ring of fairylike creatures.

"That's a fake," Lukas Blasczkiewicz said. By way of explanation, he added, "That photograph you are looking at now: I didn't take it. I bought it for nothing."

Veronica said, "I like the shade of yellow." Freddie stood behind her, his hands on her shoulders.

Lukas set down his cat. "Those fairies aren't real"—he rubbed his chin—"but I thought they were. Oh well. It's some kind of trick photography. Still, the lemons are lemony."

The cat rubbed against my calf. "What's the cat's name?"

"Cat. *Katė.*"

I knelt to pet the animal.

Lukas said, "I feel that you're what's blown in from the east." I was feeling the same thing. We all were.

The Old Man answered Lukas by pointing speechless at a photograph hanging above my head. I turned to see where he was pointing. It was a photograph of a woman with wings. She was naked, both arms and wings spread horizontally across the frame, like if you were close enough to the picture, you'd get buoyed up by them. This woman was fierce. Right away, I recognized her, remembered her from beneath the waves, her long arms disentangling me from the pier's pilings.

Lukas spoke up. "She was very real." He said to the Old Man, "Do you like that one? She is my life's inspiration." His eyes were a steely blue. "A vision sent by God to give me sight."

The Old Man pointed at the picture and then at Lukas Blasczkiewicz. His finger was bulbous, yellow from cigar smoke. "This is my sister in this photograph." I wasn't surprised by his proclamation because I knew her.

Lukas Blasczkiewicz said, "I am seventy-five years old." His butterflies flitted and his dragonflies zipped overhead.

"How?" the Old Man asked. "How? You are young. When was this taken? This is my sister, I tell you!"

Lukas tapped his lip, counting half seconds. "I met her thirty-eight years ago. On the eighth of January, 1951. I was thirty-seven."

At last, I felt my ghostly wings move, the tips tickling my back from within.

"Where was she?" the Old Man asked.

"I have a dozen pictures."

"Where? Where was she?"

"I remember everything about that day," Lukas said. "There was a new moon, and like today, it was snowing." We followed Lukas to a small enameled table. Opening the drawer and taking a seat, he rifled through photographs. "She was to be deported as an enemy of the state, but then they discovered her wings, and the Lithuanians wanted pictures before the Russians had her."

Despite his only having two, his legs reminded me of spider legs, long and spindly.

The Old Man interrupted Lukas. "Where?"

Lukas Blasczkiewicz didn't answer. He continued with his story. "At first, the wings were flat against her back, but then she saw something." He held up a photograph. "I could see that she saw something or someone because she looked through me. She murmured 'Saint Casimir,' or I heard it anyway, somehow, and then her wings moved. They extended. You could even say they suspended her off the ground. There were only two of us in the room with her."

The Old Man put his hand on his heart. "Where was this? What if she's still alive?"

"She'd been picked up by KGB." Lukas shook his head. "I don't know how she would've survived an order from Moscow." He crossed himself.

We were all stunned that we'd found Daina here on a side street in Vilnius, and I remember feeling nostalgic for my own childhood, for those missed years with Freddie. Lukas stood up. I watched him closely, thinking right away that he should take a photograph of my wings.

He slipped between an opening in the red drapes, and when he emerged, he presented the Old Man with a large manila envelope. He said, "These are copies of the photographs. No one told me her name. I don't know her name."

"Daina," the Old Man said. "Her name is Daina."

Even sixteen years later, I remember the sensation that I felt during this exchange. My body was raw, the nerve endings exposed, like I was being made over from scratch, handled adroitly by a new maker to be set on a new course. I wanted to ask him, *Can you take my picture?*

Lukas Blasczkiewicz had a lot to tell us, beginning with the story of how Daina had changed his life. Before meeting her, he'd had no hope. He trudged through life, taking his photographs, perceiving men and women, his subject matter, as sad, pathetic creatures moving from filmstrip to filmstrip until the film ran out and they left this world. After he met Daina, hope was like white chalk on black pants. There was no getting rid of it. On this chilly afternoon in Vilnius, Lithuania, a stone's throw from the Museum of Atheism, his hope passed to us. He was part of our constellation now, an important star never to be forgotten.

He told us in detail of his salvation, how birds came to him in red, ocher, blue, and tan, landing in his courtyard, resting on his head—how the starlings had done with me—drinking from his palm, perched on his arms and legs. He told us that when he was granted permission to return to Russia, he chose to move here, near the university. Lithuania was his home.

It was ours too.

When I was sixteen, I felt fortunate and blessed, and now that I am twice the age I was then, and the Old Man is apparently on his deathbed, I feel cheated and sad, and I know what Lukas Blasczkiewicz would say to me. He would tell me that everyone has a time to meet his maker. I am not Lukas Blasczkiewicz. I am selfish.

In Lithuania, the Old Man spoke in the present tense. He said, "Daina is our songbird, the youngest and most adventurous in our family. Her precociousness is encouraged because she is the baby."

Lukas made a sad *taa* noise, a verbal resignation that she was gone. I spoke up, telling him, "I was born with wings like her." Nervous, I slipped my hands in my pockets. "Would you take my picture, please?" This man was like Wheaton. He saw what others failed to see. Maybe through his camera lens, he would see my wings.

Freddie said, "No, Prudence. You don't need to have your picture taken."

Lukas said, "I will take her photograph."

I pointed my finger at Freddie, probably how the Old Man used to point his finger at my father, and I said, "You have no say-so here." It was too late for him to start acting like a doting father. One of the zipping dragonflies caught in my hair.

"You're trapped," Lukas said.

I struggled to free the dragonfly from my hair while explaining to Lukas that my wings were taken when I was a baby. "I must've inherited them from my great-aunt Daina."

"Your birthright," Lukas said. He flung the red curtain back and said, "Come this way. Follow me." I was afraid, but not of Lukas, his cool eyes and willowy gait. I was afraid that he wouldn't see my birthright. I wanted someone else to see. Not just me and Wheaton. The cat ran ahead of Lukas.

There was a short hallway. I followed Lukas to a doorway that led to a room situated beneath the stairs. From the opening, which required Lukas to crouch, the room stretched back to an exposed brick wall. As we walked farther into the room, it expanded. The ceiling was tall and growing taller. Lukas Blasczkiewicz's voice echoed when he asked me, "How about here?" He pointed to a white screen on wheels.

"Here is good." It is all very familiar still, like it could've been yesterday when he took my picture, but it wasn't yesterday. It was 1989, and I was a girl desperate for beginnings, as many as I could gather and hold in my arms, stuff deep in my pockets, tangle in my hair. I didn't know if the Old Man's sister was alive. Truthfully, I thought she had to be dead, if not from the police, then from old age. I remember thinking that what had made Daina special wasn't just the gift of wings, but the fact that they still existed in pictures. Forever, she'd be a photograph, a score of photographs. Forever, there'd be the story of the girl in a jail cell in Palanga, a girl with wings. There'd be the story of the blue-eyed photographer who took her picture. And then there were the photographs and the copies of the photographs and the copies of those copies that proved she existed. They proved that she hadn't died in 1941 as the Old Man thought. Pictures, I understood, were important. Daina would live on forever in this way.

I wanted to live forever. At sixteen, you think you might be dead by the age of thirty. Fortunately, I did not die at age thirty. I grew up.

We were in a big room with high white ceilings like a glass of milk. The exposed bricks were mossy in spots and purple in other places.

Lukas called it the Great Room. I pulled my shirt overhead and un-hooked my bra. "Do you want a stool?" he asked.

"No thank you." I turned so that Lukas could see my scars. My back. Maybe my wings.

Lukas clicked on one light and put the camera strap around his neck. My hands were tucked beneath my arms, covering my breasts. I felt vulnerable, but it felt good. I thought he would see my wings, but all of a sudden, I could not feel them. It was strange.

After ten depressions, Lukas stopped. Letting my hands fall to my side, I looked at him. I was angry. Sad. He put the camera to his face and started taking more pictures. I remember feeling like I'd been possessed, like one of those forest bears, fierce and growling, had taken hold of me. Why? Because this man couldn't see me for who I was. He couldn't see my wings. I knew it. And what did he see when I stared at him, when I turned angry, baring my teeth, on the verge of pouncing?

I couldn't think straight, and then he clapped his hands together. "We are done. That's enough."

It was like waking from a dream. I felt confused. My clothes were at my feet.

He tapped his foot, the cat encircling his calf. "I wonder if your wings are with God."

"I don't know what you mean."

"I wonder if he's holding them for you." He tapped his lip.

"I don't know."

"Me neither. It's a thought."

Lukas had things to do, so it was time for us to go. The Old Man embraced him. Lukas gave Veronica a smaller print of the lemon picture with fairies. "For the lemon-yellow color," he explained. "You can hang it up somewhere, I bet."

Ingeburg kissed Lukas's cheek. He said, "You are a beautiful woman." I felt that he could see my Oma for the girl she'd been before the war. I'm sure of it. He shook Freddie's hand. Lukas said to my father, "Not every good story needs a fool." I think Freddie was offended, but he said, "It was nice to meet you."

To me, Lukas said, "You are with the birds. Soaring. Flying. Don't worry about what used to be. If you lose something, you let it go. Do you understand?"

I nodded that I understood, but I didn't. Not then.

Lukas ushered us into the white night, bolting the door behind us. He was wonderfully smart and strange.

As we trekked back to the hotel, the Old Man said, "I'm sure that my sister is still alive. If she was alive in 1951, I'm sure that she's alive now." There was never anyone as optimistic as the Old Man.

When I was twenty-four, Lukas sent me his first published collection of photographs. It included multiple images of my scars. In stark black-and-white, they were rendered as seams. In soft blues, as zippers. In red, as knife wounds. My aunt Daina's photographs also appeared in the book. Treated with milk, they were white like Wheaton's eyes when his visions came. It was only after Wheaton disappeared that I realized how similar he and Lukas Blasczkiewicz were.

25

The Old Man

*T*he Old Man told Natasha Sluska, "We have to go to Palanga."

"It's not on our itinerary."

"Put it on our itinerary."

"Why?"

"I don't know if I can say the truth to you."

She rolled her eyes before blowing her nose. "What is it?"

"I want to see the Baltic Sea."

"In November?"

"Please, Mrs. Sluska. I beg of you."

"And you lie to me. You don't want to see the Baltic. Why do you want to see the Baltic?"

The Old Man was not in the habit of begging for anything. He put his hands out in front to steady his footing and crouched down, trying to get on his knees. He would convince the Russian official with the sniffly cold to change her mind, but the Old Man was off balance. With one knee on the floor, he toppled over, his burning cigar singeing his beard. In the fetal position, his black socks and garters showed. He reached for the rolling cigar.

"We're going to Kaunas," she said. "That's on our itinerary."

"Please."

"In November, comrade? What is the real reason you want to go to the Baltic?"

"Can you ask for permission, please?"

"Palanga is not on our itinerary."

"But it's important."

"Why?" Natasha coughed.

"It just is."

The Old Man was still on his back on the floor, but he'd gotten his cigar and put it to his lips.

Natasha Sluska lit a cigarette and frowned. "Tell me why. Tell me the real reason why you want to go to Palanga."

"I can't."

"Why not?"

"In confidence?"

"In confidence," she agreed.

"There is someone I need to see. Someone very important to me."

"Who is it? Was she a girlfriend of yours?"

"I have no girlfriends." The Old Man rolled onto his side.

"Who is it?"

"I can't," the Old Man said.

"I can't either," she said. "I can't help you." She stubbed her cigarette in the ashtray and, pulling a handkerchief from her pocket, blew her nose. "I'm sorry to disappoint you."

The Old Man rolled onto his back. "Good night," he told Natasha Sluska. He couldn't tell her the truth. If, God willing, his sister was still alive, if she'd somehow managed to escape the KGB, they might go after her again. They'd be suspicious of an American brother. The KGB wouldn't care that Daina was old. They had never cared about such things. She'd be the same age as Ingeburg: sixty-four. It seemed impossible that she would've survived, but the Old Man now believed wholeheartedly in impossibilities. He had to go to Palanga. He had to know what became of her.

The next morning, they rode in a van toward Kaunas. During the Polish occupation of Vilnius, Kaunas had served as Lithuania's capital. The Old Man had no use for Kaunas. He remembered it as a nice-enough city, but he needed to get to Palanga. He had been up all night strategizing. Perhaps when they returned to Moscow, he could petition the government for another tour, and they would assign him someone new and allow him to visit the seaside resort. His wife was talking about a future trip to Berlin. "Yes, fine," he told her. They would go to Berlin in the future, but for now, he had to figure out how to get to Palanga. In the van, his granddaughter read aloud from a small pamphlet about the Ninth Fort in Kaunas. " 'Built by Russia's tsarists, it was later used as a Nazi extermination fort.' " Prudence looked up from the pamphlet. "Will we visit the Ninth Fort?" she asked Natasha Sluska.

Looking back from the passenger's seat, Natasha said, "No, we will not go there. We are not going to see the Ninth Fort because we are not going to Kaunas. There has been a change of itinerary."

"Where are we going?" Ingeburg asked.

"To Palanga for the salt air. It's been terrible weather, and I've felt very poorly. I arranged our lodgings last night."

The Old Man couldn't believe it. He had been wrong about the Russian woman. She was a fine person. "Thank you."

"Don't thank me. For what? I didn't do anything." Natasha Sluska turned back around.

"Thank you," he said again.

"Just leave it."

In Palanga, the Old Man walked a cracked sidewalk that he remembered from when he was a boy. There was an herb store and a fish market. These places were familiar, but they'd taken pictures of their Palanga vacations, and his father had kept those in a book, so the Old Man might be remembering a photograph and not an actual time. He knew that memory could be tricky like that.

They were far from Moscow, and Natasha Sluska had ventured off on her own. The Old Man could not stop thanking her, and she told him that if he did not stop, she would change her mind. He didn't say another word. Walking the seaside streets, the Old Man tasted the salt on his lips. He was excited but scared. He didn't know what he'd find. He told his family that he would have to search for her on his own. This was something he alone must do. A whole group of foreigners would certainly attract suspicion, and besides, only he knew Daina.

Before he left the others, the Old Man kissed Ingeburg and joked with Veronica and Freddie that they never should've divorced. Prudence had a worried expression on her face. "Be careful," she advised.

The Old Man's first stop was the police station, where he found an old police captain named Vincentas. The on-duty officers told the Old Man that Vincentas had been at the station since it was built. "If anyone would have information about an arrest in 1951, it'd be him." Besides, they were too busy to help him. No one had time to search for some old file that had probably been destroyed. From 1951? Yeah, she'd be long gone.

No longer of use to the police force, Captain Vincentas sat in the back room drinking tea and pretending to be of importance. He had a tan face and green eyes. His salt-and-ginger moustache was curled up at the ends. Vincentas informed the Old Man, "Of course, I remember the girl with wings. She lit up. It was a miracle, and then she was supposed to go to Moscow or Siberia or somewhere, and there was a telephone call saying we were to release her. Just like that."

"I knew it!" The Old Man made a fist and bit his knuckle. "I just knew it."

The captain continued. "Things never happened like that. She is the only one ever released. But how often do you see a girl with wings? Never! Right? Of course! So it isn't so surprising that she was released, not when you think about it that way. Of course it isn't." Vincentas smiled then, remembering her. "Do you have another cigar?"

The Old Man did not. "No. Sorry."

"What do you want with her?" the captain asked. "She'll be an old woman now like I'm an old man."

"We were friends," the Old Man said, "before the war." He was afraid to tell *anyone* that Daina was his sister. He didn't know if that might raise suspicions of some sort.

Rising from his chair, Captain Vincentas said, "Let's take a look." The captain limped down a dark corridor, the Old Man trailing. Then dropping his keys, the captain stopped at the last door. "This one," he said, reaching down for the keys. "There should be something in here." He struggled to separate the keys and looked back at the Old Man. "How did you say you knew her?"

"We were friends."

The captain found the right key and turned the lock. Before the light switch was flipped, the smell of dusty old paper met the two men. Then the sound of fluorescent lights coming to life. "I hid her in here," the captain said. "I think I did. We were supposed to throw her away." He looked into the Old Man's hopeful blue eyes. "Who throws people away? She'll be here somewhere." The captain slid the keys into his front pants pocket and surveyed the room. In the back corner, atop an old wooden table, there was an unlabeled cardboard box. He sorted through the folders, his fingertips gray with dust. "I remember that there was a man who picked her up. He was her husband, although she seemed destined for something greater than marriage. Not me. Did you know my wife?" He looked at the Old Man.

"I don't think so," he said.

"How would you? . . . Your old friend was a beautiful girl. My wife made food for her." Captain Vincentas was nostalgic, while the Old Man was anxious. "My wife was good-hearted, always wanting to feed the prisoners because none of them were guilty of anything except maybe stealing a piece of bread or bad-mouthing Stalin."

"Are the files in alphabetical order?"

The captain laughed. "Of course not. That would make sense."

"Sorry," the Old Man said.

"Who are you again?" the captain asked, his fingers moving from file to file.

Before the Old Man could say anything more, the captain said, "I found her: Daina Valetkiene. I'll write down the address for you."

The Old Man didn't know the name Valetkiene, but he trusted the captain. "Thank you so much," he told him.

The captain pulled a scrap of envelope from the file cabinet and jotted down the Valetkys address from January eighth 1951. "Of course, you mean her no harm?" he asked the Old Man.

"Absolutely not. Of course not. She was my good friend."

"Here." Vincentas handed the address to the Old Man. "I hope that you find her. And if you do, tell her that I'm sorry she had to come here. It wasn't my fault."

The Old Man did not know what to say. He was holding his sister's last known address. His sister Daina had survived! For a second he considered that Nelly could have been wrong. Maybe all three sisters had survived.

The captain flipped off the light switch and pulled the records room door shut. They went back to his chair. "I never got to tell her that I was sorry. You didn't do that then. If you find her, will you tell her for me?"

The Old Man said, "Of course. I give you my word."

The captain grabbed on to the Old Man's forearm. "My wife died five years ago this month. It started me thinking about the angel who was here." The captain's eyes drooped. "About the afterlife, if there is one. I'm waiting now, biding my time to join my Lila. We have no children. I wanted children, but Lila didn't. She said there was too much death for children. I miss Lila." Captain Vincentas dozed off.

The Old Man sat for a minute watching him sleep, glancing at the scrap of paper, his sister's address. His heart felt like it might explode. He was elated but also sick to his stomach. Folding and unfolding the address, he perspired. He couldn't lose it. He couldn't rub the ink out. He slipped it into his coat pocket.

Out on the street, the Old Man had to steady himself against the brick exterior. A car sped by and splashed slush on his shoes. He had to think straight. It was hard. Pulling a tourist brochure from his back pocket, he searched for his sister's street on the map. It was nearby, less than a mile probably, and the Old Man liked walking, but now he walked slowly, afraid of what he'd encounter. Daina might've moved. It'd been nearly four decades since she'd been arrested. She might've passed away. The Old Man made the sign of the cross. Probably, she moved. He rolled the piece of paper, now moist, in his pocket. He remembered Daina's wings responding to the sun, his mother singing arias, her voice carrying over the dunes. The birds flying overhead. He could picture Danutė and Audra playing music. And tag. Running on the beach and in the surf. He remembered his mother as silly and wonderful, chasing after her girls. All at once, he longed for Ingeburg. He was grateful that he was not an old man alone. There was someone who loved him unconditionally.

The Old Man's feet and heart pounded faster and faster as he approached his sister's address. He breathed heavily, stopping and looking at the two-story walk-up. The Old Man paced a good ten minutes before knocking on the door. He waited, his palms sweaty. *Can she actually be here? Will she know me?* He brushed his fingers through his beard and cleared his throat.

When Daina opened the door enough to see beneath the chain, the Old Man, no longer feeling like an old man but feeling like Frederick, the boy he'd been, recognized his little sister. She, however, did not know him. She was not born where he was born—on the outskirts of Vilnius in a well-appointed brick home. Daina was born two decades later in a jail cell when Saint Casimir came to her in a vision.

In Lithuanian, Frederick said, "May I speak with you?"

"What about?"

"I knew your family."

Daina unlatched the door and called for Stasys, who was editing a hygiene pamphlet.

"There's a man here who knew my family."

Removing his cap, Frederick smoothed his hair. "Am I familiar to you?"

"No," she said. "Should you be?"

"I hoped." He felt the address in his pocket.

Stasys said, "How can we help you?" His features had remained small. His hair was thick and moppy. The scar above his left eye was barely visible. "Who are you again?"

"I am a friend of the family."

"I don't know you," Daina said. Her face was weathered from walking the sea, but her eyes were as big, as filled with orange starbursts, as Frederick remembered.

Daina wore her hair long, how Frederick remembered it. She had it plaited beneath a red kerchief.

Frederick said, "I am pleased to meet you." He rubbed his palms down the front of his slacks. Despite the damp cold, he was sweating. Addressing Daina, he said, "I saw a photograph of you. I'm traveling here with my wife, and when we were in Vilnius, there was a picture of you and your wings, and I knew your wings." He hadn't known what to say, where to start. Despite his nerves, he hadn't rehearsed what he'd say as he thought he should've because it seemed a jinx, like if he imagined seeing her again, it would not come true.

"What do you mean you saw a photograph of her? What do you want with us?" Stasys asked the Old Man. "How do you know about my wife's wings?" His face reddened.

"He doesn't know about anything," Daina said. "No one knows."

The Old Man couldn't hold it in. He was desperate. "I am your brother, Daina. It's me, Frederick." He hadn't meant to confess his identity so suddenly.

"You are a liar."

"I met the photographer. He will be so happy to know that you are well."

"I am making dinner." Turning to Stasys, Daina said, "Please show this gentleman to the door. I am making dinner."

"And I met the captain at the jail. He said to tell you that he is sorry." Frederick followed Daina into the kitchen.

Stasys said, "You need to leave," and tried to block the way. Frederick was stockier and nudged him to the side. Frederick continued, "I'm sorry, but please, Daina, this is important."

Daina's wings, which hadn't extended in years, pressed against the wool fabric of her blue shift.

Stasys said, "Are you all right, darling?"

"I don't have a brother," she said, adding a pinch of salt to the boiling pot. "And I'm fine except for the stranger in our house. He should leave."

"I am your brother," Frederick said. "I can prove it."

"He should leave now." She turned to the stranger in her house, her expression like a wild animal about to pounce. "The Russians shot my brother alongside my father."

"No, not me. The Germans took me," Frederick said. "Everyone said that you had died. Everyone said that the whole family was murdered."

Daina's wings pulsed against the blue shift.

Frederick said, "I knew you by the orange starbursts in your eyes."

Daina picked up two plates, one in each hand.

"I'd know you anywhere, Daina." Frederick showed her his palms. "Do you sing like Mother? I don't know why I was surprised to hear that you were in Palanga. I remember how much you loved the sea. I still remember that first time the sun shone on your wings, and we all saw them move. Do you remember?" He could show her his family portrait. It was in his back pocket.

Daina held on to the plates even as she trembled, pink water creasing her brow, potatoes sliced, piled on the counter, a pungent cheese beside them. On a wood block, a sheet of pastry and pile of red currants waited to be wrapped and baked. Daina's blue shift was stiff and suffocating, the room warm with steam. The window ledge, piled with snow, insulated them from everything beyond.

"You should go now," Daina said.

"Do you remember Nelly? She was our neighbor. She was your age. You must remember her, Daina!" Frederick dug through his pockets. "I have a photograph." He couldn't find it. "Nelly brought me potatoes and broth, some bread. The family hid me before the Nazis came for them."

Daina looked pleadingly at Stasys. She held on to the porcelain plates embossed *Made in Klaipèda* as if they were her hands.

Frederick said, "I didn't know you were alive until we were in Vilnius. I brought my son and my granddaughter to see where I am born, where we are from." He was still searching his pockets, sweating more profusely in the warmth of the kitchen.

"You aren't from here," Daina said. She slammed the plates into the sink. They splintered and cracked, the name *Klaipèda* remaining among the shards. "You don't know what it's like."

Stasys's voice boomed: "Get out!" He took hold of the Old Man's wool collar. "You have to leave. Now." Stasys was a slight man, but his stature belied his strength and love for Daina. He practically carried the Old Man down the steps and onto the street. "Leave her alone," Stasys said. "She doesn't want you here." He locked and chained the door, turning to rest against it. He could hear Daina crying upstairs.

On the street, the Old Man was crushed. He pressed his palms to the latched door. His sister was beyond that door. His sister was beyond his reach.

26

Prudence

*T*he Old Man returned defeated to the hotel room in Palanga's resort district where I was waiting. Ingeburg, Freddie, and Veronica had gone for a late lunch, but I'd remained behind, anxious to hear what the Old Man had discovered. My Oma had tried to convince me to go with them for a bite. She kept saying that this was a time for champagne and parties. Didn't I know that the wall was coming down?

When he returned, the Old Man's look was one of resignation. He explained that as much as he wanted his sister to know him, to see beneath his white hair and lined brow, he would not persist. After all these years, he could not defy her wishes. She did not want him there. She did not want to know him. He claimed that it should be enough for him to know that she had survived the war and an iron curtain. It ought to be enough to know that she was well, that she'd married and returned to her beloved seashore.

I had only known my grandfather since June, but this was not the man I knew. "No," I told him. "You can't just give up."

He kept insisting that he couldn't bother her if she did not want him there. He would not do that.

"But you have to try and know her," I explained. "She's your sister."

He sat on the bed, dropping his chin to his chest, and started to cry. "I am a fool. I left her behind." He wiped his face with his shirt's collar.

I didn't know it at the time, but a few short blocks away, Daina was confessing to her husband that she shouldn't have sent her brother away. She told Stasys, "What if he doesn't return? How will I find him?"

The Old Man told me, "She doesn't want to be found. She doesn't want to know me. Can I blame her? I am her big brother, and I do not see her for forty-eight years. Why should she know me? I failed her. I failed all of them."

"You have to go back." I was going too.

While I knocked, the Old Man looked skyward. From the force of my knock alone, the door blew open. The Old Man remained beyond the threshold while I entered, perching on the bottom step and looking up. Daina and Stasys were poised on the top step. I saw them. In the darkness, I couldn't see her eyes. Nor could I see her wings, but I knew her. I even felt that I knew him. It made no sense, but often life is like that. That's the miracle of all this.

I didn't think. I didn't have to. I remember saying, "I'm Prudence. I'm like you." The Old Man came up behind me. In Lithuanian, he told his sister, "This is the granddaughter who wants to meet you. She was born with wings."

Daina descended one step and I saw her eyes in the dim light. Over and over, I'd been told that my eyes resembled hers, first from the Old Man and then from Lukas Blasczkiewicz, but now I could see for myself. Except for my hair, which I got from Freddie, I resembled no one in my family. But now I did.

I moved behind the Old Man to pull the door shut. We were letting in the cold. "Go on," I told him. "They haven't told us to leave." I nudged him, but he was a stalwart, and he didn't budge until Daina said, "Please come upstairs."

"I don't want to bother you," the Old Man told her. "Are you sure it's all right?" Later, he would translate everything spoken between them.

On the landing, Stasys reached out to take our coats. I handed him mine and hugged the old woman I knew through the Old Man's stories.

I felt her stiffen. I had her gooney legs and starburst eyes, but she was sixty-four and not the young woman who'd freed me from the piling.

She turned toward the kitchen, and we followed. Stasys pulled two chairs out from a round table indicating for us to sit. In Lithuanian, the Old Man told Daina that he was sorry, that he hadn't known she was alive.

Steam encircled Daina's face. She was making dinner, pounding dough for currants, small beads of sweat at her temples.

The Old Man asked if she recognized him now. He wanted to know if that was the reason she'd changed her mind and let him in. He began to cry. "I wanted to save you. I wanted to save everyone. I failed you. I went for help, but Father was killed." The water on the stove boiled and bubbled up to the edge of the stainless steel pot.

Even without knowing the language, I could infer what Daina said next. She asked the Old Man if he'd abandoned them. "Did you run and hide while I watched Audra and Danutė die?" Her voice cracked. "Did you leave us to die, brother? *Mirtis?*" She bent forward and I saw serrated tips, sharp as knives, cut through the blue shift she wore.

The Old Man was Frederick now, a poor beast, and for the second time in less than a week, he tried to get to his knees, but off-kilter, he fell over. "I didn't run away. I didn't know. I would never run away," he told her.

I got up from the chair.

Stasys returned to the kitchen. "Daina?" He was scared. His wife's wings were like two fat butcher knives cutting through her shift.

From the linoleum, Frederick said, "Father was killed. I tried to save him. When I came home, the neighbors told me that they'd taken Mother away and that your bodies had been put in a wagon." Pressing his palms to the floor, he got to his knees. "I went to the house. There was no one there." He folded his hands together. "I beg you to forgive me."

Daina went to Frederick and placed her hands on his shoulders. With her wings extended in the warm kitchen, she looked like a visiting angel. "Nothing is your fault, brother."

He pressed his tired face against the inside of her forearm. She told him, "I hid. I built a nest and waited. And then I met Stasys. Remember your story about the bear? I thought that Stasys was a bear. Do you remember your bear, brother?"

Of course he remembered his bear. He kissed the inside of her forearm. Daina turned to me. I stood beside her kitchen chair. *I have wings like you*. Five syllables, thumb to pinky.

Her hands fluttered above her chest like she was trying to keep her heart in place. Her wings unfurled even further, like her father's accordion, a sweet, high timbre, the glint of a stainless steel knife spreading layers of steam through the kitchen. She stroked my cheek. Her rough fingertips reminded me of Freddie's, but their coarseness was not from music, but from labor—needle and thread. She felt my face, my jawline, the swoop of my nose and the shape of my eye. Everything was new and strange. I told Daina that I had scars but no wings.

The Old Man used a cabinet to rise to his feet. He repeated to his sister what I had just said. "Prudence has scars. The doctors removed her wings."

I reached back, rubbing my thumb between my shoulder blades, beneath the cotton of my sweater. "I have the scars where my wings used to be." Inching my sweater and thermal undershirt up my back, I asked her, "Can you see them? The scars?" I didn't consider it at the time, but thinking back, there was no one in the room who hadn't been scarred. In that way, I was the same as everyone else.

I told Daina that the man who'd taken her photograph had also taken mine. "He's still alive and he lives in Vilnius." She pressed her fingers to my scars and said, "I remember him. He was in the room when Saint Casimir came." Her wings opened and closed more quickly. As she took her hand from my back, I pulled my shirt down. She said, "I wanted to live."

The kitchen pulsed with steam. She continued, "Our mother brought us here to the sea every summer. She doted on us. Do you remember, Frederick?" In Daina's Palanga kitchen, the Old Man was just a boy. His sister was playing angel or bird—flapping her wings, momentum building. Steam rising. Her blue shift split horizontally at her shoulder blades and vertically down her back, the sign of the cross, the fabric dropping to the floor. Wrinkled skin sagged from Daina's triceps and forearms, the curse of age. She reached to feel the fullness of her own glorious wings, turning her head to admire them, knocking over a kitchen chair. She was giddy. In Lithuanian, she told Stasys that everything was changed. She knocked a sugar bowl and fancy cake plate to the floor. At first, it was an accident, but then she used her wings to whack commemorative Soviet Union anniversary plates, gifts from the propaganda offices, off the wall. It was heavenly to hear them shatter. Daina sent copper pots rattling to the floor and toppled a rose vase and pot of coriander from the windowsill to the sink.

I covered my mouth, my hands fluttering, how Daina's hands had fluttered to keep her heart from departing. How her sisters had kept silent lest they murder the world with their voices. But this time the fluttering hands were different, because this time no one had to hold anything captive. No one feared for her life. Because this time, the fluttering hands mimicked freedom and flight. They were their own. I stepped forward to feel one of Daina's wings and as my hand made contact, the wing swelled. There were no feathers. Fully expanded, the wings were soft and malleable like cartilage, like the rays I'd witnessed flopping on the Los Vientos pier, slick like a waterbird's, but bigger. Daina went to the window and pressed her palms there. The glass was cold. She flapped her wings deliberately, knocking pans and pots, bread and muffin tins, a metallic symphony, a cacophonic reprieve. Aunt Daina turned to face me, her wings silenced, pressed against the glass window. We met in the center of the kitchen, where she wrapped her sinewy arms around me. We were chest to chest. I felt Daina's sagging breasts against my full ones. Her arms were at my waist. The wings pulsed and flapped and quickened, and is it any wonder after all of this that I am an ornithologist? Bird girl. Girl bird. I felt something in my chest, something bigger than my heart. I felt my own ghostly wings struggling to emerge. I felt Daina's heart. The two of us were seamless now, each full up and spilling into the other. Then my big feet and Daina's small feet were off the floor, and Stasys, who apparently never used bad language, did just that, cursing out of surprise before dropping to his knees. Men are always falling to their knees around strange birds like us.

The window's frost cast a blue hue, dreamy and musical, Daina's wings, our wings, flapping, pulling down ancient cobwebs. The old woman and the young woman hovering beneath the ceiling. There was nothing but air beneath my boots. Nothing but air under Daina's slippers. Frederick sat entranced, a boy before a purging and a world war, a man on the verge of everything.

We stayed aloft for as long as Stasys could hold his breath.

The flapping slowed. Our feet touched down. The wings folded in like a Chinese paper fan, the tips touching. I fell in a heap to the floor while Daina pulled her ripped shift from the linoleum and covered her breasts. "To be born a bird," she spoke in Lithuanian, "doesn't mean you get off any easier."

I understood. Life would be life for anyone who felt different, apart from the pack. Wings or not. Life would be no better and no worse, but perhaps more inspired, but that was up to the individual, not a pair of wings. On my hands and knees, I crossed the floor to my messenger bag, returning to Daina with the gold timepiece. "My dad gave it to me, but I think it belongs to you."

"*Tėvas*," Daina said, admiring the timepiece, "Father." She cupped both hands around the watch. In Lithuanian, she said to Frederick, "How?"

"Father hid it between his bound wrists. He kept it from the Russians."

Unlike her, the watch had not aged. Unlike her, all its parts still worked the same. I imagined the Old Man's father. He used to slide the watch from his waistcoat and flick it open with his thumb. I wondered if this timepiece had foretold how much time was left. I imagined a candle burning, the wax dripping, the wick shorter. Had Petras known how much time they had left? Had anyone known what was coming for them?

Daina pressed the timepiece to her lips before passing it back to me. "This is not mine. It is rightfully Frederick's." On the stovetop, the potatoes had boiled to soup. The dough rose halfway to the ceiling. The steam spread like so many layers of cake throughout the house.

Daina later told me that she'd glimpsed her mother dancing atop ceramic shards and popping red currants from the countertop into her mouth. Daina had been longing an entire lifetime to see her mother, so it was no wonder Aleksandra had chosen this time to make herself known. Probably the kitchen was crowded with the Vilkas clan, but it was just like Aleksandra to steal the spotlight.

Palanga, Lithuania, November 1989. Kitchen. This is where I was born.

PART FIVE

And when the sun goes down and the mood comes upon me, I'll watch the play of the colors on the water, yield to the fleetly dissolving images, and turn into pure feeling, all soft and nice . . .

—Günter Grass, *My Century*

27

Prudence

My wings are with the birds now. I gave the ghost of them up. I freed them, released them to the sky to traverse the warm Gulf Stream waters with my ancestors; Aleksandra and Aušrinė I know by name, but there are others. All year, waterfowl stop here on the eastern coast of North Carolina on their way south and north. Ducks flock to the white-capped waters, hundreds basking in the light. We tag different breeds and watch the next year to record their return. We want to know if they're going to grow old. I mourn quietly for those that don't return. As much as my colleagues love the birds, they do not regard them as kin—as I do, because I was born to it, because I gave the birds my wings to carry. Because when I see the birds, I think of the Old Man's mother. I picture her spilling from a boxcar and sprouting wings to escape the frozen Siberian landscape.

It was 1992 when I gave them up for good. I had spent too many years thinking only of myself, focused on my scars, pining for my wings to return. This craving for something I did not possess was a reminder that I had been wronged. It was futile. I would never carry more than the ghost of my wings, my body's memory that they'd been a part of me. My brain was wired to know them, to mind and protect them, but what for?

In 1992, I was a sophomore at the University of Florida, auditing advanced biology and ornithology classes. This same year, I went back to Lithuania with the Old Man. It was no longer the Western Province of the Soviet Union. Freedom had evolved from a struggle to an inevitability.

Dubbed the Singing Revolution, Soviet musical festivals were transformed by one voice and then another. The performers, who'd rehearsed the state anthem of the Soviet Union, sang instead their national hymn. At first, only the performers sang, but then the crowd joined in. Television cameras rolled. The crowd expected the maestro would be shot by Soviet officials. Next the performers, and then the crowd. But they were not. The cameras were not behind a curtain, iron or otherwise.

Our Latvian and Estonian brethren did the same. As a group of nations, we opened our mouths to sing, never again the state anthem of the Soviet Union. Despite the threat of bloodshed, we sang the songs of our ancestors. More cameras rolled. The Soviets in attendance were in disbelief while the world watched us sing. Freedom was palpable. You could reach out and hold it in your hand.

During our 1992 visit, the Old Man and I recalled that glorious day in 1989 when we were part of the revolution—when everyday men and women stopped in their tracks, raising their eyes and voices to the Lithuanian flag. I think we knew it then: independence was on our heels.

During our 1992 visit, we made sure to call on Lukas Blasczkiewicz. The Old Man thanked him profusely for helping to find his sister. He relayed that Daina was beautiful and happy. The Old Man gave Lukas American trinkets: plastic replications of the Statue of Liberty, chopsticks, and an *I Love New York* T-shirt. It made me laugh to imagine Lukas in that T-shirt. The Old Man told Lukas to go see his sister. "Daina will be glad to know you."

"In due time," Lukas Blasczkiewicz said. He told us that he had recently acquired an apprentice, and they were busy with new endeavors, selling flying machines at festivals and parks. He said that we had better take our leave. There was much for him to do. He was never rude, just forthright.

At Daina's walk-up, we feasted. My Oma laughed, her chipped tooth like a diamond in the afternoon sun. Stasys was learning English. The Old Man and Daina reminisced. They spoke of their sisters and parents. They spoke without fear. The windows were open. Happiness spilled onto the street below. I remember the Old Man's joy. Like Lithuanian freedom, I could hold it in my hands. I could feel it in my bones.

When I returned from Lithuania, I was sitting on the sand, watching pelicans dive-bomb the waves. The sun was low in the sky and I felt a presence, an energy, a breath on my neck. It had the speed and motion of a whisk broom, running *swish swish* up and down my back. My wings, this birthright that I simultaneously possessed and mourned, as the Old Man had with his homeland, suddenly scattered to the wind. It took half a second. They were gone. Only my scars remained. A flock of grackles, obsidian and iridescent emerald beneath the sun, alighted from the dune. It was October. It had been a full year since Wheaton's disappearance. Dozens of grackles multiplied into hundreds and then thousands. Too many to count. I got to my feet. Already, I was lighter. The birds blotted out the Indian-summer sun. The sky shimmered black as they sang, a symphony of calls, their own song, a splash of light slipped between two A-shaped tails. John Lennon. Take these broken wings and learn to fly. All my life, *I* was waiting to be rid of the birth defect that never was. I ran parallel to the surf. Under the balls of my feet, the sand made an inky sound, felt, not heard, and the birds accompanied me. I screamed, my voice swallowed by the grackles. I gave it up: the angst and bitterness. I gave them up. I gave up everything that had weighed me down. I reached for the sky. I was without my wings and only once before, holding on to my aunt in her kitchen filled with steam, had I felt this light.

Now I have to give up the Old Man. I seem to have no other choice. I keep thinking, *You'll always have the stories. You can share the stories. You can write them down. You can sing them.* But I don't want the Old Man's stories or songs. I want him. I want to be able to pick up the phone and know that he'll be there puffing away on his cigar, asking, "What do you want?," which is his way of saying, "How can I help you?"

As soon as we exited the elevator on the tenth floor of Saint Gertrude's Hospital, Veronica felt sick. I went to the Old Man's room in the intensive care unit, while Veronica went to the bathroom. "I'll be there in a minute," she said. I was relieved to be on my own. I had to get myself together. *Don't cry. Don't fall apart in there.*

The Old Man always said, "It is a blessing to grow old." Too many people don't get to grow old. He used to tell me that young people are stupid because they pity the old. They don't see themselves humpbacked or weak. They can't imagine themselves bald or with hair coarse like bulgur wheat.

His door is open. I am here now with my back against the wall. His eyes are open, but I think he's flown. He stares at nothing, his lips a faint blue—the color of an uncertain sky. It could rain or the sun might peek out. Ingeburg sits on one side of the Old Man's bed, her collarbone visible beneath a flower-print shirt. She is too thin. Her pie face seems to dangle from her cheekbones like uncooked dough. Freddie sits on the other side of the Old Man. There's a fly buzzing in a caulked window that wasn't built to open. If the windows here *could* be opened, patients might leap to their deaths to avoid the needle pricks and beeping contraptions that accompany sickness.

The Old Man is attached to some type of machine. A white crustiness is caked in the corner of his mouth—which is hinged open like he's suffering from lockjaw. I expected to see Ingeburg crying, but it's Freddie whose tears dot the Old Man's bedcover. Ingeburg laces a silver cross between the Old Man's fingers. I press my palms to the wall. The room looks gray. The curtains are pulled back to reveal an equally gray day. From this vantage point, I can imagine the window gone, not open, but gone, this room connected to the dismal sky. We're in a rolling fog. It reminds me of the wardrobe in C. S. Lewis's *The Chronicles of Narnia*. This is new territory. If I step forward, I might plummet. I wonder if this is how Ingeburg and Freddie feel too. Sometimes, life is very difficult, like now. The Old Man would tell me that part of living is dying. I'm not as wise as he is. I'm not ready for him to go. The fly is incredibly loud, buzzing over the humming machine that monitors the Old Man's blood-oxygen level. Veronica arrives, her hand over her mouth. Freddie and Ingeburg see us, and suddenly being seen makes this more real. I can't hide. There is a knot in my stomach. I press down to the left of my belly button and feel it. Something is seriously wrong with me. I don't want to cry. Freddie gets up, pulling me to his chest, his lips pressed to my neck, and inhales deeply. "This is hard," he whispers. I know that it's hard. My father is soft. He's too much of an artist. Too sensitive. It's impossible not to love him. His face is moist on my skin. I'm sweating as he takes my hand and leads me to the Old Man's side. I can't stand seeing the Old Man's mouth hinged open, hearing him struggling to breathe. He blinks, but I can't see the light in his eyes. His baby blues have lost their luster. "He's DNR," Ingeburg informs me. There is an iciness to her German accent. Freddie explains: "Do not resuscitate."

"That's how he wants it," she adds. It's obvious that she doesn't want it to be this way. According to Freddie, when the Old Man was still conscious, they wanted to sedate him and put him on a ventilator, but the Old Man wouldn't hear of it. Of course not. That's *not* how he rolls.

His hand is gray like the fog around us. My hands look oddly pink, the color of bubble gum, fat against his. I had hoped to see him sitting up, telling me that he is all right, telling me that he doesn't mind getting off the Ferris wheel, but I don't think he's here with us. I hope he isn't, because of how he's breathing. Between jerky motions and gasps of breathlessness, there are seconds of peace. Freddie says that the Old Man's organs are failing. It's only a matter of time. And then Freddie gives up trying not to cry in front of me. His tears fall in quick succession. I can't witness my father crying and not succumb to the same. We're all trying not to cry in front of each other. Freddie's blue eyes glisten. The pit in my stomach has grown roots, and my abdomen seizes. *His blue eyes glisten* is five perfect syllables, thumb to pinky.

If only everything made sense. I have to go to the bathroom. This is worse than I'd anticipated. I'm not good at watching the Old Man die. I'm not good at accepting things I don't want. I want to tell Freddie, "It's all right," but it's not all right. Veronica has taken Freddie's hand in hers. In the bathroom, I pull the heavy door closed and flip the stainless steel lock. I stare at the mirror, blowing my nose, trying to recall the clarity and truths I've learned these past sixteen years. First and foremost, the Old Man will always be a part of me. I have my aunt Daina's eyes, my father's hair, and by proxy, the Old Man's thick locks. Stories can last forever if you share them. I can be strong, and I know it. I can do this. I smile at my reflection because none of this seems like enough. I'm angry, and I have to be strong. I can't fuck this up, but what's to fuck up? On the other side of this door, a hero is dying. My stomach knots up again. What am I going to do when I can't call the Old Man for advice? What am I going to do when I am sad or angry, and he's not a phone call away to tell me that everything is going to be okay? No one can put things in perspective like the Old Man. No one can make everything better like him. Where is Daina? Is Daina coming? I wash my hands, soaping them three times like death is contagious.

Things feel small now, like there's nothing left to look forward to. We're at an impasse in this hospital room. One of us is going away. The most important person in my life is leaving.

I splash water on my face and breathe deep before returning to the Old Man's side. His oxygen levels are dropping. It's a matter of hours or minutes. There's a nurse with us now. For all I know, she could be Miss America. Everything is whitewashed. The fog is changing into a blizzard. The Old Man's body convulses. My Oma covers her mouth, her scarred lip and chipped tooth. Veronica starts to cry. I remember the Old Man telling me about his sisters' hands covering their mouths, how they resembled wings. I remember Daina's wings expanding in the white steam of the kitchen. I remember Lukas Blasczkiewicz telling us that he saw a white light when he took photographs of Daina's wings. The hospital walls are plaster. The Old Man's bedcovers and beard are white. Like milk. Like Wheaton's crazy gone eyes. Like a saintly light filling a cell.

The nurse says, "I think it's time." The Old Man's shoulder and head jerk. We're crowded around him. With our hands, we try to hold him still. I slip three fingers inside his beard and think for a half second of Wheaton's curls. *Please don't go.* With all of this machinery, the nurse has two fingers on his wrist, feeling for a pulse. My eyes flit from his eyes to the beeping machine to the fly still trapped between plaster and glass. If I'd known that he was actually dying, I would've been here sooner. I would've said, "Good-bye" when he could still speak. I would've said, "Don't go!"

When he exhales his last breath, I'm holding mine. Not one of us is stoic. Not one of us is dry-eyed. My Oma is speaking in German to him. Her hands are on his face, which has softened. The nurse closes his eyes. I feel angry that death is a constant part of life. This is a hospital, and people die here every day, and no one here, except us three, can possibly understand how special and wonderful the Old Man is—that he was born across an ocean, marched across a continent, sailed to a new world to learn *another* new language, raised a son to know the past, sought me out to give me my homeland. The Old Man returned home after forty-eight years in exile and found his sister. He is brave. He is a survivor. The Old Man is not just a man, and he never was, not in life or death. I can hear his music now.

"He's gone," the nurse says. *Wait*, I think. I want to keep listening. She repeats, "He's gone," and I'm wondering where. I'm like the innocent child tugging at the priest's robe, looking for Jesus on the altar. If that's his body and that's his blood, why can't I see him? Everyone is talking about him, saying that he's here with us. Where?

The Old Man is gone. It seems that the deadbeat has let him off the ride. Gone but not forgotten. It's too cliché, too small and too stupid.

A doctor has come into the room. The fly is belly-up on the window's ledge, his green luminescence fading.

Just last week, the Old Man ate Pat's Deli sausage links and made speeches. He'd been sick for the better part of a year, but my Oma was under strict orders not to tell anyone.

Before he was hospitalized, he spoke to Daina every day. He was jubilant three hundred and sixty-five days, and then on the three hundredth and sixty-sixth day, he was dying. He could not breathe. No bullet to the brain for him. Just a great sigh, a submission of sorts that he was done. It had been a good fight. How many years did we have together? Sixteen. Half my short life. Last week, he stroked his beard and told my Oma that it would be hard for her to get along without him. She laughed. Then she cried. He scolded, "I can't leave if you will blubber."

"Then don't leave."

He told my Oma, "You are as beautiful as the day I met you."

"Don't start acting sweet now, Old Man."

28

Wheaton
June 2005

*W*hen I pulled the chain that opened and closed the wings, the motion produced a guttural sound. I looped the canvas straps over my shoulders and galloped through the warehouse, the noise like a dying lawn mower. It was my first semester at Saint Mark's College: 1991. I took up creative space and residence in a warehouse, majoring in painting and printmaking but working with metal and fire, constructing massive wings and smaller things. Heating the metal with my torch, turning forks into ballerinas and waffle irons into skyscrapers, building other wonders for the ballerina to gaze upon. I worked small except for the wings, which grew larger and less manageable.

I'd bought a WWII flying helmet at an antiques shop and wore it as I hurtled across the warehouse, pulling on my chain. I should paint a foolish picture of a young man constructing the heaviest, most cumbersome machine with thoughts of flying. I have.

The last time I spoke to Prudence was October of 1991, when I told her, "I will never be the leading man." I can't remember what she said in response. It did not matter. The statement was shy one syllable of the ten I needed, representative of our relationship. Prudence Eleanor Vilkas was whole in 1991, and I was like one of my flying machines, noisy and useless. The voices that had once overwhelmed me spoke to me now of men with work unfinished. Hugo Valentine, who'd built half a parking deck attached to a sand heap in Boston, Massachusetts. Ban Bulawayo of Harare, Zimbabwe, who'd planted fifty acres of crops, his farm burned before the first harvest. I heard the voice of my father. *The next idea will be better. Genius is never recognized in its own lifetime.*

I made wings with paper clips and glue. I made them with Post-it notes and glossy potato chip bags. I pinned them to my corkboard with multi-colored pushpins, and the irony of pinning wings to hold them in place was not lost on me. When I built the wings bigger, with carpet remnants and Styrofoam, my art instructors were intrigued, making mention of Da Vinci's Vitruvian man, how everything seemed dissected, surgically rendered with precision. With each scrape of my putty knife, the wings became less real. With each brushstroke and smatter of ink, less willful. With each pounding and beating, I made wings less like wings. No matter what medium I used or how many forms I mixed, my wings were sterile. As I began working with sheet metal, I understood my own failings, knew that I would never fly. These wings with rivets and wires for opening and closing made a creaky metal sound. I imagined jumping off a cliff with them. Not to die. Just to see. My roommate reported that I stayed up all night, kept him awake, talked to myself in five-syllable phrases.

There was talk among the professors that my eye was not my own, that I was a forger, a cheat, a copycat, and then there was a flimsy book, pages dog-eared and water-damaged, produced as evidence. I sat across from my academic adviser, the book between us. Already I had gently, painlessly, like a clean splinter, removed myself from Prudence's life. I hardly wrote to her. She hardly noticed. I was going elsewhere. Doing something on my own.

The book presented as evidence was a paperback titled *Wings*, a book of black-and-white photographs, of metal and bird wings, of girl wings and scars. "Have you been copying this man, Blasczkiewicz?" the adviser asked.

I flipped through the self-published book. *Never.* "I'm not." The adviser did not believe me. I had never seen the book. Looking through the photographs, I did not recognize the two scars that belonged to Prudence Vilkas. How would I know? It was too strange to fathom.

"You're allowed to be inspired. You're expected to draw from the work of others."

"I haven't."

Sitting in that cramped office, I dropped my fingers like mallets striking a xylophone, hearing *I need to be where somebody loves me,* picturing a girl from an old black-and-white film twirling and skidding across a waxy dance floor. White knickers in bloom. Five neat syllables. Another five. I wanted a cigarette. When I held her in my arms, I smelled vodka on her breath and wanted to inhale her.

My eyes had turned white.

It was not my intention to disappear on that warm October afternoon in 1991. I remember my adviser sitting there across from my teacher, Mr. Wilkie, who was summoned to give his opinion on the matter.

I was remembering what Prudence had said to me just three years before. She said, "Wheaton, this has nothing to do with you." She meant her family and her wings. And I had stopped asking her questions, limiting my sight to as little as possible. I twirled across the dance floor with the girl in white knickers, her face unreal, her hands like phantoms in mine. Something would have to change. Mr. Wilkie thought it would be important to take this evidence to the dean of the arts program. The adviser, whose name I can't recall, agreed with him. They would need another opinion, one greater, more important than theirs. "There's a similar sensibility in their work," Mr. Wilkie noted, "but nothing to imply theft."

I was not going to meet with the dean of the arts program.

In November 1991, Lukas was expecting me. I handed him a photograph of my metal bird and he sighed, opening the door wider, the early-winter sun glinting off the wings strung from the ceiling. His hands were like willow branches with leaves long and spindly enough to count multisyllabic strings, like beads of sound. Face-to-face, his ears were the size of cauliflowers, his head big enough for any number of voices. And his heart was not on his sleeve but worn like a cloak, how I've seen a man's aura. He spoke to me without words. He spoke with emotions, specifically assurances that I had found my home. When I produced his book from my knapsack, he took it from my hands like he'd been expecting it, and as it disappeared somewhere between the sunlight and his black stride, I followed him inside. Imitation is tribute, but I hadn't been imitating. I'd been making art, my art, my sight, my wings. The clunky monstrosities of my birth. They weren't for flight. They weren't Prudence's wings. They weren't for dreams. My wings were for weight, to hold me down, keep me safe. They were my mother's arms, the ones that had been taken. They were my father's arms, the ones that had never held me, fumbling with plastic typewriter keys. My wings were a behemoth. What else would they be? Assurances. Setting the metal down. Letting the hammer fall. Nothing needed soldering, not anymore. I could be still somewhere without a pushpin or paper clip, without the memory of my father's typewriter, how everything he wanted had nothing to do with me.

I was home.

It's June 2005, and I can remember my 1991 homecoming with the greatest clarity. Lukas has sharpened my sight. I can also remember another June, in 1989, when I stood useless on Prudence Vilkas's lawn, not understanding or knowing then that despite all appearances and efforts to the contrary, I was tied to her. Whether she loved me or not, there would always be a tether stringing her to me and me to her.

I apprenticed under Lukas for six months before my eyes were opened wide enough to see the obvious: the scars from the book *Wings* belonged to Prudence. Even then, I did not speak up. I did not want Prudence because I did not think she wanted me. I remember that in October of 1992, she and her grandparents came to see Lukas. I slipped out the back just as they came through the front door, the sound of the bell tinkling corresponding with the gasp of the back door opening. I could not face her.

Back then, I needed a father, and Lukas needed a son. I am not a copycat, or a thief of any man's life or art.

I am thirty-two this year, a bit of a local celebrity—the American with snowy eyes in Lithuania. My paintings have been displayed alongside Lukas's in local museums and restaurants. We throw parties and headline parades. Lukas is the stilt walker without stilts and I am the swami. We churn ice cream. I swirl pink sugar around paper wands and tell futures. I think we've attended every birthday party in Vilnius, my fingers sticky with cotton candy, the children yelling excitedly, tugging at Lukas's long pants. They beg him to send another metal bird soaring above the lawn.

The children want to know their futures, and I try to tell them, centering my silk turban over my curls, but the visions and voices hardly come anymore. They have been replaced by the immediacy of living, of building, of gleeful shouting. Even my fingers are too sticky sometimes for counting.

Last night, Daina Valetkiene telephoned Lukas to tell him that her brother the Old Man is dead. Only Lukas knows that I am an old friend of Prudence's. Only Lukas knows that I knew the Old Man. For fourteen years, this is how it has been, but then last night, I did not sleep. I thought about my old friend Prudence. I distinctly felt the absence of her hand in mine and realized that although I had belonged here with Lukas Blasczkiewicz, I might also belong elsewhere.

I rose before the sun. Lukas was already awake. He knows that I'm going. When the birds were only beginning to sing, we pulled my paintings from the beams and rafters, replacing them with blank sheets of canvas, creamy shades of nothingness, speckled fabric bleeding white and brown.

I love the Old Man. This truth is not in past tense.

I love Prudence. This truth is not in past tense.

For the fourteen years I have apprenticed with Lukas Blasczkiewicz,

I have quieted the voices of men with lives left unlived. I have made all manner of flying objects, including wind-up angels with eyes blue like the sky. They hover for seconds and fall into the hands of waiting children, who press them to the breast. I have danced and sung, letting my fingers count sleek black and white piano keys. I have climbed high steeples and never thought of jumping.

I am wrapping the slick polyester of a secondhand necktie over and under and anticipating a long flight and drive. I do not know what else the future holds. Lukas, who has no gray hair, reminds me that there is no death, only a passing over. He closes my eyes with his long fingers and keeps me still, my mind clear. There are too many canvases left unfinished in this short life I have chosen and dubbed mine. My canvas, I realize, is among them.

29

Prudence

In 1992, we went back to Lithuania. She was now an independent country. Germany was reunited. In three short years, the world had changed. On this trip, Freddie and Veronica stayed home. I was able to spend a full month with my aunt and uncle. First, we visited Vilnius and Kaunas. In Vilnius, we met Daina and Stasys's daughter, Audra. She was blond, and according to Daina, she looked like my great-grandmother, Aleksandra. We spent a week at the university where Audra taught political science. Audra told me that she'd always known that Lithuania would gain its independence during her lifetime. "Maybe because of my parents and my upbringing or maybe because some things are inevitable, or maybe because I knew my people could only remain silent for so long." Audra is an amazing woman. After a week in Vilnius and Kaunas, we returned to Palanga. I remember the windows open in Aunt Daina's flat, a warm ocean breeze drifting from the west, their apartment smelling of the sea.

Every morning and evening, we walked the long stretch of dune and played in the Baltic's shallow tide. I was mourning the loss of Wheaton, but I did so quietly. My aunt Daina still worked at the button factory, but my uncle Stasys was now a reporter for a Lithuanian newspaper. I could've remained there forever. For me, it was like hiding out, not the same as being home.

Next, we were off to Germany. It was my Oma's turn to go home.

My Oma had gone to Berlin in 1990, by herself—to visit cousins she hadn't seen in forty years—but on this trip, we were going to see her girlhood home, to see if it still remained. In 1990, my Oma hadn't wanted to go. She couldn't bring herself to see the home where she'd lost everything and everyone, not when she was filled with so much hope about the future. In 1990, she'd gotten to know her cousins, her mother's brother's children and their children, and they loved my Oma. How could they not? They described life behind the iron curtain, waiting in line for bread, being told that their fellow Berliners and Germans were suffering under capitalism, while they were thriving, but who was thriving? No one. They were hungry. They told my Oma what she already knew: before the wall, young people and educated people left in droves. The workforce dwindled. How could the communist leaders stop people from leaving? Build a wall and claim that the wall was to stop people from entering East Berlin. White is black and black is white. Two plus two equals five. Lies. Power has no conscience.

My Oma's girlhood home still remained, but in 1992, it was no longer a single home. It had long been divided into three apartments. I remember that she ran her fingers along the brick facade. Out front, there were roses in bloom, but we'd brought our own to leave on the spot where her mother had been buried. My Oma hesitated at the front steps, bending down to feel the bricks with her hand. The Old Man steadied her with his left arm. She kept looking around like she expected to see her father or brother run past. Instead, a young girl with straight black hair darted up the steps. At the front door, she turned back, speaking in German, asking if everything was okay. My Oma grinned, showing her broken tooth. "Everything is fine," she told the girl.

At the left side of the house, we passed through the same wrought-iron gate my Oma had known growing up. It was a beautiful day, the kind of day that makes it hard to imagine my Oma's last day at home: soldiers and burials. Past the gate, there was a gazebo overgrown with a white star–flowered vine and a neatly trimmed hedgerow. Around the gate's interior, there were dog and sweetbriar roses, the roses Ingeburg remembered from her youth, her mother's roses. Even with black hairs poking from a mole on her jawline and wrinkles carved deep beneath her eyes, my Oma was youthful.

We placed the flowers on the grass at the site where the Old Man and my Oma agreed the grave had been dug. With the Old Man's help, my Oma got down on her knees, slipping her fingers between the blades of grass. The black-haired girl came out through the back of the house and told my Oma that her mother and grandmother were curious to know what we were doing. My Oma told the girl that she was sorry to bother them. She was an old woman. She had lived in this house as a girl. "My mother wants you to come inside," the girl said. It was nearly the Old Man's Lithuanian homecoming wish come true.

The little girl's apartment was at the top of the stairs and to the left.

Nothing was as my Oma remembered. The space was cramped, everything divided as her country had been divided. In retrospect, I don't think she wanted to be there in the small apartment. I don't think she could breathe. We had ginger cookies and tea, and everyone spoke German. There was barely enough room for the five of us in the tight kitchen. According to my Oma, the apartment had once been her parents' bedroom.

Later that summer, when I was still on break from university, the Old Man took me to Coney Island. Apparently, he sometimes went there alone. I think he people-watched, but I don't really know. We drank cherry Cokes with real cherries and noshed hot dogs and popcorn. There was ketchup and butter in the Old Man's beard. It was comical and endearing, so I didn't tell him. We rode the Ferris wheel. On the way up, I nudged him in the side. "There's a deadbeat operating this ride." I smiled and touched his tennis shoe with my boot heel.

The Old Man rattled the metal bar latched over our laps. "I'm afraid, Prudence." He was being funny. "What do we do?"

I don't think the Old Man was afraid, not in the hospital, not at the very end.

I suspect that he was ready. His stories play in my head like an epic film with a great score. He's studying at university and playing violin with his father. He's courting a beautiful German girl at the beer garden. There's music and a parade. He's riding his bicycle across a field. The sun's setting. He's anxious, but hopeful that one day this war will come to an end. He's on a ship bound for the United States. He has a beautiful son. He teaches the boy about Lithuania, about home. He works hard. He loves hard. He treasures his father's pocket watch. You know his story.

There was a short Mass inside the church. Now, there is a gaping hole in the dirt. The backhoe that dug the grave is within sight. Earlier, it rained for the flowers. On the hillside, forsythia and gardenias bloom. The sun came out for the Old Man. It's June fifteenth, nearly summer in Bay Ridge.

Daina and Stasys arrived yesterday for the funeral.

Today, Daina wears a white cardigan dragging the ground, stained green by summer grass. An orange scarf holds back her white hair. Her wings are unfettered, but like the rest of her body, they have shrunk and are barely noticeable. She could be any other eighty-year-old woman. Stasys wears a blue suit. Last night, he was dressed all in black. He and Daina nodded off on the sofa while neighbors and friends of the Old Man came to the house, carrying casserole dishes that Oma refused to serve. I don't know why she wouldn't put them out, but no one asked because no one wanted to upset her. They remained covered on the kitchen counter. I heard Veronica whisper that Oma won't be long for this world without the Old Man.

Right now, there's no food to think about, just a big gaping hole, a grave. Oma holds a handkerchief to her eyes. Occasionally, she sobs. There was no eulogy. The Old Man left specific instructions. Daina looks up at the sky, blue and fresh after the rain. When I grow up, I want to be like her. The only problem is that I am grown up. I'm wearing an A-line silk jacket, the same blue as Stasys's suit, over capri pants. The jacket is a floral print. It has pockets and silver buttons down the front. My hair is loose and the back of my neck is sweating. There are thirty people at the gravesite. I know because I've counted them. We match the summer grass and sky. No one is dressed in black. It's strange, but good. I am waiting for a sign. I think that if the Old Man is in a magical place, he'll send me a sign that he is all right. *Stop it with the worry, Prudence,* he'll say. Lukas Blasczkiewicz believed in miracles. So did the Old Man.

So do I. I try. I did. I do. I used to. I do. I think I do.

Daina pulls an embroidered handkerchief from her pocket and opens it to show me a pile of dirt. I understand what it is. We couldn't take the Old Man's body to Lithuania, so she's brought Lithuania to him. I wonder if she'll let me throw a bit of the dirt into his grave. I think it will help me to *do* something, to actively say good-bye. Then I hear a plastic rustling. Stasys has been carrying a grocery bag, which I thought was strange, but he speaks very little English, so I left it alone. He reaches inside the grocery bag and starts handing plastic Ziploc bags of dirt to everyone around the gravesite. It's too funny: Lithuanian soil in plastic bags. Yellow and blue zipped together make green. The priest says, "We commit the body of Frederick Vilkas, husband to Ingeburg Rosemarie Kischel Vilkas, brother to Daina Vilkas Valetkiene, father to Frederick Peter Vilkas, and grandfather to Prudence Eleanor Vilkas, to the peace of the grave."

Stasys hands the priest a plastic bag of dirt. It's lovely to see thirty people at a funeral opening Ziploc bags. The priest is opening his. I'm opening mine. This is pretty good. Basically, it's the kind of sign I would expect from the Old Man. Staring down at the simple pine box the Old Man picked out, we toss our dirt on the coffin. "From dust you came, to dust you shall return. Jesus Christ is the resurrection and the life." The priest smiles at us before making the sign of the cross. No one is crying now. In fact, it's hard not to laugh. The Old Man would've liked this. He really would've liked this. Stasys walks around collecting the Ziploc bags, smoothing them, piling them back in his grocery bag. Of course, he'll reuse them. We Lithuanians are not wasteful. The priest says, "Lord God, our Father in heaven, Lord God, the Son and Savior of the world, Lord God, the Holy Spirit, have mercy on us. At the moment of death, and on the last day, save us, merciful and gracious Lord God."

The sun is up and the sky is blue. The watch in my pocket ticktocks. The Lithuanian soil has been tossed. "We thank you for what you have given us through Frederick Vilkas. When the time has come, let us depart in peace, and see you face-to-face, for you are the God of our Salvation."

"Amen."

This place of death smells like birth, like honeysuckles and hyacinth. On the hillside, jonquils are in bloom. I hug Oma first. She has slipped her handkerchief under her bra strap. In German, she thanks Stasys for the dirt. It meant so much to everyone. There was no one, not even the priest, who didn't know where the dirt was from and what it meant, how much the Old Man would've appreciated it. Oma reaches for my head to have me bend down. She kisses my hairline and says, "I love you." I think Veronica is wrong. I don't think my Oma will die right away. The Old Man teased that she couldn't get along without him, not after so many years together. Oma will prove him wrong.

The Old Man was a grumpy old man, a charming curmudgeon who didn't waste one hour of his long life. He enjoyed his cigars and his cheap Black Label beer. He reunited his family and returned to his homeland. He made peace with the world. Dying is part of the adventure.

I realize today that it doesn't matter how many people in your life die because it doesn't make being without them any easier. This is what the Old Man would tell me, and as usual, he'd be right.

Daina and I hold hands. We're two little birds, grounded for now, walking along a grassy path, passing older graves, the good kind with statues and discolored stone, with angels and dogs and dates faded by the elements. Daina says, "We talked on the phone all the time. He was proud of you. He loved you very much."

I would like *never* to let go of her hand. As we pass a statue of the Virgin Mary, I see a man up ahead with curly hair down to his shoulders. The watch ticktocks in my pocket. I can practically feel time passing in my bones, especially in my knees, which seem wobbly today, like I could fall over any second. I can't imagine how Daina must feel. The Old Man told me that pocket watches used to be a status symbol. They were expensive, complicated machines, each part—wheels, springs, and pinions— handmade. Not like today. Our watch has its own key. It's not the original, but a key that the Old Man had specially made to keep the watch ticking, to keep our family moving.

The curly-haired man wears a loose-fitting yellow oxford and faded jeans. He's just standing there. Oma is telling Freddie that there are things at the house, things that were his father's, things he'll want. Freddie doesn't want anything. Robins peck the ground for worms. It's a good day. The ground is moist. The worms are easy to find. Up ahead, the curly-haired man crosses his arms. He's just standing there. As we get closer, he turns and trots to a green four-door in the parking lot. I know that the man is not Wheaton, but there's the possibility of Wheaton. There's no reason to think that I won't see him again—one day.

I am ready to go home now, hungry for the coast of North Carolina. Before I left, pelicans were perched on my dock, their pouches like double chins. Translucent green frogs clung to the sliding glass door, their hearts visible beneath moist skin. It's a miraculous thing to see. My home is my solace. I know that Daina and Stasys feel the same way about Palanga. Oma and I have made plans: next year, we're going back to Germany and then to Lithuania to see Stasys, Daina, and Audra. Probably Veronica and Freddie will want to go. Probably the Old Man will be with us in spirit.

30

Prudence

At night, the moon is bigger than it has any right to be. Over the phone, Daina and I compare notes. We think the Old Man is inflating it for our sake. We think he's shooting stars across the sky. I dream of him in the dense pine forests of Lithuania, taming bears and slaying beasts out of reach in this life. His loony-gooney mother is perched on his shoulder, coming and going, her face to the wind.

It's July 2005, a month since the Old Man's funeral. There's a full moon tonight reflected off the water. The sky is a silky magenta, like skies I remember from my youth. I'm sorting through the Old Man's record collection. Oma asked me to look through the records for what I might like. Right now, I'm listening to a violin recording, a sonata written by Johann Sebastian Bach. So far, I really like it, but I wish I knew more about classical music. I move my hand like a maestro, how I remember the Old Man gliding his cigar through the air.

The man who resembled Wheaton at the Old Man's funeral is standing at my screened door, blotting out the light.

I'm barefoot in jeans and a cruddy T-shirt.

Over the sonata, I can't hear him, but I see him. He's wearing a white oxford and jeans. He's appeared out of nowhere. What's he doing here? His curls are familiar, as are his eyes, like sappy pines. He's smiling, his head tilted to the right, his knuckle on the wooden doorframe. I turn down the record player.

Wheaton Jones is standing on my front porch. There's a confidence in his stance that's unfamiliar, but there's no mistaking him. Not now. Even though we're staring at each other, he knocks. I rub my hands down the front of my jeans and walk to let him in. I feel light-headed and strange. As I draw closer to the door, I stop. For all I know, Wheaton Jones is dead and buried. How would I know otherwise? He disappeared on me.

I'm moving in slow motion. He's on one side of the screen and I'm on the other. The wind clacks the latched door between us.

Slipping my hands into my pockets, I wait for him to say something. I rock heel to toe.

Instead of speaking, he reaches for something in his back pocket. It's a yellow pocket edition, some kind of book. He licks one finger and turns from one page to another. He's fumbling, but then he stops and presses a page to the screen. "It's a picture of your scars," he says.

I move in closer to get a good look. I haven't seen the book, the picture . . . I always thought there'd be wings. Wheaton shows me the cover. *Sparnas, Wings, L. Blasczkiewicz.* I have no words.

He says, "I'm sorry about the Old Man."

I point to the record player on the counter. The thick black album is still turning but the music is barely discernible. Gertrude, my resident egret, flies past. I always thought there'd be wings. I don't know what to say, what to do.

He says, "I see them in the photograph—the wings." His eyes are the same as I remember.

"Where did you get the book? Where have you been?" I'm angry. "You disappeared." Confused.

He says, "It's a very long story. I want to tell you."

"You ran away."

"I want to tell you. I need to explain."

I'm nervous, sweating, tucking my hair behind my ears. I don't know that

I want to hear what he has to say. I don't know that I can listen. I rub my left big toe across the top of my right foot. "Were you at the Old Man's funeral?"

"I was there," he says.

"You didn't say anything."

"I was scared."

"What if I don't want to hear what you have to say?"

"I would understand."

"Five syllables."

He presses his right palm to the screen. In his left hand is the book of photographs. I match my left palm to his right. Behind him, I can see the moonlight trailing like liquid silver across the water. I lean into the screen. Wheaton's candy curls look and smell how I remember, and I want to dip my fingers there, keep them there, still them there, stop counting years since I've last seen him. Stop missing him. What did the Old Man ask me? *What number of years will make you happy, Prudence?* I slip one finger beneath the latch.

> *"Hope" is the thing with feathers—*
> *That perches in the soul—*
> *And sings the tune without the words—*
> *And never stops—at all—*
>
> *And sweetest—in the Gale—is heard—*
> *And sore must be the storm—*
> *That could abash the little Bird*
> *That kept so many warm—*
>
> *I've heard it in the chillest land—*
> *And on the strangest Sea—*
> *Yet—never—in Extremity,*
> *It asked a crumb—of me.*
>
> —EMILY DICKINSON

Sources—
Of Inspiration and Otherwise

We all know how babies are born, but not so much novels. I started this book with one image in my head: a teenage girl climbing onto a bus with cardboard and faux-feather wings in her arms. I imagined her awkwardness looking for a place to sit. I wrote fifty pages. I knew that she was born with wings, but I knew little else. Then slowly, as she (Prudence) came to fruition, so did the Old Man, her Lithuanian grandfather.

I wasn't sure what I was doing or where the story was going, but once I trusted the characters to speak, the story began to unfold. Eventually, I understood how this novel was born.

When I was pregnant with my son in November of 2004, Valys Zilius, a Lithuanian-born professor of linguistics and Russian languages and literature, passed away. I had known him as an adolescent and I admired him very much. I would listen to his stories of Lithuanian exile and eventual refuge in the United States. He was a man unable to "go home."

Then, in January of 2005, when I was seven months pregnant, my surrogate grandmother Ingeburg Rosemarie Kischel McGarrity (Mac, as I knew her) left this world. She was born in Berlin, Germany, and lived there as a nursing student during World War II. For most of her life, she too was a refugee in the United States. She was my mother's best friend, and I very much looked forward to her being a great-grandmother to my soon-to-be-born son. Her death came as a terrible shock.

Just as my son was about to enter this world, a beloved exiled generation was leaving it. And then, as a new mother, I was afraid for my child, haunted by the realities of war and oppression. At the same time,

I started rescuing injured birds. Not on purpose or anything. They just kept finding me. I remember driving one across town to a special veterinarian, telling it to "hold on," and even though it died right there beside me, I couldn't believe it. I carried the fledging into the vet and needed confirmation. I bawled. All of the sudden, my character Prudence was an ornithologist. What else would she be? She was a girl born with wings.

In November 1989, with the fall of the Berlin Wall, Mac was able to return and visit her former home, her family, and friends in what had been East Germany. In the early 1990s, Valys was able to return to Klaipeda, Lithuania, a city ravaged by Soviet industrialization. His former home, as he told me, was one dull high-rise apartment building after another to house as many workers as possible. Mac and Valys were seeing their homelands after five decades. I wondered, "Can anyone go 'home' again?"

"What does 'home' actually mean?" Mac and Valys planted a seed in me to tell this story. This is a fictitious imagined story, but a story inspired by many things, including family, nature, history, and the human longing—with or without wings—to find Home.

Other sources include *Lithuania in Retrospect and Prospect* by Jonas Šliupas; *The Soviet Story*, a film by Edvins Snore; *Ukrainian Minstrels* by Natalie Kononenko; *Odyssey of Hope* by Joseph Kazickas with Valdas Bartasevicius; *DPs, Europe's Displaced Persons, 1941–1951* by Mark Wyman; *Estonia, Latvia and Lithuania*, DK Eyewitness Travel, 2011; "Lithuanians by the Laptev Sea: The Siberian Memoirs of Dalia Grinkevičiūtė," translated by Laima Sruoginytė, from *Litanus: Lithuanian Quarterly Journal of Arts and Sciences* 36, no. 4.

Acknowledgments

Thank you to my family: Christopher Robin, Danny Stone, Peter Young, Rosemary Young, and Desiree Davis. I am especially indebted to my husband and son, without whom I couldn't do what I do. Because of your love and support, I know that I can always come home.

For a myriad of wonderments, including sources of research and much-needed emotional support, thank you to Sara Jo and Charles Arthur, James Zilius, Kim Lavach, Alisa Esposito Lucash, Amy Simmons Larson, Loretta Sanders, Vicki S. Bray, Gemma Driver, Dr. Carl, and Susan O. A special thank-you to Rebecca Joines Schinsky, who read *three* versions of this novel. I am deeply grateful and indebted. Thank you to my editor, Sarah Knight, for believing in me and for taking me with her. Thank you to Michelle Brower, the most wonderful, cupcake-loving, fiercest agent out there.

Thank you to the city of Richmond, Virginia, for supporting my first novel, *The Handbook for Lightning Strike Survivors*, with such fervor and warmth. Thank you to the Outer Banks of North Carolina for being kind and welcoming and small and beautiful. And to the birds, to all of them, the chickadees perched outside my door, the ospreys flying overhead, and the egrets wading in the marsh. I love it here.

About the Author

Michele Young-Stone was a public school teacher for seven years before returning to college to pursue her life's dream—writing a novel. She earned her MFA in fiction writing from Virginia Commonwealth University in 2005, the same year her son Christopher was born.

Her first novel, *The Handbook for Lightning Strike Survivors*, was published in 2010. Garnering great reviews, her debut was also selected as a Target Book Club pick in 2011. *Above Us Only Sky* is her second novel. She has a third novel under contract with Simon & Schuster and is happily at work on a fourth book.

Michele currently resides on the coast of North Carolina with her amazing son, supportive husband, obsessive-compulsive cocker spaniel, and humanlike bearded dragon. When Michele is not writing, she is crafting in some form and doing Zumba. You can learn more about Michele at www.micheleyoungstone.com.